CW00666369

HOKEY POKEY

ALSO BY KATE MASCARENHAS

The Psychology of Time Travel
The Thief on the Winged Horse

HOKEY POKEY

KATE MASCARENHAS

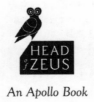

HEAD of ZEUS

An Apollo Book

First published in the UK in 2023 by Head of Zeus,
part of Bloomsbury Publishing Plc

Copyright © Kate Mascarenhas, 2023

The moral right of Kate Mascarenhas to be identified
as the author of this work has been asserted in accordance with
the Copyright, Designs and Patents Act of 1988.

All rights reserved. No part of this publication may be reproduced,
stored in a retrieval system, or transmitted in any form or by any means,
electronic, mechanical, photocopying, recording, or otherwise,
without the prior permission of both the copyright owner
and the above publisher of this book.

This is a work of fiction. All characters, organizations, and events
portrayed in this novel are either products of the author's
imagination or are used fictitiously.

Floor plans copyright © Kate Mascarenhas

9 7 5 3 1 2 4 6 8

A catalogue record for this book is available from the British Library.

ISBN (HB): 9781789543858
ISBN (XTPB): 9781789543865
ISBN (E): 9781789543841

Printed and bound in Great Britain by
CPI Group (UK) Ltd, Croydon CR0 4YY

Head of Zeus Ltd
First Floor East
5–8 Hardwick Street
London EC1R 4RG

WWW.HEADOFZEUS.COM

Dedicated to Eileen Jeffcoat, because she always enjoyed a horror story.

FLOOR PLAN OF THE REGENT HOTEL

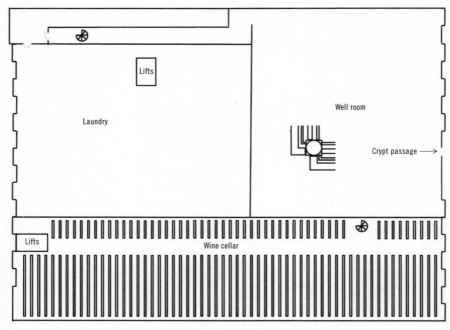

BELOW GROUND

Lifts

Laundry

Well room

Crypt passage →

Lifts

Wine cellar

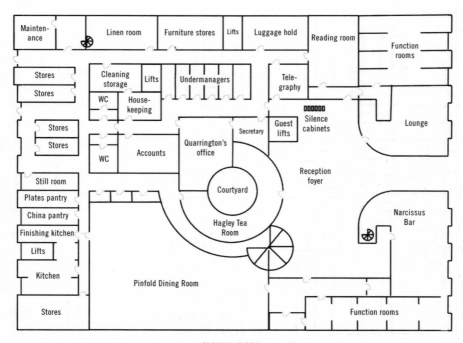

GROUND FLOOR

Maintenance

Linen room

Furniture stores

Lifts

Luggage hold

Reading room

Function rooms

Stores

Stores

Cleaning storage

Lifts

Undermanagers

Tele-graphy

WC

House-keeping

Stores

Stores

WC

Accounts

Quarrington's office

Secretary

Guest lifts

Silence cabinets

Lounge

Still room

Plates pantry

China pantry

Finishing kitchen

Courtyard

Reception foyer

Lifts

Hagley Tea Room

Narcissus Bar

Kitchen

Stores

Pinfold Dining Room

Function rooms

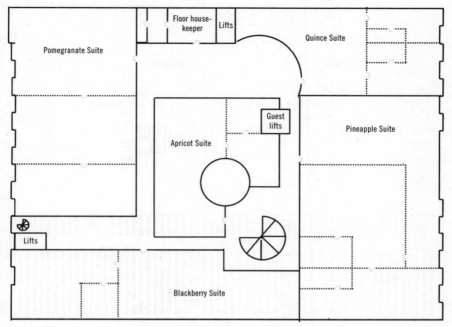

BERENICE'S FLOOR

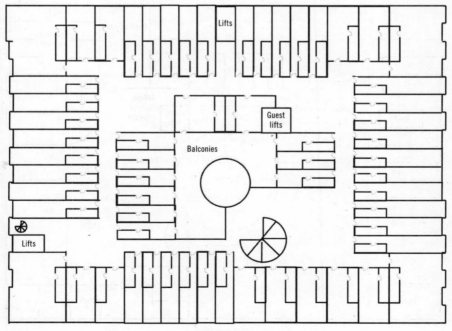

NORA'S FLOOR

**TO MAKE A
HOKEY POKEY
COCKTAIL:**

2 MEASURES
OF PERNOD FILS ABSINTHE

2 DASHES OF HONEY SYRUP

I DASH OF GARNIER CRÈME DE ROSES

I DASH OF MARIE BRIZARD AND ROGER
ANISETTE

THE WHITE OF AN EGG

SHAKE AND
STRAIN.

PART ONE

THE REGENT HOTEL, BIRMINGHAM, FEBRUARY 1929

I

Nora was not a liar, by nature. She was blessed with a prodigious skill for mimicry. If she chose, she could open her mouth and repeat every word she had ever heard, verbatim, in the style it was first spoken. Because of this ability she saw herself as truthful: she was a recorder of truth, as true as any phonograph.

At dusk, guarded against the cold by a fur coat and a mulberry red cloche, she arrived outside the Regent Hotel. The sky was opaque with the coming snowfall. The building was cream stone, half a dozen storeys high, and European in style: rectangular columns and iron balustrades abounded. Floral carvings and decorative heads, positioned in shrine-like niches, ornamented the spaces between the windows.

A red-jacketed porter carried her luggage up the central steps. He had met her at the railway station, which was a few minutes' walk away. She entered reception, blinking at the blaze of electric light. Her footfall softened on a Greek key carpet. Green marble clad the walls. She could hear the strings of salon music, coming from a distant room.

Psychoanalysts favoured luxurious accommodation, and Nora was no exception to that particular professional snobbery. But she hadn't chosen this hotel. Leo Cadieux – her fellow analyst; once her friend, and something more than a friend – had asked her to follow his wife here. He suspected promiscuity. Nora would watch, and send reports back to him in Zurich. The watching would come naturally. Despite never having met his wife, Nora was used to observing her from a distance; Berenice was a famed singer, of noted beauty, who Nora found compelling and hateful in equal measure. But the need for stealth made her feel furtive. She must appear entirely at ease, lest someone say: "Surely *you're* up to no good."

Signs pointed the way to the Pinfold Dining Room, the Hagley Tea Rooms, the Reading Room, and the Narcissus Bar. To the left was a great staircase; to the right, a long mahogany desk. Behind the desk sat a neat-moustached man in a dark suit. Beside him stood a woman with an unmade-up face, a blonde shingle cut, and a sensible demeanour. He addressed her as *Harvey*. She was likely a housekeeper. In sizeable establishments you could count on one per floor. By the hotel's rules, a woman travelling alone must have an advance reservation, and a housekeeper must be there to receive her on arrival.

"Good evening." Harvey consulted her list of that night's arrivals and departures. "Might I have your name?"

Nora was English. Despite spending her adulthood abroad she could still switch easily to the soft King's English of her mother, from her father's Czech, or her colleagues' Swiss German. With her pale blue eyes and pale brown hair she looked unremarkable in an English crowd. And the reservation was in an English name: her mother's before marriage.

Nora Čapek said: "My name is Dr Dickinson."

To be English in England was to be less conspicuous. That was valuable when you were watching someone.

Once Harvey had left her to the privacy of her room, Nora sat upon the bed, her back straight, in the dying light. She removed her gloves finger by finger and considered the task ahead. Dinner would be served at six. Nora wasn't hungry, but she must attend, because she had to watch the woman she'd come for.

There was time to wash away the taint of travel. The bathroom was strictly in accordance with the hotel's standards: the mirror was highly polished, mounted on a wall of jadeite and black chevron tiles, and the bathtub recessed in the alcove was deep. The rail bore three perfectly aligned towels. A bar of lavender soap, in stiff paper, sat perpendicular to the sink tap. Nora tore the paper away and disrobed to wash. She always regretted turning the sharp edges of new soap soft.

Clean but shivering, she returned to the trunk in her room and knelt to open it. Uppermost was a yellow silk evening gown that was formal enough for the dining room. Fully unpacking could wait until after dinner. She donned her undergarments, and the dress, which felt slippery against her skin. The bell sleeves were long and elegant. She must attain the correct presentation, neither ostentatious nor dowdy. It was necessary to blend in while she gauged the best means of gathering information on Berenice.

By the time she had locked her room, and taken the stairs, and found the Pinfold Dining Room, she was breathless yet still, officially, on time. Some two hundred guests were awaiting sustenance. Nora hated to be in the midst of this many people. So many conversations to hear, to fill her head, and leave their mark.

A waitress, in an immaculate serving smock of dark blue, indicated Nora should follow. She was shorter than Nora, around five foot six, and Nora noticed with a glance at the other servers this was one of the higher class places that insisted waitresses all be of the same height. It lent the room an uncanny air, to be served by young women of identical physique in identical clothes, as if any one of them might be swapped for another and no one need notice or care. Nora wondered if each evening they lay down in identical boxes and the maître d'hôtel placed a lid on each one, to keep them spotless for the next day. It was a silly, macabre thought, and Nora dismissed it by reflecting that waitresses probably didn't live in. They would go back to their lodgings in one of the city streets, regaining their individuality with every step towards home.

Nora was shown to an unoccupied place at the end of a long table. To her immediate left was an elderly lady, in a long mourning dress, with a white bun spun over each ear. Opposite this Old Victorian was a slight man of Nora's approximate age – probably a stockbroker or commercial lawyer – with wry hazel eyes and black hair falling in waves from a side parting. He looked at her a beat too long, almost as if he were surprised to see her there. She hoped it wasn't a sign of flirtatious interest. Attention from another guest would make her task harder. But he gave a polite nod of greeting, before returning to conversation with their neighbour, and Nora relaxed.

The place across from her was empty. She glanced about the room, reviewing the gathered hotel guests, looking for her quarry: Berenice Oxbow. Her name was anglicised too. Often Nora thought of Berenice as simply *the Icon*. For now the Icon was nowhere to be seen. Nora fidgeted with the hem of the linen tablecloth.

The room was high-ceilinged, thick with cherubs made from rose-hued plaster. Immense arched windows lined one wall. A series of blue glass lampshades swung from above: they were reminiscent of upturned goblets. The dark-haired man was talking of architecture to their elderly companion. Nora realised she had guessed wrongly; he wasn't a stockbroker after all. He was a public works architect. As the waitresses approached with plates of pâté de foie gras, the architect finished talking about the features of the Cathedral across the road. He moved on to the wonders of the hotel's water system – every guest now had access to hot and cold running water in their own suite – which, unusually, ran from the hotel's own private well.

"It's in the cellar," he explained, spearing his pâté with a small silver fork. "There's an old passage underground leading from the cathedral crypt. Before the hotel was built, locals had all sorts of ideas about the water source; they half considered it a shrine, I think. If you drank of it, you were supposed to be forgiven for your sins."

"*Really?*" the old woman replied appreciatively. "Can guests walk the passage?"

"No, there's a structural issue that's worsened with time; you could be halfway through and it would collapse on you. Hotel management keeps the door locked. But it's safe to visit the well by the hotel back stairs. Not just safe, an attraction. Think of these guests," he said with a smile. "Each bringing a guilty secret. All going home – redeemed."

She chuckled.

"Come now," he teased her. "What have you been up to? You're here to be forgiven too, aren't you – feign to deny it."

"Me?" she said in mock disbelief. "What could I possibly have to be ashamed of?"

"Yes, you're the picture of innocence! Remember appearances can be deceptive. When I was young I knew a schoolgirl who confessed to murder. She was a mere slip of a thing."

Nora winced; she didn't like this topic. But the old woman gasped, enjoying herself immensely. "You must tell me more about that. Wherever I stay, I do so love to hear of the local murders!"

The architect had apparently noticed Nora's reaction.

"What about *your* secrets?" he asked. "Are you here to be forgiven?"

"No," Nora said gravely. Her tone invited no further conversation, and he looked at her a moment longer, his smile waning at the hard ground his banter fell upon. The uncomfortable gap in conversation lasted until the pâté was eaten, and the commis cleared the plates.

"Oh look!" the old woman said then, her voice hushed. "There is Berenice Oxbow!"

Nora looked sharply at the entrance, to where a large-eyed young woman with a platinum crop was simpering apologetically at a waitress. Grey chiffon was wound around her shoulders. Yes, this was Berenice. The soprano, lately of the Zurich Opera House and now on tour. She was late, always late. A few other guests turned to note her arrival, and watched as she was led down the room. Nora dropped her head, taking new interest in a fleshy smear of pâté left upon the table linen. Her heart quickened as she sensed the waitress pass by – she could smell Shalimar, Berenice's fragrance, and for a moment she thought Berenice would take that last, empty seat at their table. But instead she sat at the table immediately behind. The two women must be three feet apart, back to back. Nora would be able to hear Berenice speak, though they were obscured from each other's view.

And speak Berenice did. As everyone digested their first course Berenice regaled her unseen dinner companions, in those twittering, half American, half Russian tones, which was the type of foreign accent people might tolerate when they were starstruck. Her conversation flattered the other guests that they were equals, no doubt… Berenice remarked that she'd missed the pâté; dreadful of her. Wasn't snow going to fall that night? The train had been comfortable but oh so unfriendly, with no one interested in conversation at all; she'd heard that the old horse and carriages had been much more congenial, in her grandmother's day – at journey's end you'd be lifelong friends with your fellow travellers.

Nora heard every banal word. The Old Victorian and the architect were listening too, with the studied expressions of people pretending not to eavesdrop. They probably thought Berenice was vivacious. Instead she was an imbecile, albeit one gifted in social niceties.

The waitresses returned bearing plates of pork, pale beneath a brittle shell of fat. Nora was starting to feel queasy. It was the clamour of the hall – all this discourse, making marks on her brain like grooves in a recording cylinder. But Berenice chose that very point to fall silent. To sate her appetite, Nora assumed briefly, before she heard the scraping of the chair across the polished floor, and the toppling of the chair to the ground. Berenice backed into her, her breathing laboured, and yet Nora still didn't turn. Nora bunched the linen cloth either side of her plate, her knuckles whitening. After a moment's bafflement, the rest of the table were watching as though this were one of Berenice's performances, with the stillness, the anticipation, of any audience at the Zurich Opera House. They were intent on understanding Berenice's actions. The Old Victorian, her eyes rolled upwards and her napkin poised mid-way to her mouth, was agog.

"A tragedy's coming," Berenice murmured.

The architect signalled for the attention of a waitress. One hastened to his side, and the architect whispered a few words to which the waitress nodded. She looked anxiously at Berenice and departed.

"A tragedy's coming," Berenice said more loudly, with greater urgency. "One of the guests here is in terrible danger. I see her! I see her in my mind's eye! She has a tattoo!"

Nora's hold on the cloth relaxed. Berenice was pretending to be in a clairvoyant trance; she did so often. She liked the attention and she used her fake reveries to manipulate people. Once she'd feigned a vision halfway through an aria, while Nora was in the theatre. Leo knew such visions were merely showpieces because Berenice had confessed to him before their marriage. She confessed just once, and resumed her pretence henceforth, as though she could overwrite the truth if she only lied more forcefully. Most people believed her – and enjoyed believing her. That made Nora's jealousy smoulder. To be taken at one's word was enviable. *Charlatan*, Nora thought.

Through her yellow evening gown Nora could feel Berenice's warmth.

A pair of housekeepers entered the room. Harvey was one; the other was doughy cheeked and stolid. As they advanced, Nora turned to see how Berenice reacted. The Icon held her hand to her heart, the better to show the swift rise and fall of her breath. Fleetingly, she met Nora's eye. They were strangers as far as Berenice was concerned. She'd never seen Nora's face before. Nora supposed she'd be taken for an avid spectator.

The housekeepers reached the spot where Berenice stood. She addressed them *sotto voce*, perhaps for added intensity. "Find the lady with flowers tattooed on her forearm. A *horrific* fate awaits her here! She must leave to save herself."

The stolid housekeeper, who quietly introduced herself as Geraldine Frye, murmured: "You'll be more comfortable in your room, Miss Oxbow."

Although Berenice was married, opera singers were always addressed as *Miss* in public.

"Our chef will prepare dinner to your liking, anything you wish," Frye continued. "We can serve it to you in your suite."

"I couldn't eat," Berenice replied, on the verge of tears. "Not after what I've seen."

Harvey placed a guiding hand upon the singer's elbow. Berenice did not resist – she let herself be led away, her face anguished. Nora rose from her chair to watch her go.

The other guests regained their garrulousness.

"What remarkable behaviour," the architect said.

"She's a spiritualist of some kind," the Old Victorian replied. "Very highly strung. She has visions – of the future."

"Don't take any of that too seriously, Mrs R. She seems a typical hysteric to me."

Nora looked at Berenice's abandoned plate, with its intact meal. An expensive cut of pork – succulent, pale pink – was quickly cooling into greasiness.

"The other rumour I've heard – " the Old Victorian was gaining enthusiasm – "is that she escaped from revolutionaries in 1917 by disguising herself as a cabin boy and hiding in a trunk. But I may be confusing her with another Russian singer?"

"One can verify the details of an escape from Russia much more easily than spiritualist powers."

"Oh, Mr Crouch, I didn't take you for a sceptic! That voice pierced me to my soul. Those were the words of someone who has seen things beyond our understanding. I may have forgotten how she escaped from Russia but I know the sound of the otherworld when I hear it."

Berenice had capitulated to the housekeepers, so was presumably walking to her suite now. Nora should follow. Once she knew which room belonged to the Icon, she needed to keep track of who entered, who departed, and when. That was the information Leo wanted about his wife, above all: who kept her bed warm.

Without bidding the old woman or the architect goodbye, Nora hastened from the restaurant, into the dimmer lighting of the corridor. Apparently Berenice had already given her guardians the slip. One housekeeper was checking side rooms for her; the other proceeded to the lift in case Berenice had gone on to her room unaccompanied. By the grand steps, Nora caught sight of a blonde woman in grey, just before the woman disappeared into the shadows beneath the stairway. Why was Berenice going that way, and not to her room? Nora drew closer to the alcove under the stairs, where she found a closed door, papered in the same swirling decorative pattern as the surrounding wall. She checked no one was watching, twisted the handle and craned to see inside. A plain white corridor stretched out, quite empty of other people; but it was clear a number of other doors lay ahead, providing staff with their own short cuts between private and public rooms. Berenice would have her own deranged reasons for exploring the hidden spaces of the building. She was of a defiant character.

Nora strode ahead. She saw signs, again, for the Reading Room, the Hagley Tea Rooms, the Pinfold Dining Room – she cracked the door each time, enough to check whether Berenice had exited there – and past those three, the corridor branched, forcing Nora to go down each path and return before trying the next one along. She saw portholed doors to the kitchens. The glass allowed her to see the steam and commotion. Men were shouting in Italian. Nora didn't think Berenice would be in the kitchen – the domestics would detect her, and expel her, in polite pretence she had lost her way. Next was something called a still room, then a suite of water closets. Nora rounded another corner (the corners seemed endless) only to see, up ahead, Berenice dive into a store room. Nora drew near the entrance. She looked through the porthole onto barely illuminated shelves, bearing stacks of tins. Berenice took a tin down and opened it with a key, too engrossed in her purpose to note Nora's eyes upon her. With the tin opened Berenice scooped her hand inside, raising the contents to her lips. It looked like potted meat – corned beef, probably. A hot meal was surely preferable. But Berenice would feed in secret, because she insisted on the illusion, even before the hotel workers, that she was too drained by her vision to eat. What a deplorable woman.

Another door opened further down the corridor – from outside, admitting a draught. It shielded the entrant but Nora could hear she was mid-conversation, curt with a companion: "*All right*, James, don't harangue me, please. You have to uphold your part of the bargain."

Harvey's voice? Nora retreated before the housekeeper could see her. She didn't want to explain why she was lurking outside the tinned meat supplies. Her observations of Berenice could resume shortly – in the bar, perhaps, after the Icon was sufficiently fed, or failing that at breakfast the following morning.

Just one encounter was enough, in Nora's experience, to cement the geography of a place in her mind; she couldn't recall ever getting lost somewhere she had visited before. And yet this time she repeatedly doubted herself as she retraced her steps. The winding, blank whiteness of these corridors unnerved her. She remembered the route she'd taken. But she did fear, quite irrationally, that the path had shifted and relaid itself while her back was turned. She scolded herself not to think such nonsense.

Back in her own room, soft with the flickering of the gas lamps – which still served for bedside illumination at the hotel – she methodically put away every item of clothing from her trunk. She did not change from her yellow evening gown, though she did shiver, and wrapped a shawl around her shoulders.

A petite bureau was positioned beneath the window. She sat there now. Her room overlooked the city's cathedral – a baroque yet surprisingly small building, with a series of stained glass windows illuminated from within, and a clock in a domed tower that was visible by the moon. It was soon to strike eight o'clock. The streets were already deserted. A few flakes of the threatened snow drifted diagonally by.

She spoke into the darkness. She said, with Berenice's voice: *I've missed the pâté; it's dreadful of me. Isn't snow going to fall tonight? The train was comfortable but oh so unfriendly, with no one interested in conversation at all; I've heard that the old horse and carriages were much more congenial, in my grandmother's day – at journey's end you'd be lifelong friends with your fellow travellers!*

Nora repeated every sentence, exactly as it had reached her ears. She came to the last few words of the vision. *Find the lady with flowers tattooed on her forearm. A horrific fate awaits her here! She must leave to save herself.*

There would be more words to come before the end of the trip, and Nora would enact Berenice's words for Leo once she was back in Zurich. Leo, who called Nora his *ozalid*: his photocopy. Sighing, Nora rolled up her silken sleeve, to expose the skin of her forearm. A tattoo, of a yellow chrysanthemum, among pale pink spots like nettle rash. It was fortunate she'd brought panstick. She'd cover that little flower before she left the room again.

15

2

At nine, Nora checked the hotel's public rooms one by one in search of Berenice. The last place remaining was the Narcissus Bar, on the ground floor, so Nora followed the signs. Sitting just outside the entrance, on a velvet upholstered banquette, was the public works architect. He inhaled his cigar and narrowed his eyes at her.

"They won't let you in," he advised.

"I'm sorry?"

"You're alone. They won't let you in. It's a hotel of standing, they have to keep out the wrong sort of woman, you understand, and only the wrong sort of woman would be drinking alone."

"Are you saying I look like a prostitute?" she asked, but she was resigned; so many hotels did hold onto these antiquated notions.

He laughed. "No. Although I bet the prostitutes serving the Regent are quite well turned out, as a rule. In any case I'm offering a solution – I can go in there with you."

Nora rapidly calculated: if unaccompanied women were turned away, then Berenice wouldn't be in the bar either.

Unless Berenice had male company, just as Leo suspected – and how could Nora check, without seeing for herself? Should she tolerate the architect's company for a while?

"They'll know we're not married," she pointed out, meaning that any hotel representative who bothered to check would see they didn't share a room. She didn't specify as much, anticipating some of the solutions he might offer to *that* problem.

"We can say I'm your brother," he countered, brushing a speck from his cuff. "They'll believe me. I'm a highly valued guest."

"Fine. I'll expect your conduct to be entirely becoming of a brother. Your name's Crouch, isn't it?" she said, remembering how the Old Victorian had addressed him.

"Arthur." He stood up, and offered an arm to link with her own, which she ignored.

"Pleased to meet you. Lead the way," she suggested.

They passed under the stone arch that served as the bar's entrance. On the other side was a walnut panelled room, lit by gilt chandeliers and sconces, with a carpet that put Nora in mind of scintillating scotoma: white wavy lines on a black background. Bottles of spirits were backlit across one wall, and the bar itself beamed light.

Most of the small round tables, with their pairs of deco tub chairs, were taken. She was busy scanning for Berenice when Arthur placed a cocktail menu in her hands. She glanced at it, and then looked again more closely. It was an attractive enough menu, of the sort you expected from these kinds of places; the cover was a Barbier illustration, or in his style, depicting with muted greens and blues a lady of the French court, taking a drink from a servant's tray.

Two pages listed the cocktails available. In addition to the standard Fizzes, Cobblers, Slings and Sours was the name that had caught her eye. *Hokey Pokey*. The menu didn't say what it contained. Her arms prickled with heat, as though afflicted with a sudden rash. *Hokey Pokey*. She saw, in her memory, light playing on furred, green leaves, pointed like spears. And blood on the earth beneath, black in the soil.

"What is this drink, please?" she asked Arthur, her finger on the line.

"I haven't the faintest idea – must be a new addition."

"Hokey Pokey means stinging nettles. It's what my mother used to call them."

He plucked the menu from her fingers. "I'll ask, shall I?"

When he'd gone, she saw Berenice on the far side of the room, standing with her coupe glass aloft, encircled by a clutch of adoring guests. They were all laughing uproariously. Berenice must be over her disturbance at dinner. Without looking away, Nora sat down in the nearest available spot. A few minutes passed, as Nora watched Berenice's mouth and imagined what she might be saying, her own lips moving in silent imitation. One of the devotees was more privileged than the rest: the fair young man recognisable to Nora as Carlo Merlini, the tenor who often partnered Berenice. Nora watched Berenice touch his collar, his wrist, and lean into his chest.

"You were right about the stinging nettles," Arthur said, suddenly present again. He placed a luminous green drink before her, in a glass that reminded her of a corseted woman, so extreme were its curves. "The barman was quite voluble; the cocktail is made with absinthe, and he explained at length how stinging nettle is one of the botanicals used in absinthe's production. Officially they produce it in Spain now but there are a few illicit distilleries dotted about France since the ban."

Nora tasted the cold green mixture. It was strong, and she liked the flavour, but she refrained from drinking it in a single draught. She needed to keep a clear head.

Arthur sat down, and drank from his own, clear, conical glass. A pickled onion, run through with a crystal lance, shone like a pearl at the base. "I did wonder if you'd live to regret your choice. We can exchange, if you like."

"No, thank you." She returned her attention to Berenice, and kept her eyes trained there.

"Absinthe is only a kind of brandy."

Nora didn't reply.

"Infused with herbs."

"Sing!" one of the guests near Berenice shouted, then begged again: "Sing!"

Nora could see Berenice shaking her head, that platinum bob swinging from side to side as she blushed, one curled hand coyly raised to her mouth. A performance of humility. She wouldn't refuse for long.

"You're quite taken with her, aren't you? With Miss Oxbow?" Arthur commented.

"I have no personal feelings about her either way. None whatsoever."

"No *personal* feelings?" he pressed. "Are there any other kind of feelings?"

Nora laughed. "Professional regard, perhaps? Respect between colleagues? The compassion of a medic, or a priest for his flock of sinners? Are those things personal?"

"I see. So you're Miss Oxbow's colleague – a fellow singer? – or her doctor, or her priest?"

"Not one of those, actually. Well, I am a doctor. But not her doctor."

"A lady doctor! No wonder you try to enter bars on your own."

"Yes. I'm *that sort*."

"General practice, or an infirmary?"

She hesitated. "Neither. Psychoanalysis."

"Good lord. What brought you here?" Arthur asked.

"I wanted a drink, Mr Crouch."

"I don't mean the bar. What brought you to the hotel?"

"I used to live in this part of the world," she said, which had the advantage of truth. When she was a very little girl, she'd lived in an English wood with a stream. This city was known for its smoke and soot but the woods were just beyond the boundary. The woods were never far away, in England. They were never far away, in Nora's head.

"I gathered you had some local connection, from that little snippet of slang for nettles." He smiled, but they both knew she had evaded his question. When she didn't provide any further information he drained his martini. "My apologies. It isn't my intention to be a pest. I'll be retiring now; perhaps I'll see you in the dining hall again before the end of your trip."

"Wait," she said, as he stood. His departure would be annoying. Berenice didn't show any sign of leaving yet, which meant Nora still needed Arthur as a chaperone. She would have to at least pretend to appreciate the company. Recollecting the droves of train passengers who had disembarked early, to shelter in Birmingham's hotels, she

20

added: "My mother's memorial is in Warwickshire. She died at this time of year. But the train terminated prematurely."

"That wasn't so hard, was it?" He returned to his seat. "You never mentioned your name."

"Dr Dickinson."

"Have you had to come far?"

"London," she said, wary. London was her most recent stopping point, after the long trip from Zurich. To steer him from further intrusiveness, she asked: "And you? What brings you here?"

"This is where I live – in the Regent."

"Oh! For how long?"

"Years. I'm practically a permanent fixture. I know the Regent down to the last square inch."

"That must be strange; to be here, constantly, with everyone else coming and going."

"I like the traffic. I like the assortment of humanity, how very mixed it is. People are willing to show themselves in a hotel because it's an in-between kind of place. Normality is suspended. One is repeatedly exposed to strange, even dubious, phenomena."

"Dubious? Who is dubious?" Nora kept her voice light. Remembering the spring beneath the hotel, and the superstition it might redeem you, she asked: "Do you mean those people looking for forgiveness?"

"Among others. There's something snivelling in their guilt," he said. "I prefer the travellers who are without remorse, who believe the only rules that matter are the ones they set. Particularly if they are honest about that fact. I don't like people who delude themselves."

Nora shifted in her chair, regaining her view of Berenice.

Carlo Merlini was no longer in attendance. If only Nora could hear the words she was saying. If only there were a seat closer to Berenice's table. Nora watched Berenice hold one hand up, palm outward, to silence the adorers in her immediate circle – to signal she would satisfy their plea and was about to sing.

With the first note, Nora jolted in her seat, the verdant liquid tipping from her glass to spatter her dress. The others in the bar jerked too, unsure in the initial seconds whether they heard a siren or an alarm before they realised it was a song. As the note expanded, their chests relaxed and they sank deeper into the velvet of their chairs. They listened, lips parted, without returning to their conversations.

Nora didn't know the song. It wasn't in the Italian one would expect from Berenice's repertoire, nor in the German that dominated the programme of the Zurich Opera House. The language was Russian, which Nora could recognise but not understand. It made no difference that it wasn't in her native tongue; did a gramophone record have a native tongue? For the rest of Nora's life she'd be able to sing it as Berenice did without ever knowing what it meant. The song swelled into the air above them and everyone present breathed it in. Nora believed Berenice was staring directly at her. How strange, that Berenice's hair should be so light – a sheath of platinum armour reflecting every electric ray that lit the room – and yet her eyes were so black. Depthless. Nora kept watching Berenice's eyes. They grew like ink drops on a marbled page. They grew, and they grew, until there was nothing else of the room left. Nora was swallowed by them. She floated through their expanse. Inside the blackness was not empty, as Nora had thought. She saw a wreath of nettles twisting in the darkness, drawing closer until Nora thought they would rest upon her head like a crown – but she sailed through the wreath like an acrobat through a circus hoop.

The song stopped. Nora was in the bar again, wearing a stained dress with a head starting to hurt from the lights. Berenice looked around at the hotel guests, her expression almost girlish, shyly hoping for approval. The audience recovered from its silence and began to clap, except Nora, who hated Berenice, in a hungry kind of way. She placed the half full glass back upon the table and licked her fingers clean of absinthe. *Like a child*, she thought, *sucking an open cut.*

"Quite a performance," commented Arthur Crouch.

Was he still there? Everything inessential had melted away over the past few minutes. How disappointing to feel it return. How disappointing to see Arthur Crouch had never gone away: solid, generic Arthur Crouch, with his tireless dispensing of information about brandy or the hotel's water system. Nora asked: "Don't you like opera?"

"I don't mind a good show. The hotel's own salon quintet is rather fine. Run by a young Italian violinist. And there are plenty of other good musicians in this city. There's one chap does the piano for the Elite Picture House – he's good enough for any symphony orchestra." Arthur rubbed his forehead with his thumb. "I don't know. Miss Oxbow sings well enough. Perhaps it's that spiritualism business our dinner companion mentioned."

"You don't believe she's a seer."

"Of course not. Do you?"

"No. There are analysts – like Jung – who say precognition is a very real phenomenon." She stared into the green shallows of her cocktail glass, considering her encounters with Jung's wife and protégées. "But I don't think he'd like Miss Oxbow very much. She hoodwinks people."

"Is she intelligent enough to hoodwink people? I think she's hoodwinking herself. She's too enamoured of her own mystique. And everyone here colludes…"

He waved vaguely at the other guests, who had returned to their drinking gayer, and more excitable, after Berenice's singing. The room was notably louder than it had been when they arrived. The huddle round Berenice was thicker too, granting Nora only snapshots of her quarry. Nora speculated whether Arthur Crouch was criticising Berenice as a way to curry her own favour, having realised her antipathy for the singer. His strategy was futile. If Leo were here, he could tell Arthur that the fastest way to secure Nora's interest would be to fall in love with Berenice; to think of no one else; to measure every other woman against her, and want them to the degree they matched.

Yet Arthur's criticisms were correct. Berenice thrived on the collusion of others in her spiritualism. Could Nora lower herself to collude? If Nora presented herself as a believer, Berenice would preen. Nora could try to befriend Berenice; that might make it easier to finagle a confession, or at least be present when Berenice let slip some clue of her infidelity. Such a strategy would take time. Perhaps Nora could engineer an urgent situation to hasten Berenice's dependence on her. Fortunately, from Berenice's psychoanalysis with Leo, Nora knew which situations would constitute an emergency for the singer.

That very minute Berenice was breaking away from her companions, in a flurry of kissed cheeks and called goodbyes. Nora twitched inside.

"You know, I think that drink was too strong for me after all," Nora said, newly grateful for spilling so much. "You must think me fickle, to keep you here then leave this soon, but I really think I should be going."

"Oh, I won't take offence; on one condition."

"What might that be?"

"You'll come back tomorrow?"

She nodded as she stood. Berenice was halfway to the door.

"Assuming your train's still delayed," Arthur Crouch prompted.

Nora wasn't sure whether she imagined that his tone was meaningful – that she was a poor liar, it not coming naturally to her, and he had seen through her falsehoods.

"Assuming I'm still here," she agreed.

Nora kept pace with Berenice, all the way into the lift which was full enough for Nora to be merely one nameless stranger amongst many. But then guests trickled out floor by floor, until only Nora, Berenice and the liftman remained. They reached the top. The Icon exited first; she tripped on the threshold. People had been buying cocktails for her, too. This was all to the good. Alcohol would lower the woman's guard. She righted herself and walked on. Nora stepped out and the lift doors closed behind her.

They were now in the grandest quarters of the hotel. Nora swiftly turned up her sleeves, so that anyone could tell, with a glance, no tattoo was visible upon her. She saw Berenice reach a smooth, pink door. Up here, the richest guests reserved suites rather than the single, by no means humble, bedrooms of the type Nora was staying in. There were no room numbers. Instead each suite was marked with a different fruit; in Berenice's case, a pineapple.

Nora called out: "Miss Oxbow?"

Berenice looked back, her hand raised with a key in her grip; her expression was blandly appeasing in the usual manner of someone fielding attention from a stranger. "Hm? Yes?"

"Miss Oxbow," Nora said again, to give herself chance to draw level. At a conversational distance, she said: "I wondered if we might talk."

"Oh angel." Berenice smiled sweetly, her hand still aloft. The key was large and brassy; one end was wrought into a miniature version of the pineapple upon the door. "I'm tired as heck. Is it an autograph you want?"

Nora should lead with flattery.

"Yes, of course I'd love an autograph – but – I also have something to discuss with you."

"Is that right? I hate to disappoint you, but I have to be bright eyed and bushy tailed for my performance tomorrow. We can catch up at the theatre door. Bring your autograph book." She returned her attention to the lock.

"Miss Oxbow, the matter isn't suited to the theatre door. It's rather more grave than that."

The door swung open. Berenice looked at Nora with a hint of condescension. "Sorry! I don't tell fortunes."

"That's not what I want. Might I have just a quarter of an hour, to speak privately?"

Faced with Nora's persistence, Berenice frowned and gestured to the empty corridor. "You've got privacy, angel. There's nobody here but us chickens. What do you want?"

"To discuss your health. Miss Oxbow—"

"My health? I've never even met you!"

Nora must offer more to obtain entry.

"I'm a doctor. When you were singing in the Narcissus I noticed something." Knowing how much Berenice feared the loss of her voice, Nora raised a hand to her own throat. "You have a lump."

Berenice blanched. Silently she felt the corresponding patch of her neck, her fingers pushing at a very ordinary gland. In a more subdued tone, she asked: "How do I know you're a real doctor?"

"You don't," Nora said. Taking a gamble, she added: "You can ask for the hotel physician if you prefer. I'm sure, if he isn't resident, the manager will do his utmost to arrange an appointment once the snow's cleared."

"You really think I need to worry?"

"A short physical exam will give you more information." So far, Nora had said nothing she considered to be false.

Conflicted, Berenice glanced through the open door into her apartment. She looked back at Nora. Did her gaze flicker towards Nora's arm? Nora thought it did. Good. Berenice would see there was no tattoo.

"A quarter of an hour, you say?" Berenice asked.

"Yes."

"All right. My schedule's a harsh mistress and I've *got* to perform tomorrow."

Nora followed her into a drawing room with a circular

recessed floor at its centre. Miniature lamps on every table cast a gentle light. She noted the deep pink carpet, the low-backed, curving sofa, the shining curtains that fell from ceiling to skirting board. Berenice kicked her shoes off. From the drinks alcove, she poured herself a glass of crème de menthe, and knocked it back in one gulp. For nerves, probably.

"Might I have one of the stirrers?" Nora asked. She glanced about for any sign of prior visitors. Male visitors, specifically, though she was unsure what such evidence would consist of; an abandoned jacket, perhaps. "My medical bag's in my room, but I can use a stirrer to depress your tongue."

Berenice picked one from a silver tumbler. "Where do you want me?"

A man might be quietly concealed in one of the other rooms. As a pretext for seeing the rest of the suite, Nora improvised: "I need the brightest available light. I assume that will be the bathroom?"

Berenice led Nora down a wastefully wide hallway, lined with bouquets of orchids. They reached a bedroom, papered with an embossed, geometric pattern of midnight blue. No man awaited. Regrettably Nora had no time to look more closely at Berenice's sleeping quarters; they immediately passed into the adjoining bathroom.

Nora gestured that Berenice should sit on the edge of the tub, and placed the stirrer on the shelf above the basin, beside the toiletries. She hoped in vain for a man's razor; a shaving brush; a bottle of cologne.

She stood before the Icon. This was the closest they had ever been to each other. Berenice upturned her face. Her left eyebrow had a single fair hair which refused to rest in line with the others. Her skin was downy and poreless. Where her burgundy lipstick had worn away, Nora saw the pale pink lip beneath.

Nora placed the pads of her fingers below Berenice's chin. How soft the Icon's skin was; could Nora's ever be so soft? She stored the sensation as she stored everything about Berenice. Nora felt beneath Berenice's jawline, as she'd learnt to do long ago – earlier than medical school; at the knee of her father, for he'd also been a doctor.

"Are you expecting company?" Nora hoped the question passed for polite conversation as she walked her fingertips back towards Berenice's ears then down the neck.

"At this hour? You must think I'm an incorrigible sinner," Berenice said flirtatiously, albeit with an undercurrent of apprehension. "I told you I'm going to bed. My husband's in another country."

"Open your mouth," Nora instructed, letting her hands drop.

Berenice did so, closing her eyes simultaneously. Her mouth was clean as a cat's. Nora grabbed the stirrer and placed it on Berenice's tongue. Everything looked perfectly healthy, just as Nora anticipated. She firmly jabbed the back of Berenice's throat, pulling the stirrer back out again just as Berenice began to gag. The Icon pushed Nora out of the way, her eyes streaming as she coughed, to turn on the cold tap.

"There there," Nora said softly. "All done."

She wasn't sure the Icon heard. Quietly, Nora stepped back into the bedroom. As she waited for the coughs to cease, her eyes darted for signs of masculine company, and found none. A single crystal tumbler stood empty on the dressing table, suggesting Berenice had been drinking alone earlier that night; a gown lay in a silken pool by the closet door, but if there were any items of men's clothing in the room, they must have been safely stowed. No love letters were discarded in view. No photo but Leo's was displayed, in its small travel frame, at the bedside. In fact Berenice appeared to be playing the part of devoted wife rather well. The running water stopped. Berenice muttered something in Russian before emerging from the bathroom.

She sat on the edge of the bed and sank backwards into the blankets.

"Everything's spinning. Did you finish the examination? Do you need to check anything else?"

"No, that'll be all. I'm happy to say the lump isn't serious," Nora said. "You have an inflamed lymph node, which suggests you may have fought off a cold or another trivial infection."

"Hallelujah," Berenice said with relief. "You were none too gentle back there. What do I owe you?"

This was an opportunity for collusion. "Half a crown – unless—"

"What?"

"Do you really never tell fortunes?"

"Oh!" Berenice laughed. "I've still got one eye on the clock, baby, and your time is up. Maybe later in the week. I *knew* you were a devotee."

"Well, I heard you at dinner." Quoting the Old Victorian, she said: "You're someone who has seen things beyond our understanding... I know the sound of the otherworld when I hear it."

"That's sweet." Berenice sighed, then giggled, as she sat up. The back of her hair was mussed into peaks like a duck's tail. She reached for a fat ceramic bear on the bedside cabinet.

With no remaining rooms to search, Nora felt suddenly flat at the lack of evidence. For the first time since her departure from Zurich she let a worm of doubt enter her mind. Leo had confided his suspicions about Berenice's loyalty, and Nora had her own reasons for seizing upon those doubts as truth. But was it plausible that Berenice – with all her passion for scandal and limelight – would conduct an affair *discreetly*?

Berenice removed the bear's head and withdrew half a crown, which she offered to Nora. "You never told me your name, you know."

Nora thought, once more, how they had this in common: the use of pseudonyms. Berenice understood the slipperiness of naming. She was Вераніка on her documents. She was Vieranika, or Weronika, or Berenike, depending on the territory, because she had been much harmonised. She was once Nika, to her dead father; Vroni to her friends in Zurich; Véro to her husband. Oxbow was simpler for American tongues than Luckiewicz, or Luchesk, or any of the other English transliterations of her true last name. Nora wondered which of those names felt most true to Berenice. For here, in this hotel near the woods where her mother was born and died, Nora didn't feel like a Čapek. Her mother's maiden name felt most right. So she claimed it again, as she had with the receptionist, and with Crouch.

She said, feeling the name was faithful and true: "I'm Dr Dickinson."

"It's lovely to meet you, Dr Dickinson, but I really need you to skedaddle."

Berenice rose unsteadily from the bed, and walked Nora back through the apartment.

3

In the ground floor lobby, Nora passed by the waiting room chairs and front desk to the row of silence cabinets positioned in the far right corner. They were nearly all occupied. She stepped inside the sole empty kiosk. It was narrow, with a telephone book suspended from an s-shaped wooden holder on the wall. A page had loosened from the centre, listing local companies in the middle of the alphabet. *The Pacific Steam Navigation Company, 86 Colmore Row. 8340 Central. Parker Iron and Steel Merchants, 39 Corporation Street. 1869 Central. Parkes and Son, 16 and 18 Cherry Street. 6210 Central. Patent Borax Company Limited, Ladywood. 3572 Central. Payton, Pepper and Sons, 3, 4 and 5 Vyse Street. 7 Jewellers.*

Nora spoke to the operator; Leo would be expecting her call. As she waited, her eyes settled on the next cabinet. Carlo Merlini was deep in a telephone conversation of his own. Their gaze met through the glass, and Nora looked swiftly away.

"Well?" Leo greeted her. The line was dreadful. She could barely hear him.

"Nothing yet," she said as loudly as she could.

He didn't answer, she guessed from a combination of impatience and irritation.

"It's only the first night," she pointed out.

"I know."

What would she do if the evidence he was anticipating never materialised? So ready was he to believe, she could invent whatever she liked to discredit Berenice. Couldn't she describe a parade of lovers, as luridly as she wished, each of them brazenly encouraged by Leo's depraved wife? Nora realised how easy she found it to imagine a train of people in love with Berenice.

But Nora wasn't a liar.

"I'll be watching her all the time," Nora reassured him.

"And listening?"

"Always."

"Tell me what you've heard?"

She let her eyes meet Carlo Merlini's again.

"*Angel.*" Nora spoke with Berenice's voice, her lips moved as Berenice's moved. "*There's nobody here but us...*"

Far, far away, she heard Leo say: "I've missed you, being her."

She had missed being her too, with the validation of an audience. Alone in her room wasn't enough. Should she believe Leo missed her mimicry when he had the real thing? He was paying her to spy, but he must realise that, more than the money, Nora wanted to hear she was indistinguishable from the Icon. *I've missed you, being her.* It was a victory to hear him say it. It made her want to cry. She counted the buttons on Merlini's waistcoat to stop herself. He had his key in his slim waistcoat pocket. A brassy key, the top just peeking over the seam.

She could see it was wrought into the shape of a pineapple.

Straightening, Nora said: "Leo – I think there's something I need to ch—"

The line went dead.

She assumed they were cut off through the vagaries of long distance calls. But Merlini was looking bemused at his own telephone, speechless. People were stepping out from the other kiosks. Nora pulled back her cabinet door, and walked to the reception desk to report the difficulty. Harvey was attempting, and failing, to reach the operator on the desk phone.

From his office to the side, Quarrington, the manager, approached the desk.

"All down at once?" Nora asked him.

"So it seems!" His hands were clasped apologetically. "A temporary problem, I'm sure."

"The snow?"

"Very likely."

From the corner of her eye, Nora saw Merlini ascending the grand staircase.

"We'll establish how much of the area is affected," the manager was telling her. "It may still be possible to send telegrams from the post office. If you have urgent communications, instruct our usual telegraphist and she will check—"

"Thank you," Nora cut in, with a small nod of thanks.

She strode to the stairs. Merlini had passed out of view. If she had interpreted his possession of the key correctly, rather than alighting at the first floor he would have kept going on to the next flight. So much for respectability and chaperoning. Quarrington or Harvey must have sanctioned the extra key to Berenice's suite; a famous opera singer wouldn't have to toe the same line as their other guests.

Hoping to close the gap, Nora picked up speed. By the time she'd gained on Merlini, on the third flight, she was flushed but trying to maintain an outward impression of composure.

She watched him turn a corner, towards the hotel suites where Nora had already followed a guest that evening. By now she was feeling quite the old hand at spying. Nora lingered at the edge of the wall, peeping round as Merlini audibly shoved a key into a smooth, pale pink door. It swung open before he had successfully turned the key.

Berenice stood in the doorway.

"You're very late," Berenice told Merlini, and pouted. Her Russian accent was stronger with drink.

"La lontananza è come il vento. And it's a taste of your own medicine."

She tutted, leaning against the jamb. "I had company anyway. It was good you weren't on time."

"Company? Who?"

"A lady come to venerate! My audience, they love me."

So Merlini wasn't someone Berenice would tell about a doctor's visit. Still, he pulled her waist towards his, his hand on the small of her back. Nora watched them kiss. Then they went in, and the door was closed.

Nora exhaled. Leo had guessed right; his wife was faithless. Now Nora could tell him so, and name the culprit into the bargain. An unaccustomed sensation engulfed her:

glee. She hadn't been happy for months. She hadn't been happy since Leo got married. A smile spread, slowly, across her face.

Nora worded a telegram for Leo, succinctly confirming Berenice's infidelity and partner in crime, which was left with a telegraphist for despatch. There was nothing left to keep Nora there now, but on enquiry at reception, the snow was still preventing all trains from leaving the city. Five days remained until Nora's scheduled voyage home, weather conditions permitting. She was not disappointed. What was it Leo had said? *I've missed you, being her.* He didn't miss Berenice – how could he, guessing at her treachery? He didn't miss Nora – he didn't love her, nor she him. But he missed Nora being Berenice and it was this she thrived upon. So she should take the opportunity to watch, and imitate, the true Icon, to perform the role better in Zurich. For now she returned to her own rooms. She diligently recited Berenice's speech of the evening; beginning with the Russian song, which Nora mimicked perfectly with no understanding of the meaning. With that done, she repeated every line of English Berenice had spoken under Nora's surveillance.

"My audience." Nora pouted between the last words. "They love me!"

She readied herself for bed. She drew the curtains only for the time it took her to change into her night things and extinguish the lights, for she disliked sleeping in a stuffy room. The snow was falling now in earnest, which was all that prevented her from also opening the windows for the fresh air. The embers in the fireplace were dying as her head touched the pillow. No sooner had she drawn the blanket over her than she fell asleep. The rest of the hotel teemed without her. Both the lounge and the bar remained busy. The dining hall was open till midnight, serving supper, and was often more crowded in these final hours than at dinner; the kitchen likewise was hot and bright with activity. The chef de cuisine concerned himself with the quality of the goods and the discipline of the kitchen: he instructed the soup cook, the glacier, the fish cook, the sous chef, the sauce cook – and they instructed their assistants. The menu that night was consommé Alexandra, filet sole Cléopâtre, contre filet de boeuf, petit pois au beurre, céleri au jus and pouding saxon. Midnight came. The commis cleared the tables of the evening's debris, and guests one by one made their way to their suites. The bar, and the lounge, fell silent. Of those workers who retreated to bed, some drank nightcaps in the privacy of their rooms, and one took a delicate morphine syringe from a locked drawer. The night staff continued working with quiet industry, but for the next few hours, the hotel's atmosphere would settle into dormancy.

Nora never dreamed; not once in her life had she recalled a dream on waking. This was a conundrum for a psychoanalyst, who spent much time contemplating the content of other people's dreams, yet had only the dimmest understanding of what they may be like to experience. She speculated sometimes that the dreaming process was a means of expelling extraneous matter from the mind. Her impressions throughout the day were never reworked into dream symbolism, and she often wondered if this was because she needed them, to mimic as well as she did. For she reimagined little that passed through her senses; she observed, recorded and relayed exactly what she heard.

When she woke, she felt a weight upon her feet, and dazedly believed herself to be at her great aunt's house, fifteen years before, with that old dowager's dog asleep over the covers. She recollected her true surroundings then her breath caught as she made out the silhouette of a beast curled at the end of the bed. Something black, or dark brown, the heat of his stomach radiating through the blankets to where her feet were crushed. Yes. A dog, though not her aunt's.

Nora saw through the window that the snow was still falling heavily and it was half past three by the cathedral clock. She wriggled her feet from under the dog, cautious of provoking him. He was watching her. Tentatively she stroked his head and he submitted to being petted. He seemed an amiable fellow.

But how did he get in?

She glanced at the door; the key was no longer in the lock, where she had turned it the night before. It lay on the ground. Odd.

She lay on her stomach and slowly, very slowly, let her head hang over the side of the mattress to see what lurked beneath the bed. Nothing beside her trunk. She resumed breathing. However the dog got in, he was apparently the only other occupant of the room.

Shuddering elaborately from the cold, she got out of bed. She changed from her nightdress into the first pair of trousers and blouse to hand in the wardrobe, the wooden hangers clattering. Then she laced her boots.

"Come on," she said to the dog, with a pat. "Off!"

He settled deeper into the blankets. She tugged him gently from the scruff of his neck, but he refused to budge. And he really was of phenomenal size. That would just have to be the housekeeper's problem.

She stole into the corridor, shutting and locking the door behind her again. Then she leant against the door for a moment. Across the hallway, in 426, a guest had a painful coughing fit. But it was otherwise quiet enough to think.

The mystery to be solved, with a cool head, was how the dog had entered. He was too large to have concealed himself in the room before her arrival, only to re-emerge when she fell quiet in sleep; the only possible hiding place had been under the bed, and she would have seen him there when she stowed the trunk away.

So someone with their own key had let him in afterwards. The maids could enter, of course. But this was the difficulty with hotels. They implied privacy, and retreat, while any number of strangers could invade your sleeping quarters. Yes, a maid or, worse, a porter had silently entered and let this dog in. Nora could not fathom their intent.

Around the corner, Nora found the rooms of the floor housekeeper and knocked lightly for attention. The woman who answered was the same housekeeper who'd taken her reservation: Harvey. Nora quickly explained the difficulty, and Harvey frowned in concern. The housekeeper appeared fluish – a sheen glistened on her skin and her eyes were watery – but she reacted promptly.

"A dog? In your room?" She unhooked her own keys from the wall, in readiness to follow Nora back.

"Maybe it's a prank," Nora said. "But I'm sure you see

why it would be alarming, to be intruded upon while I slept."

"You were quite right to alert me, Dr Dickinson."

They returned. Harvey entered Nora's bedroom, and lit the gas lamp. Nora hovered in the doorway, as Harvey looked to and fro. The dog was nowhere to be seen. The housekeeper checked under the bed and in the wardrobe.

"I don't understand," Nora muttered. "I locked the door behind me."

"It sounds very distressing, Dr Dickinson – perhaps you misunderstood? A pile of blankets, in the dark – maybe you were still waking up?"

"No," said Nora definitely. "I wasn't dreaming it, or making a mistake. A dog appeared in my room. And now he's gone."

"I'll alert Mr Quarrington. Rest assured we will get to the bottom of the mystery. In the meantime, I can arrange for you to stay in a different room, if that would put your mind at ease."

Did it matter which room she was in? Whoever had access to this one presumably had access to the others.

"I won't get back to sleep again now," she said. "Is the lounge open? I would rather just wait there until the problem is resolved."

"You may sit in the lounge, of course – but refreshments are not available at this hour."

"I'm not hungry. A comfortable place to sit will suffice."

They parted – Harvey in search of Mr Quarrington, and Nora to the lounge, where at least a fire was lit. She sat in the nearest armchair. She had the room quite to herself, and was somewhat sorry for that. It seemed that, whenever she was by herself, the hotel liked to trick her: she thought of chasing Berenice the preceding evening, down passageways that sought to rearrange themselves, or so it felt. Now her bedroom had contorted, while she wasn't looking, to admit a strange animal, and whoever owned him. Her thoughts turned to Arthur Crouch. He said he knew every inch of the hotel. Reluctantly she realised talking to him again might be helpful. If he lived here, he would surely have heard tell of unwelcome guests making appearances in the bedroom, four-legged or otherwise. She would honour her promise to see him in the bar that evening.

Snow was piling at the bottom of the window ledges, white and soft as a cat's belly. Nora leant back against the easy chair, settling in for a period of reflection and watching the blizzard. She spent a considerable time thinking back over her observations of Berenice, a topic which, though aggravating, could never be said to bore Nora. The sky was just beginning to lighten – by Nora's reckoning that meant it was half past six or so – when Harvey came to speak to her. Through the open door of the lounge, Nora glimpsed the young girls with mops and brooms, cleaning the reception floor. Every one of them wore a brown apron. They swept back and forth in time with each other, putting Nora in mind of a stage number where they might leap into a dance at any moment. However, the door swung shut behind the housekeeper, putting the cleaners out of view again.

"Dr Dickinson," Harvey began, "we have searched the property, and are quite certain that there is no dog on the premises. I cannot account for the dog you saw. You have our sincerest apologies; we can, if you wish, still arrange for you to move to another room. Needless to say there will be no additional charge and I believe you will find the new room to your satisfaction."

Nora was *not* satisfied. It was clear that the hotel, having conducted minimal investigations, meant to imply she had confabulated the tale of the dog; or else they knew entirely how the dog came to be in her room and were concealing their fault in the matter. How would a new room help? It would be no more secure against the entry of the hotel's own staff.

"I'll make arrangements to stay at another hotel," Nora decided.

Harvey closed her eyes with a shake of the head. "They are all quite full, Dr Dickinson. Stranded travellers – the snow."

Of course Harvey had an incentive to keep Nora there, but in this detail she was convincing. Indignation had led Nora to forget she wasn't the only stranger confined to the city. So for now Nora's options were limited. What could she do? If she were stuck here, she would have to push the dressing table against the door before bed, as a barrier against intruders.

"Very well," Nora said tightly. "I'll stay and ensure myself that the room is secure."

Harvey inclined her head, indicating they had brought the matter to a close, and turned back, crossing paths with the Old Victorian.

"Good morning," the elderly woman said.

"Good morning to you, Mrs Reid," said Harvey. "What are your plans for today?"

"Ghost hunting in the cathedral! I mean to familiarise myself with *all* the local restless dead…"

43

Nora ignored the rest of Mrs Reid's prattle. Eventually the old woman let the housekeeper leave and seated herself at the grand piano, in the corner of the room, and commenced playing something comic and dated and once-popular; Gilbert and Sullivan, if Nora had to guess. Nora felt it was too early in the day for such music. But she voiced no complaint, feeling suddenly wearied by the dispute over the dog. It would not be long till the kitchen was serving. She should show some mettle and return to the bedroom, if only to dress more appropriately for breakfast.

It turned out to be a morning of inconveniences for everyone. The newspapers had not arrived, due to the severe weather; and nor had the coal van. Nobody would be leaving the city today, though the Regent was at least fortunate that the majority of staff lived within walking distance. Breakfast was busy – but Nora was acutely conscious of Berenice's absence. The singer also failed to materialise in any of the public rooms that Nora visited in a repeated circuit. By noon, she suspected Berenice of idleness, and pictured her at rest in her midnight blue bed, with one elegant arm above her head. Or perhaps she continued to be ravished by Carlo. It was only quite by chance that Nora, passing through the foyer, saw Berenice at the reception desk, coated in mink and a chic powder blue hat. Berenice nodded in greeting.

"I was meant to perform this evening – and due for rehearsal an hour ago. They know what a lollygagger I am... But the entire night's been cancelled. The Theatre Royal sent a gopher when I was about to step outside."

"An unexpected holiday, then." So much, Nora thought, for Berenice's ability to see the future.

"I hate to disappoint my audience. It's ridiculous that the city should come to a halt just because of a few snowflakes – I remember snowfalls a million times worse, when I was a child, and no one stopped singing!"

"You could always perform here. The guests would be delighted – think of how happy they were in the bar," Nora said sardonically. If Berenice noticed the tone she pretended otherwise.

"Oh, you enjoyed that, didn't you? You're a doll to say. But I won't be performing anywhere, if the theatre's closed for business. The date's cursed now. I'll go bathe all afternoon instead!" She beamed with the air of one making the best of things. To the manager, she said: "Quarrington, be an angel and arrange dinner for my room?"

Nora returned to her own room, where she checked in the wardrobe, beneath the bed and in the bathroom for evidence of unwanted companions, then propped a chair under the handle of the door. It wouldn't stop a determined intruder but it was adequate for now to ensure she was alone. She recited her most recent conversation with Berenice as she completed these checks.

Fully clothed, Nora lay on the bed, stared at the ceiling, and projected back into those long afternoons in Zurich, in Leo's apartment. For a year Nora had heard every word Berenice said to Leo. He'd made sure of that. Now she could rifle through those mental transcripts at leisure. Detail by detail flittered through Nora's mind. Berenice's love of *The Magic Flute*; her fear of rats; her dreadful literacy; an insecurity that her left eye was lazy, which no one else ever noticed but sometimes took on an obsessive quality for her. Nora remembered the day to day rhythms of Berenice's childhood before the Revolution; the pleasure she took from keeping people waiting; her professed belief in reincarnation, the cyclicality of all life, and occult knowledge of the future; her confession, soon denied, that her visions were a lie.

In the past day, Nora had benefited from only three hours' sleep. The ceiling above her was painted pale green and a crack zigzagged from the light fitting to the corner of the room. She watched a small spider emerge from the gap. Not a big enough gap for a dog, she reflected; but it confirmed there were ways into this room she hadn't previously noticed. For now, she closed her eyes. Her breathing was slow and deep. She slept.

4

Carlo Merlini checked he was alone in the corridor before letting himself into Berenice's suite. He found her in the bedroom, where she was sitting criss-cross on the floor, knees rosy beneath a sleeveless peignoir which barely concealed anything at all. Her hair was damp and the tendrils curled round her face. She clutched a tattered piece of paper covered in dense writing – a dozen more pages were strewn over the carpet – and she squinted at the words, stiltedly speaking each letter. The poor girl was a bad reader, in English at any rate, to a degree you'd never guess from how she spoke the language. She'd never mastered the Roman alphabet.

"Vroni?" he greeted her.

She jerked her head in response and returned to her papers. He removed his shoes to sit beside her, coaxing: "Vroni. Vroni. You'll ruin those pretty eyes."

"Hush, why don't you. I'm trying to read."

Merlini picked up the nearest page; the hand looked French, though the words were English. They seemed to be doctor's notes, as they contained numerous references to a *patient*.

"So much of it I can't make out," Berenice said.

He'd hoped for a keener welcome. The let-down of a cancelled performance made him fractious and in need of distraction. He was wound too tightly. Sighing, he said: "Leave the reading alone, Berenice. It's not what you're made for."

She slapped him, and he caught her wrist. His cheek throbbed. Her jaw was set and her eyes bright, unrepentant.

"What am I made for?" she challenged. "As if I didn't know your opinion."

She wasn't being fair. He didn't want her for her brain. But she commanded audiences with beauty and horror and a voice made by God. Did she want brains too? He thought himself romantic; he believed his lust was driven as much by the exhilaration of their performing together as her youth.

She jerked her wrist from his grasp. She picked up another page and said: "Tell me what this says, please."

He accepted the page she passed him. *Patient MCCLX is preoccupied with supernatural delusions*, Merlini read to himself. *She claims to believe in monstrous predators, called hyrings, that feast on human flesh. A hyring can look like any one of us, though it may also impersonate an animal. In its true form, it is a brute on all fours, with hooves and sharp teeth. It eats for enjoyment, not sustenance.* He struggled to make out the next bit – *it uuuics its prey to escape? it nunucs its prey to escape?* The word was too badly formed to understand, so Merlini skipped forward. *Hyrings can enter a mirror on the far side of the world, and arrive through any mirror in your own quarters. The patient believes even a mirror the size of your palm is sufficient and insists all mirrors be covered. With advancing maturity the hyring becomes bound to their lair and struggles to leave by ordinary means, increasing their reliance on mirrors. The bond compels their return to the lair within minutes to hours, though this is ample time in which to kill.* Merlini skimmed negative comments about the patient's state of mind.

"I'm waiting," Berenice prompted.

Merlini was loath to say the notes described supernatural matters; that might initiate one of Berenice's visions, and frustratingly, though her allure was often heightened during such episodes, she tended to be so enervated afterwards he might as well go back to his room. He said only: "They're doctor's notes, from a mad house."

"I guessed *that* much – I took them from the files in Leo's study."

"Why, Vroni?"

She shrugged. "I think he's fucking one of the women he treats. If you could just tell me what it says – maybe I can work out—"

"Why d'you care what that coglione does?" Merlini interrupted.

"Merl, don't pretend you're jealous of my husband. You and I would never be married."

True, but the match was a mystery to him.

"You could be married to a prince or a movie idol," he pointed out. "Not a doctor in an ugly city for little businessmen."

"You don't get it." She was vehement. "Doctors take a knife to you, Merl. They look down your ear or throat and you let them close because you need the help and the whole time you're holding your breath because anyone that close has the power to hurt. And afterwards it's like a secret – no one else has seen those parts. *You* haven't seen those parts of me. Leo took something that was hiding in my brain and he laid it all out in front of me. Like, like he'd hooked the innards of a fish and pulled them out. Oh, I married him all right. I'm not losing sight of anyone who knows me like that."

She was growing agitated. Merlini had erred; it wouldn't take much more to tip her into the unwanted vision.

"Just help me out here," Berenice said. "This patient, in the notes, is she a woman?"

"No." Merlini folded the piece of paper in half. "A man."

"Oh," she said, deflated, and he felt a little guilty, though not guilty enough to reveal the lie.

"A poor man..." he teased. From habit he tucked the paper in his pocket, as if it were a ten shilling note or his handkerchief, and Berenice, picking at the wool of the carpet, did not notice. "Driven mad by a beautiful singer... she made him be her secretary... he went insane with yearning..."

"You're the coglione," she retorted, but any suggestion she was worshipped made her smile, no matter how sly she thought the sweet talk. Merlini had regained her approval. He pushed the useless peignoir from her shoulders. He grabbed her breast. She let him bury his face in her neck; she smelt of jasmine.

5

Nora slept so long she missed dinner. She woke in the dark, alone thankfully – she shot a grateful glance at the chair by the door – and was rather cold. Recollecting her promise to meet Arthur Crouch, she rose and changed her outfit. Not the yellow gown this time, which was regretfully still stained with Hokey Pokey. She chose a cornflower blue dress, with a fringe that brushed her knees.

Crouch was waiting, in exactly the spot outside the bar he had occupied last night. For her, she assumed, though they had never specified a time.

Along similar lines, he said: "I was beginning to wonder if I'd been jilted."

"I came for the absinthe," she said. "Not the company."

With respect to the tricky balance men expected of women – you must be available, but just available enough, not so available they might think you were anybody's – Nora felt her mild insult was appropriate, even when she must keep on his good side to get the information she wanted. He appeared to agree her spirited comment was permissible, because he offered his arm, as he had the night before.

This time she accepted it. That was part of maintaining the balance too.

The bar was not quite as busy this evening; Berenice was nowhere to be seen, which may have contributed to the more subdued atmosphere in Nora's eyes.

"I noted your absence from dinner," Arthur said, once he had bought their drinks.

"Didn't you have company – your widow friend?" Nora asked brightly.

"Mrs Reid? I met her mere minutes before your arrival yesterday. Although she did manage to cram in a lifetime's acquaintance. She's travelling with a niece who sickened with bronchitis as the weather worsened and hasn't left her room for the duration of their stay. Mrs Reid felt at a loose end. But as it happens, this evening she didn't attend dinner, either – perhaps her nursing skills were required."

Nora recalled the coughing from the opposite bedroom the previous night. She and the Old Victorian were closer neighbours than she'd realised.

"You might just have missed her in the crowd. Easy enough here," said Nora, who divided the guests into *Berenice* and an undifferentiated mass who were *not Berenice*.

"No. She wasn't at dinner." Arthur was firm. "It's difficult to hide from me."

"That's useful," Nora said, "because I require your insights. Does anyone on the premises own a dog?"

His jaw tightened, and he paused longer than a simple question warranted. "The cinema king's wife has half a dozen Pomeranians. Dreadful things. Reddish fur, like a set of foxes who've been prinked at a beauty parlour. They rather snarl at me when they pass. Wife and dogs both."

"You don't like dogs?"

"They don't like me."

"Pomeranians are the small, yappy sort, aren't they? I was thinking of something considerably larger – owned by a member of staff, rather than a guest."

Arthur's brow lined. "What prompted your interest?"

She explained her disturbed night. He did not suggest she might be mistaken, as Harvey had implied. In fact, he did not seem at all surprised that a hotel worker might invade her room, which was at once vindicating and alarming.

"Most of the people who work here don't have accommodation which would permit a dog." He paused; half a dozen young men and women, tipsy in voice though not disputatiously so, sidled past them to the next table. "The vast majority board in the surrounding streets. But there is one chap, name of Westall. An under-manager who lives in, with the privileges to match. He adopted a stray from the streets – it was always coming to the kitchen doors here, for scraps. It's an undoubted mongrel with some German Shepherd in the mix, by my reckoning. Certainly larger than a Pomeranian. Larger than most dogs."

"With a dark coat?" Nora pressed.

"Yes."

"And this Westall – is he a prankster?"

"No, absolutely not, he's rather quiet and serious. But you don't strike me as a naive woman. Forget pranks – he might have a darker intent for invading your room. Let's say he brought the dog to intimidate you, or to keep watch. Then something interrupted him and he got out so fast he left the dog behind. When you fetched the housekeeper, were you gone long enough for him to retrieve the dog?"

"Technically," Nora said. "But I'd think a dog was more of a hindrance than a help for that particular crime. Especially if he's the only worker who owns one – surely he would be making himself easier to identify?"

"Depends how credible he thinks you are, I suppose." Nora tensed at that comment – it touched a sore spot – but Crouch continued without seeming to notice. "A policeman might believe a well-off woman over a hotel worker. But he might also have his own prejudices about women travelling alone. Westall could rely on hotel management to close ranks. They wouldn't want the scandal of admitting an employee invades women's rooms. And of course, he may have grown bold by committing crimes before."

"At this rate I'll have to spend another night in the lounge."

"Here's what I propose. Westall is off shift now. He can usually be found walking the dog in Victoria Square before his supper. He's a man who sticks strictly to the daily routine. I bet we could catch him if we look sharp. All quite accidental and informal, of course. But you could get a good look at the dog that way. When you've confirmed it's him, speak to Quarrington directly. It might be enough to convince him the problem's not going away. He'll find it harder to discount you with my support anyway." He sipped his martini. "I'm assuming you remember the dog well enough? In the circumstances fogginess would be forgivable."

"I have an excellent memory," she said, irritated.

"Shall we go, then?"

She would rest easier if the man could be named and identified. Still, it was mad to venture into the darkness of a strange city, in search of a man who may mean her harm, on the word of another man she didn't know. Crouch let the silence expand as he watched her, before he turned to the guests at the next table, twisting in his chair. He slapped the nearest neighbour on the shoulder, a young man in a cream lounge suit and lemon necktie, with black hair. Nora looked at the line of skin in the man's side parting. It reminded her of the ceiling crack above her bed.

"Charlie," Arthur Crouch greeted him. "How would your lot feel about a snowball fight? There's a nice open space up the street, just in Victoria Square."

"Why not," Charlie replied. "Ward off the cabin fever, shall we?"

"You can't decline now," Arthur said to Nora. "Not when we have the makings of a party."

Clearly he'd sensed her reticence was self-protective. So he had engineered a gathering of eight: four men, four women – to create safety in numbers, or at least the respectable appearance of it. And perhaps to wield a modicum of social pressure too. It crossed her mind that his efforts weren't entirely flattering. He might have continued to annex her attention here, in the bar; and he might have wanted her alone, out there, in the dark; but with the expanded invitation it became clear he was less interested in her than in the servants' transgression. He had sniffed some wrong-doing at the hotel. He wanted to know what it was, to file away with every other feud and violation he'd enjoyed, vicariously, under the Regent's roof. Oddly this trait enhanced her interest in him, though not her attraction.

"It will be a cold party," she remarked. "I'll come, but just until this Westall shows up."

If Westall was the intruder, she didn't want to hang about. She'd come back with a positive identification, and insist on his dismissal. Critically, she looked down at her silver-trimmed button shoes. She'd break her neck if they had to cross any ice. This outing would require boots and a heavy coat. "I'll meet you in reception when I've changed."

Outside, the street was nearly monochrome: a black sky; the deep level whiteness of the snow; the glossy railings round the cathedral; the grey stone banks, and insurers, and unions, that stood empty and dark-windowed on every side of the square. The only colour was the blazing stained glass window in the chancel. Christ ascended in scarlet and indigo robes.

Nora held herself a step away from the group, having no interest in making friends with Charlie, or *his lot*, as Arthur had referred to them. For their part they seemed singularly uninterested in her, preferring to roughhouse and tease each other as they kicked the snow ahead of them. For a while Arthur chatted to a young blonde in a Cossack hat. The coating on the ground muffled all sounds, rendering voices soft and diffuse. Halfway down the road Arthur returned to Nora.

"While you were locating suitable attire, I made some enquiries about Mrs Reid," he commented.

"Oh?" Nora was short of breath; the snow was higher than her ankles, requiring some exertion to wade through. No wonder the passages to and from the city were closed, especially where the ground was higher.

"Between you and me, she hasn't been playing nurse; she's disappeared."

"What do you mean, disappeared?"

"She's nowhere to be found. Her ill niece is beside herself."

"I saw the old woman this morning – she was playing Gilbert and Sullivan in the lounge. How long has she been gone?"

"Since lunch, by all accounts. She told her niece she was going to the cathedral, and one of the cathedral cleaners corroborated Mrs Reid was there. But she didn't return at the time she was expected."

"She's still out in the snow?"

"Apparently. The hotel notified the police, due to her age. If Mrs Reid slipped on the ice somewhere and is in danger of dying from exposure then obviously time is of the essence. And of course it's in the hotel's interests to find her before people start inventing silly reasons for her disappearance."

"So who spilled the beans to you?"

"Harvey. We scratch each other's backs from time to time. She knows I'm immune to panic."

"And me? You don't think I'll panic?"

"No. You don't seem the nervous type at all. But the women of the Regent are flightier than you, as a rule. The cinema king's wife would be horrified at guests going missing. I don't imagine Miss Oxbow would respond calmly to the news, either. She doesn't even respond calmly to the serving of pork at dinner. I expect she'd hold a séance, get the spirits' opinion on where Mrs Reid is hiding."

"You may be right. But Mrs Reid herself would be delighted at such a development, don't you think? She was very taken with Berenice's visions." Nora spoke evenly, but this was the first point in the conversation where her attention was truly engaged. She didn't care what had happened to Mrs Reid – although it seemed remarkably negligent for a hotel to admit a stranger to Nora's room, and lose an elderly guest all within the space of a day. But Berenice's reactions were a constant source of interest to her. She hoped she would be the one to tell her of Mrs Reid's disappearance. Almost certainly Arthur was correct, and Berenice would respond dramatically.

"This is Victoria Square," Arthur announced, as the street joined a moonlit open space, with civic buildings at the periphery. Ahead of them stood a Corinthian temple in miniature; its sloping roof was upheld by numerous columns, which were carved with leaves and other Roman details. To the right stood a larger, many windowed edifice with a Venetian-style mosaic above its great doors. A clock tower was just visible on its far side.

"The Town Hall, and the Council House," Arthur said.

"You're quite the tour guide. When can we expect Westall to come by?" She pulled her scarf up around her face. If Westall had been in her room, he'd recognise her, and worry she was there to get a fix on him. Much better if he didn't guess that yet.

"He should be here any moment."

A podium at the square's centre bore a marble statue of Queen Victoria, capped with snow. She held her orb, her sceptre. The girl in the Cossack hat scooped up a handful of snow and patted it into a ball between her mint green gloves. She pitched the ball at the monarch with a laugh. It exploded upon the marble shoulder.

"Not fair," said her friend, a large-toothed, pale-eyelashed girl in a brown tapestry coat. "Queenie can't fight back."

Charlie pelted her with snow and she squealed. The snowball fight had begun. Nora maintained her distance from the ensuing scrum. The party darted together and scattered back again across the white terrain, spoiling the snow's smoothness. Nora's eyes were trained on the dark edges of the square where the side streets funnelled in. She hoped that this wouldn't be a wasted journey. All she had was Arthur's word for it that Westall was such a creature of routine he would arrive as expected.

"Come on, Crouch," Charlie hooted from the Council House doors. "Don't stand on ceremony."

Arthur raised his palms and bowed his head, in a gesture of quiet refusal. A second young man, barely distinguishable from Charlie in Nora's view – these callow unformed men were so alike – took this as provocation, and fired his next snowball in Arthur's direction. It landed on Arthur's shoe.

"Who are these people, anyway?" Nora murmured.

"Nobody," Arthur said. "They're nobodies, with minor titles, tediously playing at decadence."

"We could hide by the clock tower," Nora deadpanned. "Pretend to spoon, if you want to save face. Which side will Westall arrive from?"

Arthur pointed two fingers, gun-like, at the Town Hall. "He's already here. See?"

A silhouette moved before the stone wall: the thin outline of a flat-capped man, a dog lead outstretched from his hand. The dog was indeed large, his head dropped low, his nose to the ground, but Nora could already see the dog wasn't large *enough*. She strode towards the Town Hall, no longer fearing a confrontation with her intruder. If the dog was wrong, there was no reason to suspect his owner.

"Mr Crouch; Miss," Westall greeted them as they drew near. His features lacked any hint of cunning, or concern, or shiftiness. He looked merely cold and ordinary, his pale skin just reddening at the tip of his nose. He looked meek.

"Evening, Westall," Arthur returned.

Nora dropped to her haunches, the hem of her coat rumpling in the snow. It would be wet against her legs when she walked back. For now she made eye contact with the dog. As Arthur had said, he was a large mongrel, with black hair fading to brown on his legs and stomach. His face was wolfish, which might have been alarming, had his left ear not been lower than his right, giving him a droll, lopsided look. She removed her glove, ran her hand over his head and beneath his chin. He licked her palm, then yawned.

"He's a good-natured sort," she remarked. "What's his name?"

"Glennard," Westall said, with a timid smirk. Arthur laughed.

"What's funny?" Nora enquired.

"That's the hotel manager's Christian name. He's called Glennard Quarrington," Arthur explained. To Westall, he said: "Does your boss mind the gesture?"

"No! Animal lover, isn't he. And he can take a bit of fun." Westall glanced over at the continuing snowball fight. "Out skylarking?"

"Something like that," Arthur said.

Nora stood up. "It's time I was getting back."

"Goodnight, Westall," said Arthur. "See you tomorrow, perhaps."

"Have a good evening."

Nora followed an already-flattened path across the square. Arthur ran over to Charlie, exchanged a few words, then caught up with her.

"Won't they find it odd that you asked them out here and we disappeared so quickly?" she asked.

"I told them you felt unwell."

They slipped off the square into a side street.

"Have you reached a verdict?" Arthur asked. "Was it the same dog?"

"Quite different," Nora said firmly. "Not big enough. Wrong ears."

"Not big *enough*? What kind of monster were you expecting to see?"

"Larger than that."

Arthur paused. "But our new friend Glennard is very large. Your visitor would have to be enormous. You'd just woken up – in a closed room, not the outdoors like this – perhaps he *seemed* bigger? You might be misremembering – it would be quite understandable."

"I don't take kindly to having my testimony questioned," she said crisply, because in his reaction she heard something of Harvey's tone, the growing disbelief at Nora's account. Arthur had enjoyed playing detective, and now she had ruled out his theory, he'd rather undermine her version of events than show his knowledge of hotel intrigues was flawed.

"Don't be prickly." Arthur sighed. "Haven't I been terribly obliging? But I can't abide exaggeration."

"I exaggerate nothing. You said Westall took in this dog, this Glennard, as a stray? He was begging at the kitchen door?"

"That's right."

"Do any other strays do the same?"

"I feel quite sure that a stray larger than Glennard, and an unfriendly one at that, would have a name for himself in these streets. You've described a beast, of a sort it would be impossible to smuggle into the hotel. Somebody would have seen a man with a dog the size of a pony roaming the corridors."

"I don't doubt it," Nora said sourly. "Someone knows who the dog is – whether it's a stray, or belongs to the porter's aunt. And someone knows who locked me in a room with him. But will any hotel worker deign to tell me? Or will they prefer to keep denying, because a strange man shouldn't be invading my room while I sleep and the hotel *doesn't want people to panic*?"

"They'd admit it to me," Arthur insisted. "If there's anything to admit."

Nora wondered what the workers of the Regent really thought of Arthur Crouch. His longstanding stay, in his eyes, equated to a type of ownership. He really seemed to believe he had a claim to the hotel. But what had workers to gain from being open with him? He might have had longer than the typical guest to observe the rhythms and practices of their working lives; but he couldn't compel them to say what they knew, or what they observed, among themselves.

They walked the remaining distance to the hotel in silence. At the steps, Arthur said, in a bored way, without even meeting her gaze: "You're rather a disappointment to me. I thought your suspicion of people was rooted in discernment. But it isn't. You're just another hysteric, aren't you?"

His pomposity was comical. He walked ahead of her

up the steps. She stayed where she was for a moment, to be certain they wouldn't encounter each other again in the lobby. The snow was beginning to fall once more. It would make the paths even again. She plunged her hands into her pockets and looked over at the cathedral. In the graveyard, by the light of the moon, Nora saw a familiar platinum head and a flash of fur. She crossed the street to enter.

6

"I couldn't bear to be in that building any longer," Berenice said when Nora approached.

"The hotel? Why not?"

Berenice opened a yellow box labelled *Kreteks*. Medicinal cigarettes, imported from Java through the Netherlands, because she couldn't possibly buy a normal brand from a normal shop. She lit one and sat on a gravestone. The kretek crackled as it burnt, quite unlike regular tobacco. Clove-scented smoke carried on the breeze.

"I saw policemen in the lobby." She shuddered delicately. "I feel sick around men in uniform."

"Policemen? Has something happened?"

"Some old lady's missing. I left before anyone saw me. The police will want to use my clairvoyance, to find out what happened to her. I've had premonitions of murder ever since I got off the train. I bet some wicked man killed her. Or a woman, they can kill too."

Berenice was revelling in another silly fantasy, because she loved melodrama. It was testimony to Leo's infatuation that he married her knowing the visions were a sham.

Nora had once sincerely believed in the supernatural, and did no longer, because Leo worked hard to disabuse her. He had done so rather brutally, reconfiguring Nora's mind so that certain childhood memories were lost, and others, when they arose, intolerable. An image of her mother on all fours flashed through her thoughts and she pushed it away forcefully.

Maybe the police *would* ask for the Icon's insights. Leo wasn't the only one in her thrall. Most people pandered to her. Nora wondered who was the last person to refuse Berenice what she wanted, and whether Berenice had been angry. She'd rather like to see Berenice angry, and to imitate her anger.

"Don't you think Mrs Reid will have fallen in the snow?" Nora asked. "I sat with her at dinner during your vision. She's a batty old thing, quite ordinary. I don't imagine there's any mystery surrounding her at all."

Berenice shrugged. "You can't know what she's done in her life."

"No. It's just my impression on meeting her."

"I thought you were a great believer in my clairvoyance. Or were you lying about that?" Berenice addressed the question to her cigarette. She appeared to be musing, rather than accusatory. "Perhaps you were buttering me up. I think you wanted to be close to me."

This was true, wasn't it? Although not in the way Berenice meant, going by her indulgent tone. She thought Nora was infatuated with her beauty, hungry for contact.

Berenice threw her head back and laughed. "Your face! I'm just kidding. You do keep following me. The funny thing is, Dr Dickinson, I *did* think you were lying when you stood outside my door. I thought you were lying about why you were there, and about who you were. But when you admired my clairvoyance, I never heard anything sound so true."

The accusation pierced Nora where she was most vulnerable. Of course that part sounded true. She was mimicking the other guests, and Nora was a true and faithful recorder. People questioned her authenticity the moment she stopped pretending to be anyone but herself.

"Come on now," Berenice teased. She tweaked Nora's sleeve to pull her forward. "It's nice to be admired. But I have to joke about it. You don't understand how hard it is to possess a gift like mine. People are scared of it – or they're enamoured, but see me as an entertainment, like a stage magician."

"Or a freak in the circus."

Berenice said nothing for several seconds, then laughed.

"Yes, yes, like someone in the circus." She let go of Nora with a playful shove. Nora rubbed her arm. Berenice was infuriating: she faked clairvoyance to feel the adoration of strangers, then faked stoicism for enduring it. Nora stamped her feet to warm them.

"I understand very well what it is to be gifted," Nora said.

The amusement hadn't left Berenice's features. "Is that right, Dr Dickinson?"

"I also have an ability that unnerves people."

"Whatever it is, nobody's on your tail for it. My gift precedes me. Everyone knows who I am, and what I can do, before we've exchanged two words."

Nora remembered Gruszinskaya, the Russian ballerina

in that Baum novel, crying all the time because she wanted to be alone. Everyone loved an aloof beauty and didn't Berenice know it: she'd play that part even if fame was no hardship for her. Fame was the fount of all the attention she craved.

"You're right," Nora agreed. "We aren't similar in that way."

"Tell me your gift."

"I'm a mimic."

"What? A cheap comedian?"

That was rich: for Berenice to sneer at Nora's talents, while her own were entirely fabricated.

Nora smoothed her coat. She opened her mouth, and sang, exactly as she had heard it, Berenice's Russian song from the cocktail bar. The words echoed Berenice's perfectly. Every syllable, every note. Nora relaxed into Berenice's posture. Her expressions were no longer her own. They were Berenice's. And it was blissful, to be inside Berenice, rather than watching her while being nothing at all.

The song stopped. Berenice's eyes were round and glassy. Nora recalled the images that had burst through her mind when Berenice sang in the bar. Had those images appeared in Berenice's mind now? Maybe they'd swapped places, for those short, delectable minutes.

"I'm a recorder," Nora said. "I have heard this song, once and once only, when you sang it for the guests of the hotel. The language isn't even known to me."

"Huh. Aren't you the little mynah bird?" Gratifyingly, Berenice no longer looked smug, and her speech had lost its sugar. She seemed to accept one exposure was enough, even in an unknown language. Nora knew opera singers were capable of picking up songs without prior fluency. Sure enough Berenice added: "You're definitely not trained?"

"No. Don't you think I sound like you?"

"I don't sound or look anything like you."

People didn't like to be confronted with themselves. Sometimes people recoiled as though from an unflattering photograph. Nora had learnt this early, as a very little child.

"Put it properly to the test," Nora suggested. "You're married. Shall I telephone your husband and pretend I'm you? Would he know the difference?"

"Yes, he would know."

"Prove it!"

"The telephones aren't working."

Of course they weren't.

"Your singing partner then," said Nora. If Merlini were truly enamoured with Berenice, he'd suffice. Nora would enjoy him saying she was her match. "Blindfold him. Let him tell us apart."

But Berenice shook her head and hopped off the gravestone. She drew her coat closer around her and walked away, in the direction of the hotel. The unbearable omens of doom that she claimed had driven her to the graveyard must no longer be so hard for her to tolerate.

In the middle of the road she turned, the toss of her platinum hair coquettish.

"Be careful!" she called back. "If you're so good at copying, you might copy something really evil by mistake. There's a killer around, Dr Dickinson. I feel it in my bones!"

Nora didn't reply. She stayed where she was until

Berenice had moved inside, and realised she was still unwilling to enter the hotel. Not because of Berenice's silly closing words. Rather, a person had entered Nora's room as she slept, but he shouldn't have been there and it was no longer a safe retreat. For now the snow in the graveyard was preferable.

Berenice had left her packet of kreteks on the gravestone. Nora took one out, slid the remainder into her pocket, and lit it in imitation of Berenice. She inhaled and exhaled as Berenice did. She would take everything from her, even the way she smoked a cigarette.

Moving from grave to grave to keep warm, Nora read what names she could in the moonlight. Every inch of this cemetery had been used for burials, making the earth ankle-twistingly uneven beneath the deceptive snow cover. What a lot of dead Birmingham had. Crouch had been telling Mrs Reid about the cemetery, when Nora first met them. Nora had been focused on Berenice, but some information must have taken hold, for she knew that the boundary between the road and cemetery had been moved to widen the streets without relocating the bodies. Skeletons were strewn deep beneath the cars that motored through when the roads were clear. Now the cars were as still as the dead, immobile at the pavement side in the mounting snow.

She approached a limestone obelisk near the cathedral doors. It was as tall as the building itself, and bore, in relief, the dates and places of a military feat. She was just brushing some snow away to read the name of a dead colonel when she heard the crunch of footfall. Over by the corner of the cathedral was a dog. Even in the moonlight she was certain it was the dog from her room – as certain as she had been Glennard was *not* the dog in question. He was of the same implausible size. And he wasn't alone. He was leashed by a tall thin man in a dark coat; his age and features were otherwise hard to discern, between his bowler and the raised lapels obscuring his jaw. Dog and owner kept uncannily in step with each other, as if one mind were shared between them. They didn't see Nora. The man pushed open the cathedral door, casting a trapezium of light on the snow; then he walked the dog inside, and the door slowly closed behind them.

Was it safe to confront him? She couldn't know that. But if she followed, she might catch sight of his face. Though Nora had little faith in the housekeeper, or Crouch, to listen to her description at this point, being able to visually identify him would surely stand her in good stead. She might recognise him as one of the porters or managers or even a waiter.

So she followed, with caution. When she opened the door she was met with the illumination of candles, but barely more warmth than outside. Quietly she stepped within. Beyond the arcaded porch, she saw many rows of pews and marbled columns. The stained glass window was at the far end, though the images were no longer clear from this angle, against the night sky as they were. All the seats were empty. An old woman in a fawn knitted dress was sweeping the floor.

Where was the man now? An upper gallery of pews hung above them on either side. He must be seated upstairs. Nora took the winding staircase by the door, quailing at the creak of the wood beneath her weight; she would have preferred to approach without warning. But it didn't matter, because the seats there were empty too.

She returned to the sweeping woman. The cleaner had white hair sparse enough to reveal the scalp beneath and her eyes were a milked-over blue.

"Excuse me," Nora said quietly. "I was just looking for the gentleman who came in with his dog?"

"No one here but you and me, bab," the woman replied.

Bab. They said that locally. It was years since Nora had heard it.

"I saw a man come in," Nora said.

The old woman shook her head, lips pursed. Maybe her eyesight or hearing was failing. Certainly Nora couldn't think why she would lie over such a thing.

"And there's no other exit?"

"That's the only unlocked door," the old woman said, with a nod at the entrance Nora had arrived by. "Big black dog, was it?"

"Yes, very big!" Nora leapt on the question. Maybe the sweeper had missed him this time, but he regularly came here. "I've never seen so large a dog. Do you know the man who owns him?"

The old woman laughed. "You saw Edward Markham."

At the name, Nora thought of stinging nettles. *Hokey pokey*, splattered with blood in a glade. The room slid sideways.

"Eh eh eh!" The old woman sprang forward, letting the broom drop onto the flags, and grasped Nora by the elbow to prevent her fall. "You all right?"

"I'm sorry." Nora righted herself, embarrassed. "I don't know why I felt so faint. I'm fine."

"You're not. You've gone white. You should get home. Do you have far to go?"

Nora gaped, unsure how to answer. She should have said – *I'm staying in the hotel opposite*, except then she would have to go there. "I live very far away," she said, like a child who has lost sight of her mother. "I'm trapped here by the snow!"

"What! That's no good. I'm good as done here, bab, come with me. You can have a tea at mine. I only live round the corner." A new crease, grooved deeply between the wrinkles at the bridge of her nose, signalled the old woman's concern.

Nora picked up the broom, to save her elder bending down, and to signal her own restoration to normality. She returned the broom to its owner. "I can get home. I spoke too dramatically – it's only snow."

"None of that." The old woman was decided. "You're going to have a hot drink with me at least. Just have to fetch me coat."

She took the broom into the shadows of the cathedral. Nora waited, relenting to the offer of tea, with secret relief at the cleaner's insistence.

"Now. I'm Enid," said the old woman, returning in a patched maroon reefer and a sage woollen hat.

"I'm Nora."

Side by side they left the building. By now the snow was deep enough to make a foothold difficult, and Nora felt more justified in accepting Enid's invitation. It would be terrible to let an old woman find her way back in these conditions. They passed two pairs of policemen, equipped with torch boxes, in search of another old woman needing aid: Mrs Reid.

Enid and Nora reached the road arm in arm. Music drifted from the hotel, softened by the fresh snow cover.

"You just stick with me." Enid was wheezing. "It's over this way, and the first left."

Nora hadn't taken this turning before, which was too poorly lit to make out the buildings in any detail. The two women were plunged into a steep downwards incline, which required a slowed pace not to slip. Everyone else must have already taken shelter, because they didn't encounter another soul, before reaching a mean-looking brick boarding house at the end of the street.

"Here we are." Enid let go of Nora to grasp the iron railing at the side of the steps. She pushed the front door open and stamped her boots on the mat. "Come in! Come in!"

Nora obeyed, spying the dirty face of a toddler on the stairs, who ran away as soon as he realised he'd been spotted.

"Home sweet home." Enid opened one of the doors off the corridor and Nora waited for her to light the gas lamp before entering. She saw a bedsitter, with another door off the side – to a crude kitchen, Nora guessed.

"Sit down," Enid urged, nudging Nora into a winged armchair. "I'll make the tea."

Nora, once seated, took in the details of this carefully neat room: the pale green linoleum with its trompe l'oeil rug, the cast iron bed with each leg in a bowl of water, the drop leaf table under a small window on the darkness. A faint odour of haddock permeated the air; indelible, formed by the preparation of many breakfasts.

Cautiously, Nora said: "You mentioned Edward Markham. Who is he?"

Enid laughed uncomfortably from the kitchen. Nora heard the clink of cups on saucers.

"Don't worry about that. Silly of me to mention him. In a church as well!"

"No – please do go on. I'd like to know."

Enid moved into the doorway, twisting and untwisting a worn tea towel.

"I hadn't thought of him in a while. Just coincidence that someone else was asking about him this week. Small, old-fashioned-looking, bit snooty. She wanted to know if he'd ever attended a service." Enid paused. "He used to be an accountant. Worked at a firm called Parkes, just round the corner from here. Years ago, before the war. Came up on the train each day on the Shakespeare Line. Sometimes he'd bring his dog."

"Does he still have business here?"

"Not the way you mean."

"I don't follow."

"He had a wife, back in Alspath."

Alspath. Another name that made Nora's stomach clench. Enid carried on.

"But he got some girl into trouble. He killed her. He didn't get away with it, though. He was hanged. But I don't think he knows he's dead. Not if he's still wandering the streets. Who wouldn't feel faint after seeing him, eh?"

This was the same Edward Markham, then. Nora might have known that, on returning to England, he would haunt her. Especially because she knew the woods were close, very close, to this particular bit of England. But she had never known Mr Markham worked in Birmingham.

"How – how did he kill the girl?"

"With an axe," Enid whispered. "Some parts were never found."

She retreated to fill the teapot. Soon she came back with strong sweet tea in a china cup. The steam condensed on Nora's face as she drank. She might have told Enid: only one part was never found. An arm, with a tattoo upon it, and a rash from stinging nettles. Nora's eyes were so heavy. She finished the drink and let them close. A blanket was draped over her lap before oblivion claimed her. The oblivion was welcome, blocking out thoughts of Edward Markham, the girl who was killed with an axe, and the scent of flesh cooking in the pot.

7

The Cathedral clock struck five in the darkness and most of the Regent clientele were asleep. The cinema king's wife slumbered in rose satin pyjamas. Charlie the skylarker snored in a fellow libertine's bathtub, yet to remove his cream lounge suit. Mrs Reid's niece, Pretoria, overwarm with bronchitis, cried out from nightmares of her aunt trapped in the snow. Crouch was alert and readying himself for the morning ahead. As he contemplated his lathered face in the mirror, he thought: *I'm shaving my father*. On each floor the nightworkers were handing over. The still-room maid filled the urn to make tea for everyone starting their shift. All the cooking fires were cleaned out, set and lit by the porters. In the stores, the kitchen clerk drew the sugar, flour and salt needed for the day. She noted their weights in the Daily Account. The linen keepers brought freshly aired tablecloths to the Pinfold Dining Room and billowed them over the plain oak tables. Waitresses folded serviettes while the commis arranged coffee spoons in electroplated cruets. One of the waitresses hung a printed breakfast menu by the door: Cambridge sausages; eggs fried or poached; grilled lambs' kidneys; fillet of whiting; kippered herring; broiled bacon; marmalades; and compotes of peaches and apricots. Minute by minute, the hotel was awakening.

Soon Nora was waking up too. Light slipped between the striped curtains that didn't meet in the middle. She could just see the sun above the rooftops. Snow lay thick upon the slates, thawing only at the base of each chimney. Her own breath was misting and the ends of her fingers were icy. But she was still fully dressed in the previous evening's clothes, including her thick coat, and a blanket lay over her lap. Enid must have spared one of her own. Nora glanced over at the bed, where Enid seemingly slept soundly, beneath a dome of further blankets which put Nora in mind of a tortoiseshell.

A steel wall clock ticked in the alcove. Half past seven. With the coming of the day Nora felt rather foolish for staying here at all. She had let herself be spooked in the darkness with a name from her past. But it was only unpleasant coincidence that Enid should speak of Markham. Nora didn't believe that the dead come back. Not as anything other than a vivid memory – and not while the sun was out. At any rate, she remembered Markham's dog. He was not as large as the dog in her room. She would return to the hotel, like the sensible adult that she was; make her room secure as she had previously planned; and patiently wait until the snow cleared for her passage home.

The prospect of waking Enid, if it meant discussing Markham again, didn't appeal. Silently, Nora stood up and folded the blanket upon the arm of the chair. She felt guilty for skulking away, and to assuage her conscience took the cash she had on her person and left it upon the mantelpiece. Enid slept as Nora crossed the room and let herself out.

The hallway was empty although Nora could hear the slamming of doors and the shouting of children above. On the front step she passed a black and white cat, licking his paws; she saw his prints in the otherwise flawless drifts across the pavement.

Her walk to the hotel, uphill for the return journey, was laborious. She discovered her boots were less waterproof than she had thought; wet stockings twisted round her toes. This time as she progressed she could see the variety of buildings that lined the street: more boarding houses, from the look of it, then a derelict pub. As she drew closer to Temple Row, the style and nature of the buildings altered dramatically. She passed several large finance companies. Was one of them the workplace of Markham? Enid hadn't specified the street name; only said the company was called Parkes.

He probably never worked near here, Nora thought. Ghost stories often used little local embellishments to persuade the listener of their veracity. That didn't mean Enid set out to lie. It might mean she liked repeating ghost stories more than she liked looking for holes in their credibility.

Nora could hear birdsong, and gratefully switched her attention to guessing the source. Robins, probably. The cathedral came into view – the clock was now nearing eight – and Nora turned left, towards the hotel. She arrived at the grand entrance, which was flanked by one of the red-jacketed porters and a couple of doormen in blue and gold. Self-consciously she shook snow from her toecaps before

passing through. Inside, she hoped to evade the attention
of reception before getting to the stairs, because she had
slept in her clothes; she hewed close to the walls. This took
her past the silence cabinets. On each door hung a neat
printed sign, proclaiming the telephones OUT OF ORDER.
She paused at the cubicle she had occupied when the lines
went down. Through the glass she could see the loose page
still hanging from the telephone book. Again her thoughts
turned to Markham. Parkes would be in the book, wouldn't
it, if it were a real firm? That was one verifiable detail. She
stepped into the booth, picked up the book, and ran her
finger down the *P* column. She hovered halfway down.
Parkes and Son, 16 and 18 Cherry Street...

She jumped at the clatter of the cabinet door opening
behind her, just as the draught hit her neck.

"Make room, angel!" Berenice said as she crammed
inside, pulling the door closed again. "What are you
doing in here? Did you forget again that the phones aren't
working?"

They were close enough for their fur lapels to touch.
Nora let go of the telephone book, losing her place as it
swung from the wooden holder.

"I wanted to check an address," she said.

"Oh! I thought you might be trying to telephone my
husband."

"I'm sorry?"

"You suggested testing him." Berenice laughed, to Nora's
discomfort.

"That was a joke," Nora said. "I wouldn't know where to
find your husband. Why are you so cheerful this morning?"

Maybe Merlini had put her in good spirits.

"I'm pleased to see you, Dr Dickinson. I've had time to think about your mimicry."

"Oh?" Nora said in surprise.

"It was rude to dismiss your gift. I should have taken it as a compliment – your wish to imitate me."

Nora's mimicry was neither gift nor compliment, as she understood it; it was a function, like a Dictaphone recording and replaying. When she imitated a person, she was passively relaying the truth.

Berenice said: "Now, I don't even know the point of your trip. I bet you were drawn here to meet me. Weren't you?"

Nora recoursed again to the explanation she'd given Crouch. "It's approaching the anniversary of my mother's death. The memorial is in Warwickshire. But the roads there are blocked with snow and this is a convenient breaking point."

A beefy-faced man rapped on the glass. He mouthed: "The telephones are out of order."

Berenice stuck her tongue out at him. The man blinked in surprise, and he stepped away.

"Are you going to, or returning from, breakfast?" Nora asked Berenice. It wasn't like the Icon to be up at so early an hour.

"This morning I couldn't touch a morsel," Berenice said. "There's rumours of another disappearance – the Italian servants were gossiping."

Merlini had overheard something, then, presumably between the breakfast waiters.

"Who do they say has disappeared?" Nora checked. Thinking of the dog, she said: "They didn't go missing from their room, I hope?"

"Not a guest, thank God! Oh, I forget the name. A man who works here. Lousy of me not to remember, I know – but I barely slept," Berenice said, and Nora thought of Merlini again, as she watched the Icon yawn prettily, raising the back of her slender hand to her mouth.

"I'm tired myself," Nora responded. It wasn't only the aches from sleeping in Enid's chair. It was monitoring Berenice's every gesture and utterance, and pretending to want her friendship. It sapped her as nothing else could.

"Two disappearances, Dr Dickinson! I bet the police will start a manhunt. The killer will have me next in his sights, in case the police use my gift to find him. Oh!"

"What?"

"Let's say you *do* resemble me as much as you say. Wouldn't that be a swell thing?"

"Why?"

Berenice looked mischievous. "Because the murderer might come for you instead of me. I know, I'm selfish! But we both could benefit. Two of us divides his attention."

Ah. Such a jab showed she was still rattled after all; the accuracy of Nora's imitation threatened the Icon. But Nora would parry in like spirit. It was all a chance to study Berenice's quirks. So she said: "We'd have a common enemy."

"How perfect." Berenice pulled the booth door wide again. "I saw you just as I was planning a walk through the snow. I'm going out there now. It'll liven me up. Maybe I'll find the killer on the way."

That seemed to be her farewell. Then, almost as an afterthought, she turned back and pecked Nora on the mouth. Berenice's lip was warm, and papery – chapped from

the winter weather. Nora thought of kissing the envelope of
a love letter. She was so startled by the kiss she said nothing
at all by way of farewell. But she stored the sensation away.
It would be useful to know how Berenice kissed a person
goodbye. It would be a useful thing, to remember, and to
replicate, when she supplanted her.

Nora's room was exactly as she had left it. Whoever might
have visited in the meantime, they had caused minimal
disturbance; she was certain of that, because she checked
behind each curtain, under the bed, in the closets and in
the drawers. She propped a chair back under the handle to
prevent further breaches while she was in the bath.

The hot water restored her thoroughly. She submerged
herself, letting the water run into her mouth. As her bones
warmed through she remembered what Crouch had said
about the redemptive powers of the hotel's water supply;
and she remembered a conversation with Claus Kruger, the
Medical Superintendent at the Holzberg asylum. When she
was a student he'd told her, privately, of a woman he'd once
treated for depression. The woman had suffered a tragic
bereavement. Her small daughter had died after drinking
too much Soothing Syrup. The bottle was ordinarily
kept in a locked cabinet but the woman had neglected
to return it from the side of the cot, and the little girl
drained it in the night. Kruger suspected his patient had
fulfilled an unconscious desire to kill the child, and the
depression arose from her guilt. He weighed whether to say
so during analysis, uncertain whether she could stand to
hear it without her condition worsening. Instead, when he

confronted her, she recognised and accepted the truth. With it voiced she recovered from her depression and left the hospital very soon afterwards. Nora had been struck, at the time, not by the healing capacities of psychoanalysis but by the fact Kruger hadn't discussed the matter with the police. It seemed he thought himself answerable to a different law, like a Catholic priest in the confessional. Perhaps all psychoanalysts felt that way. And not just psychoanalysts; she had personal experience of people turning a blind eye to confessions of heinous crimes, for altruistic, and not so altruistic reasons. But now she was straying close to thoughts of Markham again – none of that. She deliberately focused her mind on Berenice, and how well Nora would be able to imitate her when she returned to Leo in Zurich, surpassing the original in one important regard: fidelity. She did not love Leo, but she would be loyal to him if he worshipped her mimicry. He was the highest judge of her similarity to Berenice. *Two of us divides his attention*, Nora mouthed while the steam condensed on her face.

She sat in the water until it was tepid and the pads of her fingers had wrinkled, then dried herself and donned a simple green frock. She was just rubbing fresh panstick onto the tattoo on her arm when an envelope was passed beneath the door.

A telegram, from Leo, as if made manifest by her daydreams in the bath.

She had told him she had seen Berenice admit Merlini to her room with a kiss. Now she would read Leo's reaction. She tore the seal. Typed inside were the words: SAY NOTHING—I WILL CONFRONT ON HER RETURN—WAITING FOR YOU MY OZALID—L.

Nora sat on the bed, tracing his words with her fingertip. She would do as he instructed; if Leo wanted to confront Berenice with the advantage of surprise, then Nora would comply. She would do so happily, knowing her chance to supplant Berenice had come. Why else would Leo say *waiting for you my ozalid?*

Her stomach growled with startling ferocity. Often she forgot mealtimes, and here, unmoored from her usual routines, the need for fuel was particularly easy to overlook. She had attended neither breakfast nor, the night before, dinner. No wonder she had been unsteady on her feet and imagining things in the cathedral. She'd lacked sustenance. What a mundane explanation, when Enid was sure she'd seen a ghost.

The hour had turned twelve; the dining room would be open for luncheon. Nora returned there wondering if she would see Crouch. He might know more about the missing servant Berenice had mentioned – she wanted to know if the rumour had any basis, given Berenice's propensity for exaggeration – but his pomposity the preceding evening had been off-putting. The dining room was moderately busy and Crouch was, in any case, nowhere to be seen. Nora compensated for her long fast by indulging in all five available courses: scotch broth, grilled halibut in anchovy sauce, beef olives, roast mutton and rice pudding. The cold weather must have heightened her hunger for blood, because she could have eaten the sheep entire. And didn't she deserve a feast? She had vanquished the Icon, and that must be celebrated. She drank a glass of Chablis, of champagne, and of claret while she ate. By the meal's end she was as warm as a furnace, happily immobile, and more benevolent towards Crouch. He had said he often spent his afternoons in the Reading Room. If he were there, he might enjoy telling her the latest hotel tittle-tattle. And if he weren't, she would read the newspaper.

The Reading Room sat on the opposite side of the building from the dining room. Gridded glass acted as a divider from the hall, so that Nora saw the interior before she entered: innumerable captains' chairs (one of them occupied by Crouch), two expansive leather chesterfields and reading lamps with fringed shades. Phosphorus scallops patterned the wallpaper above the dado. Nora perused the newspapers by the entrance, ironed-smooth and folded upon the tabletop. Despite their neatness they were all a couple of days old now, because deliveries were delayed. She hovered over *Der Bund* but picked up *The Times* and strode towards Crouch, before taking the opposing chair. He looked at her, placing a thumb between the pages of his book to hold his place. *The Winding Stair*, the volume was titled in small gold type; *W.B. Yeats*. He frowned.

"Pax." She kept her voice low, so as not to distract the other handful of readers in the room. "I know you couldn't mean any of that nonsense about me being hysterical just because I disagreed with you."

"I enjoy a rational disagreement. Giant dogs don't fall into that category."

"I'm extending an olive branch – show some grace in return. Is it true someone else here has gone missing? Someone who works here?"

He tapped his fingers upon the table. "Now," he said, his tone more inquisitive, "where did you happen upon that information?"

If she said Berenice he'd snort and stay schtum. "Carlo Merlini."

"That surprises me. I had no idea of his powers of observation. He seemed to have eyes only for his duet partner."

"You noticed that, did you?"

"I'm not an idiot." He paused. "A few of the hotel's people were upset this morning. It's our friend Westall."

"What about him?"

"He didn't report for work – that's most unlike him – and his rooms are empty. The dog is gone too."

"He can hardly have gone far, not with the roads as they are – does he have family near?"

"Yes, his parents. He isn't with them. They're bewildered not to have heard from him and are assuming he's been hurt in an accident. But don't you think the timing is interesting?"

"In what way?"

"He must have gone AWOL straight after seeing us. I have a theory. You see, Harvey also thought Westall's dog was the one in your room, though she's under orders not to say as much. She questioned Westall about it but couldn't prove anything and heavily intimated she would pass the matter on to the police if he wasn't forthcoming. After all, a man letting himself into a female guest's room shouldn't be taken lightly. When we approached Westall in the square, it must have been obvious why you were so interested in the dog. Westall thought it wouldn't be long before he got into trouble for it. So he scarpered."

Westall might have feared trouble, but that didn't make him guilty. Crouch kept harping on the wrong dog.

There was no point repeating her objections. He'd be as obstinate as last time. More so, possibly, because Harvey had buoyed his theory. But Nora knew just what the dog in her room looked like. She'd pictured him perfectly outside the cathedral: a dog on a lead, following a man hanged for murder, who didn't know he was dead. Enid said Edward Markham was a ghost. Nora thought he was a memory, made vivid by hunger and the strangeness of returning to England. He was haunting her, either way. In stories, the dead returned for vengeance; or to correct a lie. They might come back to ask forgiveness, but Edward Markham wouldn't do that. She thought of the redeeming waters, running through the hotel, and the guests Crouch liked least flocking to clean their conscience. Maybe he would have liked Markham.

"What are you thinking?" Crouch demanded, at her silence.

She still didn't want to speak of Markham. Not to Enid, and not to Crouch. Better to speak a partial truth: "I was thinking of the well, in the basement. It does rather a lot of work for you, doesn't it, even though you don't believe in its powers?"

"What do you mean?"

"You like to tell people about it, and see how they react, and sort them accordingly into whether they are your sort of person. The ones that want forgiveness aren't, and the ones that don't, are. That's why you waited for me in the bar. Because – unlike Mrs Reid – I disdained the very idea of redemption as soon as we met."

"That isn't why I waited for you."

"No?"

He stood up. "You haven't seen the well yet, have you? Let's go visit now."

The cellar was unlit, and they each used their lighters to guide their path. Nora could taste brickdust. Although she couldn't see outside her small circle of illumination, she knew the room was expansive because she could hear the echo. Coming down here with Crouch was charged in a way she couldn't quite identify: it wasn't sexual – more that he had hinted at a revelation to come, and that gave her a pleasurable nervousness. She pictured those identically uniformed cleaners and wait staff, all of them precisely the same height, coming to life in the dark: seizing moments to drink or smoke, or even conduct affairs, below stairs and between shifts.

"Do the hotel workers come down here much?"

"In summer. But not in a February like this one. It's too blasted cold. They could have the comfort and warmth of a vacant room."

Nora had felt her forearms break into gooseflesh but didn't yet mind the chill. The meat and alcohol were still in effect. She startled at the touch of Crouch's hand on her elbow, but he was only guiding her from collision. Before them stood an upright stone cylinder, about six feet in diameter and as high as her chest. A smooth iron cap concealed her view of the water she could hear rushing inside. This was the old well, sustaining the hotel's plumbing system. To the left was a second cylinder, twice as wide and half as high, connected by a sloping pipe. She knew little of the working of wells, or whether they could ever flood, and assumed the pipe allowed excess to drain away. Mrs Reid, she imagined, would be very disappointed by the well's prosaic exterior.

"No one pictures this when they hear the words *local spring*," Nora observed. She touched the cast iron, and it was cold enough to cause pain in her fingertips.

"Water is water," Crouch said dismissively. "I brought you here because we need to have a conversation without being overheard."

"That sounds very solemn."

"I find you a puzzle, Dr Dickinson."

"There isn't anything mysterious about me." Nora's tone was light, but she sensed Crouch was going to ask a difficult question.

"Let's talk about tattoos."

Nora said nothing, knowing the claret might affect her judgement of what was, and wasn't, safe to mention. She waited for him to continue.

"On your first night here, at dinner, I noticed you had a tattoo of flowers and speckles on your forearm. Your sleeve slipped along your arm when you raised your wine glass – you quickly covered the tattoo again, but I'd seen. And then, before the meal was out, Miss Oxbow described exactly your tattoo in her bogus vision. Ever since then, your tattoo has been disguised. What exactly is going on with you two? I can't make head nor tail of it."

"You were mistaken. I have no tattoo—"

"It was plain as day, before my own eyes. Would you be happy to take soap and water to your arm to prove me wrong? Or should I ask Miss Oxbow instead?"

"No, don't do that," Nora said quickly. Leo had told her

to *say nothing* to Berenice; if she defied his wishes, she might damage her chances of replacing the Icon. "Just – give me a moment. I will explain, in exchange for you keeping your observation from her. Please."

"Let me hear, before I give any assurances."

Nora nodded. She could provide a plausible explanation, one which was wholly true, if incomplete. "Although Miss Oxbow is a stranger to me, her husband is not. I've known him for many years. He suspected her tour was an opportunity for promiscuity and asked me, as a confidante, to set his mind at ease."

"What kind of friendship does he keep secret from his wife?"

"An unusual one."

"You're his mistress?"

"No. He has been faithful since his marriage. No one could accuse him of anything but devotion to Berenice."

"But before their courtship? During it? Don't be mealy mouthed, Dr Dickinson; I don't want to have to tease the truth from you question by question."

"We had an affair," Nora confessed, and it felt like a lie. It wasn't an affair in the ordinary sense of the word.

"And the tattoo?"

"I've had this tattoo since I was twenty. My school teacher had one very like it – hence the old-fashioned appearance – and I wished to imitate it. Rather sentimental of me, because she died young." Nora shivered. The cold, staved off till now, was finally reaching her bones. She offered another partial truth. "Soon after Berenice and Leo were married, she saw a photograph in his wallet, of my tattoo. It wasn't a lurid photo – but it was an intimate one, I suppose. I wasn't otherwise identifiable. That tattoo is the only thing she knows about my appearance."

"How did he explain this little memento?"

In the flickering light, Crouch's lips were parted with anticipation. His tone had settled into ordinary prurience, and had lost its accusatory timbre. Yet the next part in Nora's story felt hardest to say. She closed her eyes, the half darkness insufficient for Nora to pretend she wasn't there at all: that she was nothing but a voice, speaking.

"Badly," Crouch concluded from her silence.

"Berenice either suspects or knows Leo has eyes on her, and his lover is the likeliest spy. When she faked her vision on her first night, she was trying to flush me out, by provoking a reaction."

"I'll admit I was expecting you to reveal a grift, between you and her." Crouch bit his lip. "A fight over a man is rather more pitiable."

A fight over a man? This wasn't a fight over a man. It was a fight to be Berenice, with Leo as the arbiter. But she wouldn't expect Crouch to understand and she didn't bother to enlighten him. For one who'd eschewed forgiveness, her partial confession had left her oddly light. She said, blithely: "I've succeeded in what I set out to do. I discovered Berenice shares her bed with Merlini. When she returns to Zurich, Leo will tell her everything he knows, then I will take Berenice's place in his eyes. Do I have your assurance, now? You won't mention it to her? Leo wishes to be the first to confront her."

"I've no interest in telling her. Miss Oxbow doesn't mean anything to me," Crouch said. "But you should probably remember, Dr Dickinson – there's no guarantee he'll give her up for you. She's the one he married."

He took off his jacket and draped it over her shoulders. "It's too cold to stay down here any longer," he said.

Q

They went to the Narcissus; then to dinner; then to the
Narcissus again. Cocktail hour had arrived. The Narcissus
Bar was the most profitable concern in the Regent,
and cocktails were the bar's most profitable offering.
Maintaining cachet involved labour and expense in hidden
quarters. Laundry maids washed and starched pristine white
jackets for the barmen; they had to be the brightest white,
the easiest colour to stain, as a show of confidence in the
barman's steady hand. The abundance of conical glasses,
coupes and thick-based crystal tumblers that flashed on
the shelves was worth twice the average man's salary. To
account for customer breakages the head barman restocked
glassware daily. He had a memory for three hundred
separate cocktail recipes; he knew the prices by heart too,
though he never provided those unless they were asked for.
Drinks were credited to the room. He devised new drinks
with seriousness. He experimented with vermouth, or
orange peel, or Bénédictine, and turned equally seriously to
the business of naming. The Hunt and Peck; Comfortable
Importance; Amoroso; Apple Squire; Drowsy Bess; Varlet;

Star Gazer; Roaring Boy; Lombard Fever; Chanticleer; the Hokey Pokey. That last was his favourite, evoking for him every childhood brush with the heat and sting of woodland nettles, and the scent of warm leaves; but it was a connoisseur's choice and, in the rush on the bar that night, was drunk by Nora alone, while Crouch matched her drink for drink with martinis. By the time Nora returned to her bedroom, it was late.

She'd lost some, but not all, of the bravado she'd brought that morning. Nora pushed the dressing table up against the door, because a chair seemed inadequate for a full night's protection from invasive elements. Moving the dressing table required considerable exertion and she had to lift one corner at a time to shuffle it along. Each time she released a corner it struck the floor with a thud. She hoped that, downstairs, the occupant wouldn't complain of the noise; a visit from the housekeeper would mean moving the table back again just to speak to her.

Eventually the door was blocked. Nora rubbed her palms with her thumbs, where they had suffered friction against the table. She prepared for bed. And then, in the darkness, beneath the covers, she closed her eyes, allowed her breathing to slow.

Nora's right hand rested above the covers. Her skin felt the wet, slippery contact of a tongue and Nora's eyes shot back open. *How* was that blasted dog getting—

A cry stuck in her throat.

For a terrifying moment she thought a man wrapped in pelts licked her skin. Then she saw an outstretched hoof clear enough. This was no man, and no dog. The beast breathed with a panting rasp.

She watched the creature lift his head into the shaft of light from the window. She saw his long snout, and curved teeth which he revealed in a yawn, white and glistening in a dark mouth. The truth returned to her with profound clarity. She recognised his kind: this was a hyring. His *odour* was familiar... like leaves silting. Another such beast stalked her childhood memories and Leo told her it could not exist. She had resisted Leo, then succumbed, and now saw he was wrong.

Nora was very still as the hyring dropped from the bed to the floor. He stretched his long legs before him on the rug and juddered.

Nora glanced at the bedroom door, with its barrier still intact. She sat up, and drew her knees to her chest as the beast bounded upon the bed. He lay down among the kicked-off covers, the mattress sighing beneath the beast's considerable weight. His eyes were wet and fixed upon her. His tongue flashed back out, over his mouth, as though she were something appetising.

Nora got out of bed, never turning her back on the animal. She fumbled for her coat in the wardrobe. It came down to her calves. No one would see her nightclothes beneath that. The monster watched as she hauled the dressing table far back enough to open the door. Then she flinched in the light of the corridor, her hands shaking as she drew the door shut again, keeping the threat inside. Her feet were bare. How had she come out with no shoes? To go back inside, with that *thing*, was unthinkable. Harvey had denied there was any alternative entrance to the room. Now Nora saw the hyring didn't need a concealed panel or a trapdoor. It had entered by paranormal means. It had entered by the mirror.

She shuddered, knowing no one would believe her. If only, she thought resentfully, people accepted her testimony as readily as the Icon's.

She remembered Berenice's fantasy that a killer was on the loose. Fine; Berenice could face the hyring down. Let her be eaten.

Nora strode down the corridor, clutching the lapels of her coat round her neck. Fortunately she encountered no other guests. She took the back stairs to Berenice's floor rather than wait for the lift like a sitting duck. But the staircase took on the same shifting quality that the corridors had done her first night: she was certain the hotel was moving around her, responding to her every step with a step of its own in a different direction. Stumbling in her haste, she reached the correct floor and walked to Berenice's suite.

Nora rapped on Berenice's door with force and rapidity. How noisy she was being this evening! First the dressing table, now this. She would not be ignored. It was imperative that Berenice hear the urgency of Nora's knock and respond. If she were asleep, or bathing, she must be roused by the volume of Nora's fist on the satin pink of the door. There was, of course, the risk that the cinema king or one of his privileged neighbours would be similarly roused; Nora anticipated just how he would react to her current appearance, barefoot and half asleep. But she did not relent. For what was surely a full minute, Nora knocked without ceasing. She was rewarded with the sound of Berenice's footfall and the apparition of Berenice in the doorway.

"Dr Dickinson," Berenice scolded. "What a hullaballoo!"
Nora's words burst forth like water from the mouth of

a girl pulled to shore. "There's something in my room –
There's *something* – in my—"

Berenice's eyes glittered.

"A kind of beast," Nora gasped. "I'm not going back
down there. You can see it on your own. Room 427. The
door isn't locked—"

Berenice pushed past her and walked towards the lift,
a smirk playing about her lips. She'd find out it wasn't a
laughing matter soon enough.

Nora waited half a minute. When she heard the lift doors
close, she entered Berenice's suite. She passed through the
drawing room and the orchid-strewn hall. No sight nor
sound of Merlini. She returned to Berenice's midnight blue
sleeping quarters, en route to a wardrobe large enough to
constitute a room of its own.

Nora took a dark worsted dress from the rack, a pair of
equally plain black shoes from the shelf above, and some
combinations from a drawer. It was emboldening, to swap
her nightclothes for Berenice's undergarments, to replicate
her in layers upwards from the body. Over the top Nora
fastened the dress. Her skin itched against the fibres. It
clung more tightly than it would have over Berenice's body,
but not conspicuously so. Nora decided she would keep the
clothes. When she next saw Leo she must wear them. She
wondered whether the dress was one he liked. Probably
it was too plain for his tastes. But Nora didn't necessarily
want his admiration; she wanted the reaction from him that
Berenice would have received. If he didn't like Berenice in
this dress, then it would be fine for him not to like Nora in
the dress either.

She picked up her own nightgown and carefully draped

it over a hanger. The shoes were on the floor, their toes pointed towards the door in readiness. She stepped into them, right foot first. Ten peaks rose in the leather where her knuckles bunched. She pictured the ugly sisters. But there was no need to cut off her toes. They were tolerable. Perhaps she could learn to walk in them as Berenice walked, to stand as she did, to lie, prone, upon Leo's couch without removing them, crossed at the ankle, the scuffing of the soles visible.

Nora checked, then, if the soles were indeed scuffed. They were not. They were as smooth as if Berenice never walked anywhere – merely glided.

"I found nothing," Berenice said from the bedroom door.

Nora's mouth tasted bitter. The monster was still loose, and Berenice was still here.

"Did you say you saw a *beast*?" Berenice asked. "What shape did it take – a man?" The question was laced with innuendo, suggesting a different, everyday kind of scandal.

"No. It revealed its full monstrousness." When she spoke to Leo he would tell her not to trust her senses. It would be painful, but admittedly simpler, to let him convince her she was deluded. She did not want to believe in hyrings again. Even if she could still feel that tongue on her skin. Even if—"He smelt of the woods. And like... formaldehyde."

"How disappointing that he didn't stay for me to see." She was humouring Nora, assuming that every story of the occult was as false as her own.

"I've seen such things before, when I was growing up," Nora said. "They're called *hyrings*. They shapeshift and they eat human flesh. I don't want to go back there. None of my barricades kept it out."

"You can stay here." Berenice cocked her head, looking upon Nora's theft of her clothes with a benevolent air. "We'll be like schoolgirls in a dormitory, won't we?"

She opened a door, camouflaged with wallpaper, onto a second bedroom. So much for Nora's initial reconnaissance. It seemed to be a mirror of Berenice's own room, though the walls were purple, not blue. Nora stepped inside and sat upon the bed. The door remained open as Berenice readied herself for sleep in Nora's view; she turned her back, and slipped off her gown to the waist while singing snatches of song. Not operatic in style. Less self-conscious, more homely. Nora looked at the pale arcs of her shoulder blades, the sierra of her spine. Berenice donned a bathrobe and Nora quickly looked away again, lest she be noticed watching.

"Did you go to a boarding school?" Nora called, interrupting the song.

"I did in America for a short time – not much like an English boarding school I don't think – did you go to one?"

"I went to a village school for a very little while. Then I was schooled at home."

"How lonely!"

"I liked it that way. *You* said you craved solitude."

"No – I crave love like you wouldn't believe – but I'm no one's possession. Too many of the people who follow me on tour think they have a claim on me. When they act like I owe them something, I despise company."

"Don't you have a husband?" Nora asked slyly. "Doesn't he love you?"

Berenice laughed hollowly. "*He* wants to own me too. I thought, once, that he'd help me understand myself. But he thinks I'm a painting or a china figurine. Who helps a painting understand itself? No one. I'm there to be admired and displayed. I'm there to be imitated."

"Imitated?" Nora echoed.

"I'm under no illusion," Berenice said sourly. "As soon as I am old I'll be replaced by another brittle young lady, blonde and tragic and artistic, if she's fool enough to walk into his waiting room."

This was unfair to Leo. He had shown nothing but devotion to Berenice until she betrayed him. If anything, he acted against his own best interests by showing such fidelity. And against her own interests Nora had to acknowledge Berenice's power. She remembered that papery kiss in the telephone kiosk – the transporting voice in the bar – the glowing electricity of Berenice's hair. Leo never stood a chance.

"You ever want to get married, Nora?"

"No."

"But you received offers?"

"Yes."

"But not from the one you wanted, I bet. You were disappointed in love? He made another match? So many women after so few men."

Nora laughed, and not with scorn, at this mixing of perceptiveness with misapprehension. "You're wrong. I think there's a certain degradation in marriage. As soon as you admit someone to yourself in that way you are vulnerable. Marriage is not something I would ever choose for myself, whoever the man."

"You're very independent! Not like me. I approve. You'll never be replaced by a young girl in a waiting room with that attitude. But I'm also sceptical. No one's immune to love."

"You're the seer." Nora was arid. "Look into the future; will I ever marry?"

"Sure. I promised I'd read your fortune, didn't I? And I haven't yet."

Berenice approached Nora's bedside. She looked into Nora's eyes and clasped her hands. Nora expected her to commence her usual pseudo-trance state; to predict a story with the greatest drama, perhaps a tempestuous elopement or a tragic loss. When Berenice remained steady, Nora realised, a second before it came, that a barb was coming instead, the casual assertion of a pecking order made by schoolgirls in a dormitory.

"You're right after all, Dr Dickinson," the Icon said matter-of-factly. "You're never going to marry anyone."

An hour later Nora lay awake, listening to icicles melt at the window ledge. Drip, drip, drip, on wood. That must mean thaw. The roads would open. She could escape the beast that haunted her; go back to Zurich, where Leo had banished her ghosts once before. He would do so again, and banish Berenice too.

From the creak of a hinge next door she knew Berenice was also still awake.

Nora tiptoed from the bed to the shared wall. A square crystal vase containing a single orchid stood upon an occasional table. She tossed the flower onto the floor and held the glass to the wall, bringing her ear close. It sounded as though Berenice was pacing. Maybe she was a poor sleeper. Nora could learn the rhythms of Berenice's sleep now, and re-enact the times, like this, that Berenice rose. Could Nora learn to slumber and wake according to the exact same pattern? Was it any different from anything else she had replicated, to acquire Berenice's rhythms?

The pacing stopped. Behind the very spot of the glass, Berenice rapped the wall in a succession of beats. Nora backed from the wall in surprise. It was a code, Morse code, she thought, though she didn't know for definite. Berenice stopped and laughed. Apparently Nora had not been silent enough to escape detection.

Nora got into bed. The door inched open a few seconds later.

"Dr Dickinson, I know you're just pretending to sleep!" The Russian in her voice was more pronounced again.

"I'm still awake," Nora confirmed.

Berenice ran to Nora's bed and, with an exaggerated shiver, slid between the covers. The tips of her feet brushed against Nora's calves, her touch icy.

"Can you hear the snow melt?" Berenice asked in a whisper.

"Yes. Will you leave tomorrow, do you think? If the roads are open?"

"They won't be; that much snow will turn to flood. You wait. Get closer, Nora. I mean to warm myself, I warn you."

Nora shuffled till their skin touched. The rest of Berenice was cold and soft, cold silk, cold limbs. They couldn't see each other clearly in the darkness, but Nora's thoughts turned to the earlier sight of Berenice's white shoulders, how naked her narrow back had been, how curved the hip and flesh beneath the satin fabric.

"What did you tap through the wall?" Nora asked.

Berenice laughed. "Cash or check?"

"But why?"

"It's an American expression, my baby. A little flirtation, at the end of a night courting."

"What does it mean?"

"It means, are you going to make me wait to kiss you?" Berenice taunted.

Nora digested the question. Snow, or floods, the weather could not keep them there forever, and she had been issued here a call to action. She grabbed Berenice's hair to tilt her head and kissed her. Berenice yielded; Nora swallowed Berenice's saliva, felt the slipperiness of Berenice's inner cheek, the sharp chipped corner of a tooth. So this was how Berenice tasted inside. Nora let herself merely sense, and abandoned her monitoring, until Berenice's thumb edged over Nora's areola, through the taut fabric of her nightdress, and Nora pushed Berenice's hand away. That touch had jerked Nora into common sense again. What use was it, to know how Berenice could excite a woman? Nora couldn't use that at all. But to know what Berenice was excited by, her movement and voice in that excitement, was valuable. Nora could use such knowledge. She could incorporate it into her own careful imitation of Berenice, should Leo ever take the opportunity to compare them again.

"Sit on your heels," Nora ordered.

Berenice obeyed. Nora sat similarly, facing her, and pushed the skirt of Berenice's satin nightgown up around her waist, prompting Berenice to remove it altogether. She dropped it silently to the floor by the bed. Nora felt Berenice shiver again. Slowly, against the grain, Nora stroked the down on Berenice's thighs. Bumps of gooseflesh rose palpably on Berenice's skin. Nora lightly traced their emergence, from the coolness of Berenice's knee up. The tops of Berenice's thighs were warmer. Between her legs was hot. Nora heard Berenice's intake of breath. Another breath, as Nora's touch moved back, and forth, over the correct spot, and inside her. The breaths ascended into cries. Nora was glad Berenice did not come quietly. It meant Nora could be loud, when she assumed Berenice's voice and utterances; and imitating the nuances of a silence was so much harder than imitating a cry. The sound, what Leo would be able to hear, was what mattered in Nora's performance. In the darkness, Nora couldn't see Berenice's face well, and Nora felt a passing frustration at this, before mentally scolding herself that she didn't need to see Berenice. Leo never looked at Nora's face, anyway. He never had. To assume Berenice's facial expression would be wasted on him.

The darkness was on Berenice's mind too. From the bed, she leant to the window, which was just over an arm's comfortable length away. In one fierce movement she yanked at the curtain. The velvet ripped free from the rings. The moon shone on Berenice's face and breasts. She was white and luminous as a phantom, her hair bright.

"I hate not to be seen," she said. "My husband puts his hand over my face when we're intimate. Can you imagine such a thing?"

The disclosure, the good timing of it, almost made Nora believe in Berenice's occult powers. For at the very point she needed it Nora understood something new about Leo: he had not turned her face away because she was not Berenice.

He did so because he must render a woman anonymous to take her. She saw this was his flaw, not hers.

Berenice kept her eyes fixed on Nora's. She, again, placed her hand upon Nora's breast, her expression cautious, seeking permission. "Don't you want me to please you? Don't you want me to give you pleasure?"

Nora's own pleasure was useless. It had no purpose. And the generosity of Berenice's question brought Nora the closest to guilt she had been; for the first time, she contemplated whether she should apologise to Berenice, for the slow theft of her words, her stories, her passage through the world. For these thefts were surely worse than the sexual knowledge of her husband, from a time before he was even promised to Berenice. The attempt to don Berenice like a carapace must be worse even than a plot to re-win Leo's attention.

"Of course I want you to please me – it's only – I have not been entirely honest with you," she confessed.

Berenice's gaze fell on Nora's arm. The panstick had smeared away from the tattoo.

"I never thought you were honest," Berenice said. "You lie nearly every time you speak. Do you want me to touch you?"

"Yes."

"Is that a lie?"

"No."

"Well then," Berenice said, and she pushed Nora back onto the bed.

PART TWO

THE WOODS,
EDWARDIAN ENGLAND

I

Nora remembers every conversation she heard in the womb. She remembers the sound of her mother's blood, every pulse of it, and the words that reached her through warm dark muscle, despite her not yet knowing their meaning. There were a great number of insults: in her mother's voice, *swindler* and *filthy foreigner* and *wolf*. In her father's voice, *succubus*. When Nora was born her mother cried: "I didn't want a girl." Her father merely said, upon seeing her: "She looks like the last one. A little revenant." Then she assumed her place as an only child and never learnt who *the last one* was, for they must have gone before her conception.

Nora remembers everything, including the living room where she learnt to walk: the timber beams, the flags upon the floor, the buttoned red leather armchair and the pale blue Wedgwood on the sideboard. She pulled herself up on the window seat, and looked out on the dense trees, their roots full of snarled rat nests. When the rats were poisoned, swarms of mites infested the living room. They were tiny, smaller than poppy seeds, and like dancers they grouped in rings before dispersing, slipping down cracks faster than water.

Nora remembers the years her mother was alive. Valery Čapek sat in a rocking chair every day in their small stone house by the stream in the woods. Her face was half Nora's and half somebody else's, somebody both more beautiful, and less patient. Her yellow hair had a sheen, like whale oil that had caught the light. From her neck she wore a glittering jewelled cross. She hemmed the skirts of muslin dresses, then unpicked them again, leaving a series of puncture wounds and a row of puckers where she pulled the thread through. Her skin was punctured too, with one red dot after another. She scratched the skin of her hands in a lazy, sensuous way as she talked. Nora's father, Jaroslav, accused Valery of making the dots herself, jabbing her own soft flesh with the needle whenever he wasn't looking. Valery said *he* was safe from attack; his hide would make a poor dress. She never confirmed or denied that her marks were self-inflicted. Nora had seen the spots rise and bloom only to be replaced by others. Her mother's skin reminded her of a pale underripe strawberry, with irregular pink rashes spreading from the seeds. One day, Nora assumed, her mother would turn scarlet.

Nora never saw her mother enter the village. Valery would send Nora out with a basket and a list of errands and instructions to return with the words of certain villagers.

"But be discreet," she warned Nora.

"Discreet?" Nora echoed.

"That means people can't tell you are listening. They

might complain to your father if they noticed." Valery sighed, unpicking the latest line of stitches from a skirt. "Perhaps it isn't a good idea. You are too little to keep secrets."

"I'm not!" Nora exclaimed, indignant. "I listen to secrets all the time and don't tell them to anyone, not to Father, and not to you, neither."

Valery quickly jabbed the needle in Nora's arm.

"Ow!" Nora yelped. A globe of blood welled and its perfect spherical shape rapidly collapsed into a smear and dried.

"A girl mustn't keep secrets from her mother," Valery instructed. "It's quite a different thing from telling your father."

"Why?"

"Because he owns us, that's why. He owns me and you and every mechanical convenience in the house. We are on a different side to him, Nora." Valery pulled a strand of red thread from her lip.

"You're not on my side," Nora reminded her. "You never wanted a girl."

"Because any daughter I could bear is another of his chattels. That's why I didn't want you. But neither you nor I get to pick a side. There's us, and there's him."

Nora went through the woods with the basket. She stalked a rat, but there was no need to approach with caution. It wasn't afraid of her at all. It wasn't friendly, either. She drew close enough to see mites crawling in the matted fur. Underneath, she thought, the rat's flesh must be as bloodspecked as her mother's.

★ ★ ★

Nora attended the village school. When she was eleven the old schoolmistress, Miss Banbury, died. The new teacher was ebony haired and she closed her eyes when she spoke to you. Her name was Irene Lowrie. She trained the class in penmanship, where Nora excelled because she could replicate Miss Lowrie's chalk copperplate perfectly. Miss Lowrie taught the girls needlework and Nora was reprimanded for retracing the exact sequence of her mother's stitches: a row sewn, and a row unravelled.

"You'll write lines," Miss Lowrie decreed. "'I must not wantonly ruin my work.'"

But Nora's work was executed exactly as she had wished, in close imitation of what she had seen. The length of every stitch and the speed of its unravelling were identical to her mother's. It was through her punishment that Nora learnt not all indiscretions were spoken. She must be discreet in deeds as well as in words. Her mimicry, her recordings and imitations were a private matter, as Valery had always implied. Enacted publicly they risked misunderstanding and hostility. Better they only be revealed in an intimate context. Valery took pleasure in the wanton ruining of her work; she did not want to be productive, or useful to her husband and household. She wished to needle him, and Nora believed none of that was Miss Lowrie's business. Nora wrote out her lines, and did not mimic her mother through speech or action at school again.

The reasons why her parents' marriage had ever taken place at all eluded Nora because she had not witnessed, and by necessity could not remember, their courtship.

"Why did you accept my father?" she asked her mother, the evening after Miss Lowrie gave her lines.

"He put an engagement ring in my stew," Valery said acridly. "I broke my tooth upon the stone, and the bastard kept the tooth."

Nora did not understand this explanation, but the profanity shocked her enough to prevent further questions: the only time she had heard the word before was from sly little Robert Scott at school and he had been badly whipped for it. She was startled to hear it applied to her father. She had never watched Jaroslav as closely as her mother. He was not at home, while her mother was; Valery was the more obvious study for Nora to undertake, particularly because they were on the same side. Jaroslav left for work early in the mornings with his black leather case of steel instruments and his vials of chemicals. Once Nora had asked Valery what they were used for. Chopping off fingers and toes and ears and eyelids, had come the response, but Nora guessed these must be exceptional incidents, required once or twice a year at most. Unless they were hidden away, the village housed few fingerless or earless residents. Nora imagined that maybe her father listened to hearts and looked down people's throats, as he had hers from time to time. She suggested as such, and Valery replied, her voice laden with contempt: "People can't afford the doctor for a sore throat, Nora."

The surgery was in the village. Just because he was not on their side, did that mean Nora should be ignorant of his pursuits and interests? She suspected the opposite were true. The next morning she did not go to school as she should. She set out on foot at the earlier time of her father's departure, keeping a dozen steps behind him so he would not know he was being followed. She silently registered every footfall and swing of his arm. She recorded the breaking of every twig on the woodland floor. Her own steps were as light and nimble as Miss Lowrie's. And yet he stopped at the wood's edge, when she had anticipated his onward stride, and without turning round, he said: "Nora."

She did not reply because he could not have seen her. But he spoke again, in Czech. "Nora. Show yourself."

Grudgingly she walked to the spot where he stood, her head hanging.

"Creeping behind me like a white ghost," he observed.

"*A little revenant,*" she said in his voice; then in her own, reminded him: "That's what you said when I was born."

He was cocking his head. "It's an odd mind you possess. Your mother said you would. This mimicry isn't my trait."

"Do you doubt I'm your child?"

"No. You have my chin." He proceeded along the earthen path. She tailed him again, immediately behind this time. "Nora. Does your mother ever ask you to repeat things you've heard?"

"No," said Nora, thinking of her discretion.

"And yet you followed me. Did you mean to follow me to the surgery door?"

"Mother didn't know I was doing that. I wanted to see you at work."

"You couldn't have entered without my notice."

"Will you let me?"

"Don't be ridiculous, Nora. You know you can't be present during patient consultations. It's private. I'll make sure you arrive at school myself."

The patient and the doctor was another private, intimate exchange, then, just like her imitations. She would be well in time for the start of school. When they reached the low wooden gate, one of the village children was playing two-ball; James Markham, dark curled and with a determined set to his teeth despite being only twelve, looked sideways at the doctor. If a parent came to the school it usually signalled someone was in trouble, either the teacher or more likely a pupil. Miss Lowrie herself was just arriving, one hand at the back of her hat to prevent it flapping in the wind.

"And that is your teacher, Nora? The Lowrie girl?" he asked.

"Yes."

"What a refined girl she is; I've often thought her deportment and her low, gentle speaking are the very ideal for a girl such as yourself to aspire to."

"She closes her eyes when she speaks to you," Nora complained.

"Very modest of her. Do you hear me, Nora? I want you to pay attention to Miss Lowrie's modesty. It is the most important feminine attribute, and any daughter of mine should possess it."

"Yes, Father, I am listening." She had no choice but to listen to him. He spoke of Miss Lowrie with emphasis and deliberation, as if he were giving a speech in a play, not like his ordinary speaking voice at all.

"Don't forget, now," he said. "She's the type of lady you should wish to be."

"I never forget anything I'm told," Nora said, though that didn't mean she did as she was instructed, and she didn't want to be a schoolmistress one bit, even if Miss Lowrie was less wizened than decrepit Miss Banbury. Did her father really want her to teach penmanship and needlework to motley children? Somehow it didn't seem very likely.

He meant he approved of how she walked and so on, that was what he valued her for, rather than the drudgery she undertook for pay.

Miss Lowrie was at the gate. "Dr Čapek... I didn't expect Nora to be accompanied. Was there something you wished to discuss with me?"

He surprised Nora by saying: "Yes, Miss Lowrie – if I might take a moment of your time."

Nora watched the two adults enter the schoolroom. She saw them, through the window, stand opposite each other by Miss Lowrie's desk. Her father spoke at length. He would have switched to English. Nora could lip read well enough, in ordinary circumstances, but her father's moustache prevented her from interpreting his speech. She could tell only that Miss Lowrie's face formed expressions of concern, even as her eyes closed. At one point Miss Lowrie clasped her hands to her mouth in sympathy. After several minutes the adults nodded at each other in farewell and her father left. Nora watched him leave the yard by the side gate without bidding her goodbye.

Miss Lowrie refrained from mentioning their discussion during the morning's lessons. At noon when the other children filed from the schoolroom into a drizzly and rather damp schoolyard, Miss Lowrie asked Nora to wait.

"It must be hard," she said delicately, "seeing your mother so frail."

Nora was speechless, for frail was not a word she would use to describe her mother.

"For you and your father both," Miss Lowrie prompted. "I wonder, Nora – do you help with the care of the home?"

"We have a girl in from the village."

"Yes, but there are some matters which one needs the loving attention of a mother to learn. I see better now why you have struggled to fulfil some of the more domestic lessons at school. The circumstances at home must be very difficult for your father, and you must think more on what it means to be the lady of a house. He has asked me to take you under my wing where possible. I would begin by drawing your attention to your character and attitude. It isn't wholly your fault, you haven't had the proper guidance, but there are matters of feminine conduct it would do well for you to master, not least speaking to your father with love and affection, as befits a loyal daughter. I believe that would be a great solace to him, in his, and your mother's, difficulty."

"Thank you, Miss Lowrie," Nora said neutrally.

"That's quite all right. You may join the other children now, but we'll discuss these matters again in future, you may count upon it."

When Nora repeated the conversations of the day to her mother, Valery laughed unpleasantly, dropping her sewing in her lap.

"All that was for my benefit," she said. "The admiration of Miss Lowrie; and encouraging her to belittle me to you. He knew you'd recite it all back to me. It is not enough just to own me; I must be humiliated as well. Men like to put wives in their place, and remind them of their failures."

Nora paused. "Should I not have said anything?"

"You must always tell me everything you hear. He might think to manipulate you – and upset me – but I see right through him. He is performing, Nora, a show entirely to demean me."

"I did think he sounded like he was in a play."

"He was, of his own devising, and he is a poor playwright." Valery was scathing. "The escapade will come to nothing, Nora. He thinks to make me jealous with compliments to a pretty young lady but I know he daren't anger me by doing worse."

"You're prettier than Miss Lowrie, Mother," Nora insisted. It was true. Though Miss Lowrie was younger and not covered in pinpricks.

"I know I am prettier," Valery enunciated. "And so does he."

"She told me to be a loving daughter," Nora mused.

"Yes, and you should put on a show too, doing exactly that. Let him think his ruses have worked too well, the fool. Persuade him you *are* a loving daughter, one who wouldn't dare repeat his foolishness to me, from affection for him and respect for my *frailty*. And I'll act too as if you've never spoken. But don't forget your loyalties, Nora. You will still report his real thoughts, as well as the lies, back to me."

Nora considered how to make herself a loving daughter. It would be difficult to do so at home, when he was never there. She had wished to see inside his surgery, so perhaps offering daughterly help and assistance wouldn't be so bad if it gained her admission. He had said she must not be present when he spoke with the patients, but surely she could be of help outside that capacity? She would suggest as much to Miss Lowrie first. Nora could pick flowers for vases, or serve waiting patients tea; these were domestic chores and Miss Lowrie had urged her to be more domestic.

If the suggestion reached Dr Čapek via Miss Lowrie, he would be less inclined to view it as a second attempt at stalking him through the woods. He may believe Nora had taken Miss Lowrie's instruction to heart.

She went out then and there to pick wildflowers from the wood, to practise arrangements. The ground was dense with daisies and trefoil and knapweed. The hokey pokey tickled her wrists as she bent to pick the flowers and a stinging heat spread over her skin. Now her arms looked like Valery's, marked pinkly with pinpricks and soft, round circles. Valery would no doubt place hokey pokey in the vases, to give patients a shock if they bent to sniff the flowers. She specialised in provocation. But Nora, at her mother's very instruction, specialised in discretion. It might be a lesson she would later reject, but it served her well in childhood, when much depends on adults forgetting you are there.

2

The plan to infiltrate the surgery worked. Miss Lowrie
made her suggestion to Nora's father, and he acquiesced;
Nora might spend a short period in the waiting room after
school, changing water for the flowers and bringing him
a teatime refreshment between his appointments. By these
means Nora saw her father's consultation room for the first
time. He worked in a compact room, with cream walls, a
pine floor and a square window of opaque pale green glass.
A substantial square sink with a gingham skirt occupied
one corner. The shelves above bore shining bottles of blue
and orange glass. The other corner was adorned with an
alphabet on a scroll, for the testing of eyesight. A brown
leather folding couch ran across the opposite wall. Her
father's desk sat at right angles to it, with two chairs, one
for him, one for his patient. Sometimes, when Nora brought
him his customary cup of tea and biscuit, he shooed her out
again, but sometimes he allowed her to take the patient's
chair, and watch him as he ate and drank, a dusting of
shortbread falling upon the polished surface of his desk.
When he had finished he swept the crumbs with one hand

into his saucer and wordlessly returned it to Nora, which was her cue to leave him in peace. She wondered if his silence was a strategy for avoiding Nora's repetition of his words to Valery. Once, at home, Nora carefully imitated her father eating a biscuit for her mother's benefit. Valery sighed and remarked Nora would be much better to focus on his conversations with patients, rather than his table manners. Valery had seen her own husband eat often enough. What she hungered for was knowledge of his movements through the world, the things he said to the other villagers, and, most of all, the things he said to the other villagers about *her*.

Nora had reasons of her own for wanting greater insight into the words that passed between doctor and patient. She was beginning to think she might like to be a doctor – to sit in that communion and dispense remedies, as she guessed such meetings entailed. So she did not need encouragement to eavesdrop on her father's consultations, but she did lack obvious means. She was rarely in the waiting room alone, and couldn't be seen listening at the door by any of the villagers. A side room containing clean bandages and dressings offered better concealment. Under the pretext of dusting, she could enter, and press her ear to the wall shared with her father's office. The words were always too muffled to make out. Weeks passed without Nora solving how to hear through lath and plaster.

She tried to use her knowledge of her father's shibboleths. He was fastidious about vectors, refusing to install a telephone, despite their emerging popularity for doctors' surgeries, because he insisted it harboured infection. Warm rooms, Nora had gathered, were also conducive to infectious spread.

"If fresh cool air is good for one," Nora observed, breaking the silence of their next tea-and-biscuit session, "why not allow the air to circulate, and lift the sash?"

She could then also open the side room window, to hear everything through the ether.

But her father scoffed. "And have patients complain of a chill? There's no need. We have a well-ventilated building."

He gestured, with half a shortbread finger, to the iron vent that had previously escaped Nora's notice. It was positioned at an adult's eye level – reachable by Nora, if she had something on which to stand.

That day, once her duties were complete, Nora walked to the rear of the building rather than take the path home. She took care to avoid the window, though her father was unlikely to detect her presence through the obscured glass; and she noticed, for the first time, that the pane was cracked, a single black line zigzagging from the leaded corner and ending in a tiny triangle of air. Now Nora upturned a flowerpot and perched unsteadily upon it to listen at the vent, which was wrought into decorative swirls, and painted in a fierce yellow that peeled to show the iron beneath. Despite some echoing distortion she was gratified to learn the voices within were now quite discernible. Because she had seen the patient arrive she knew her father was talking to Mr Edward Markham, a man from the village who was something called an accountant. He had not arrived with his dog today.

"She has always been plagued by minor ailments," he said. "She sabotages her duties and her appearance, as if the whole world is against her."

Nora was puzzled, because this sounded very like a description of her mother, and Mr Markham had no connection with her.

"Of late her hair has been falling from her head," Mr Markham continued. "She isn't fit to leave the house."

"Mrs Markham can be added to my rota of house calls," Nora's father responded, and Nora realised that the accountant's wife must be the afflicted woman. She had seen Mrs Markham before, with the Markhams' son James, who was near Nora's age and familiar from school. Did Mrs Markham constrain herself regretfully from physical illness, or was the illness a secret relief, allowing her to withdraw from society, if only her husband wouldn't meddle with doctors and their house calls? This was the question that most interested Nora, and she waited for her father to ask Mr Markham which of the two applied to his wife. But following the assurance of his visit the next day it appeared Dr Čapek had no further thoughts on the matter.

Nora stepped down from her flowerpot, disappointed. As she walked home she attempted to fabricate a different patient's account for her mother. Though keen to impart she had finally found a way to eavesdrop, Nora anticipated an angry reaction from her mother if the details of Mrs Markham's situation, so similar to her own, were relayed. Her mother did not like to have her individuality undermined. But Nora's imaginative faculties were poorly developed – she always believed this was, in some way, the trade-off for her preciseness of replication – and by the time she reached the cottage, she was resigned to reciting Mr Markham's words verbatim.

Yet Valery remained quite calm through the telling of it. So calm that Nora felt brave enough to venture a related question.

"Mother, why do you stay at home all the time?"

"I grew too attached to these stones." She was bitter, glowering at the walls. "It's a danger, with my kind, and yours, that we sometimes get bound to a particular spot. Like a binding curse or a glamour. I can't pass the gate to the north or the stream to the south. If I had a looking glass I could go further, at least for a while, but your blasted father won't let me have one. The windows and the water won't do, I can't see myself well enough."

Nora didn't understand half these words, but at the mention of the looking glass, took Valery to mean – like Mrs Markham – that she wasn't fit to be seen. Valery was much more comely than Mrs Markham, and the loss of Mrs Markham's hair had surely cemented the difference; but perhaps Valery was vain about her rash. She wouldn't leave without checking her appearance.

"Are you and Mrs Markham the same kind, then?" Nora asked hesitantly.

"No!" Valery laughed. "Mrs Markham is just mad and unhappy."

Over the following weeks and months Nora's appetite for spying grew. She became adept at finding spots to hide and spots to listen, making good use of vents in other village houses, but also taking advantage of the summer warmth to dawdle near open windows and doors propped wide. One Saturday afternoon she observed the attic dormer of the schoolhouse thrown open – it would be fiercely hot in the loft, Nora guessed, though she wasn't sure what business would be conducted there after the end of lessons. She climbed the overhanging oak by the schoolhouse, and rested on a branch, carefully, trying to keep from the view of the window.

The loft was occupied. It took a moment for Nora to make sense of what she heard, for there was no conversation, only the short, pained whimper of a breathless woman. It was a high, choking, recurrent sound, made ghostly by the emptiness of the loft. After a minute or two Nora heard a man mutter: "Quieter, you must be quiet."

She knew the voice, she'd heard it before, in the village and in her father's surgery. It was Mr Markham.

"But there's no one to hear," came the response, in Miss Lowrie's voice, still with that breathlessness that suggested pain.

"It was a mistake to meet you here. We cannot meet unless you are quiet. You must be undetectable."

"I'm sorry; I'll be quiet." She was meek. There was no more sound, though Nora craned so close she risked losing her balance on the branch. Several minutes later, Mr Markham spoke again. "Get dressed; hurry."

The strangeness of the exchange led Nora into recklessness. She shifted into view of the window, counting on the leaves to disguise her. Through the open dormer she saw the naked Miss Lowrie, picking up her garments to dress. The curve of her belly was like a snowdrop's sloping petals, and her skin was as white. Nora covered her mouth with her hand in shock. She saw the protruding stomach ripple as though something moved beneath the surface. Poor Miss Lowrie.

Something must be very wrong inside her; no wonder she cried out in pain. And yet how odd that she should be so shameless. Nora recollected, at the age of two, being beaten soundly for escaping her tin bath and running naked into the garden; and her father had never allowed mirrors in the house. She had taken in his lesson that modesty, and propriety, depended on the proper veiling of the body. Yet here was Miss Lowrie, naked in the schoolhouse, for Mr Markham to see.

Miss Lowrie looked up, and Nora ducked. Silently, Nora swarmed down the tree, and when she reached the ground she ran the rest of the way home. She might have asked her mother the meaning of what she had seen, but couldn't even work out what question to ask; no aspect of it was intelligible enough to her to know where to begin. The incident played on her mind for days to come and Miss Lowrie edged, sideways, into Nora's conversations with Valery.

"Miss Lowrie is getting fat," Nora commented. "Maybe that's why Father hasn't complimented her again."

For he hadn't; since that day he'd walked her to school, Jaroslav had never again praised Miss Lowrie, or another woman, in Nora's presence.

Valery dismissed Nora's theory. "Your father dislikes underfed women. Fleshiness is a sign of health."

Nora considered this. She was captivated by Miss Lowrie's changing form, which it seemed no corset could disguise. Her bosom and belly rose like the loaves in the baker's window. Her face glowed pinkly and dimpled, giving no clue of the suffering that led her to weep in the loft. Perhaps fleshiness *was* a sign of health, for she seemed to be thriving in appearance. And Nora concluded that Valery was right; Jaroslav would not consider her less charming for this.

"It is merely as I said at the outset," Valery continued. "He taunted me by comparing us once, but dared do no more. Never forget your father is a coward."

"He hasn't mentioned you either, Mother, not in any of his conversations I've heard. Should I stop listening at the vent?"

"No," Valery demurred.

"Why not?"

"It keeps me alive to the village. And who knows what titbit may one day be useful?"

Nora had no idea. The problems the villagers brought to her father took on a sameness, with just a handful of ailments coming up again and again. Mr Markham was far from the only man to complain of an indisposed wife. Nora would have minded the lack of variety less if her father had only asked the right questions of his patients. He never asked of their thoughts, or even their feelings, concentrating on the mechanics of their bodies as if he were a watchmaker tinkering with some faulty cogs. One evening, relinquishing hope of his ever noticing what mattered, she stepped down from the flowerpot halfway through a consultation and busied herself with daisy chains. She fell asleep, in the sunshine, a daisy between her fingers.

Fortunately she was not roused from dozing by her father's discovery, but by the church clock chiming seven. It was still light, and she should have been home by now, as her father's surgery closed at half past five. He often had house calls to conduct, which lengthened his working hours, but it was rare for him to still be in his consulting rooms. She stood, brushing soil from her skirts. She faced a predicament. Valery would expect a full hour of repeated conversation, and Nora couldn't provide this much. This caused considerable fretting on the way home. When she reached the house, Valery was not sewing or unpicking in her chair as usual. Nora called up the stairs and heard no response. Valery could not have gone far: she never ventured past the gate to the north of the house, nor the stream to the south. Sure enough, Nora looked through the kitchen window, and saw her mother poking a small fire with a stick by the far wall.

Nora sat on the footstool by her mother's empty chair, feet turned toes inwards, and smoothed her dress over her knees. Because her routine was to recite the conversations of the day, and the evening had sorely lacked routine, she wished to begin her recital even without an audience. The repetition of speech would soothe her. She would lose herself in it. For ten minutes she spoke to the empty room, recounting both sides of the tedious consultation about earache that had preceded her slumber. Then she paused, uncertain what to say next, having entered the phase of her sleeping. Her thoughts turned again to Miss Lowrie, naked on a hot summer's day. With minimal examination of her reasons, Nora slipped into a fresh performance; the repetition of Miss Lowrie's cries. Nora lost track of how long they took, focusing only on the accuracies of pitch and timbre.

"What are you doing, Nora?" Valery said from the doorway, her voice dangerously cold.

"I began my mimicking without you," Nora explained. "What were you burning?"

Valery looked at her palms. "The rat corpses. I wearied of the smell while they rotted. Who are you mimicking?"

"Miss Lowrie." The memory of the teacher's swollen belly returned. She realised she could let her mother think the cries were overheard in the surgery. Nora need not say she had fallen asleep and missed any conversation, risking her mother's anger. So she added: "Miss Lowrie has a stomach complaint."

"Start mimicking again from the beginning, if you please."

Nora dithered, because Valery was still to sit down.

"Didn't you hear me?" Valery demanded. "Start again!"

Nora did so. Her accuracy did not suffer from nerves and yet this time it was impossible to lose herself in the recital because a sense of oncoming trouble built inside her. When she reached Mr Markham's words, she said them instead in her father's voice, his lingering Czech accent. This maintained the pretence Miss Lowrie was at the surgery.

"*You must be undetectable.*"

Valery shot forward, her hand snaking to Nora's face in a slap.

Nursing the burning cheek with her own hand, Nora uttered Miss Lowrie's next words. "*I'm sorry. I'll be quiet.*"

A silence elapsed while Valery waited.

"*Get dressed. Hurry,*" Nora said, in her father's voice. Then in her own: "Why did you hit me, Mother?"

"Because you're a dolt. What is wrong with Miss Lowrie's stomach?"

"It's very swollen and moves like it can't contain its contents. What disease causes that?"

"It's a disease of morals. She caught it from your father." Finally, her mother sat down, and picked up the sewing, though she did not stitch or cut. She stared at the wall.

"Will I catch it?" Nora asked, nervous.

"No. You must go to school tomorrow as normal. Act as if nothing were amiss. Then tell Miss Lowrie: your father has given you a message for her. It will say he has requested her presence here, at the cottage, as soon as school is over."

"But what if she should check?"

"She will have no reason to doubt you. You can forge a script as well as you can copy a voice."

Nora nodded. At Valery's instruction, she fetched ink, a pen, paper and an envelope. The message was very short and did not stretch her powers of imitation. Her father's *L*s had two loops and two tails. His *B*s were fatter below than above, like Miss Lowrie's belly. The paper was cream and the ink was black. Valery read the words through, gave a curt nod of approval, inserted it into the envelope, and licked the seal with a flash of her wet, pink tongue. She passed it to Nora.

"Put it in your satchel."

"Why do you want Miss Lowrie to come here, Mother, if we might catch her disease?"

"We won't. I have a remedy for her particular sickness."

"What is the remedy?"

"Butchery. Did you think your father was the only butcher in the family?" At this Valery started to laugh, though Nora was unsure what was amusing about sickness or butchery, or indeed what butchery her father was involved with.

The next day was inexorable. The envelope lay in Nora's satchel, waiting to be called into use, and all the time it was there Nora failed to concentrate on her work. Never a noisy or disobedient child, she was subdued enough for Miss Lowrie to ask more than once if she were sickening. Each time Nora's eyes widened in alarm at the mention of illness. Did Miss Lowrie know her ailment was catching? At least Valery had a plan to implement. Nora must take comfort in that, even if the need to forge a letter escaped her. She reminded herself that Jaroslav was always, as Valery insisted, on his own side, and the rest of them were on the other. Nora, Valery, every convenience in Jaroslav's house. And, apparently, Miss Lowrie too.

The final bell of the day rang at last. The children filed out in line, but Nora remained, and wordlessly passed the envelope to Miss Lowrie. She looked perplexed to receive it, then flustered as she read the words.

"Nora, what did your father say to you when he asked you to deliver this?"

"Nothing, Miss," Nora said. "I can accompany you, to the cottage."

"I see." Miss Lowrie still looked anxious. "Forgive me, Nora, but – is your mother expected to be at home?"

Thinking of her mother's excursion the previous evening to burn the rats, Nora said: "She has been busy outdoors."

"I see. I'm very glad to hear that. Then, if you don't mind waiting while I fetch my coat and hat, we'll do as your father asked, and walk through the woods together."

Jaroslav was at the surgery, and would be there long after Nora and Miss Lowrie reached the cottage. He wouldn't learn of the forgery till then; he wouldn't learn until Miss Lowrie was, at Valery's hand, cured.

3

Miss Lowrie kept talking while they walked through the woods. She didn't require much response from Nora, who was supposed to listen to the advice on proper conduct and feminine duty. At one point, halfway, Miss Lowrie begged Nora that they might rest for a moment; she placed one hand on a tree trunk and the other on her middle, and took some breaths with her eyes closed.

"Are you in a lot of pain?" Nora asked, sympathetic, thinking of Miss Lowrie's illness.

"Not a bit of it," Miss Lowrie replied. "I'm merely light-headed."

They resumed their walking. The cottage eventually appeared before them, and Miss Lowrie exclaimed: "But it's quite a pretty little house! How well tended!"

There were no rats in view, to be sure, and no smell of decay, following Valery's pyre of corpses.

"Come with me," instructed Nora, who led the way to the wooden door with its diamond of glass. On the other side, Valery was in her rocking chair as expected. But she wasn't sewing or unpicking. She was steeping tea. She smiled at her visitor. Nora was so unused to Valery being hospitable the smile made her nervous. They had never, in her recollection, welcomed a guest. But Miss Lowrie didn't know that.

"You must be Mrs Čapek," was all she said. "I'm so pleased to meet you at last."

"The doctor will be along shortly," Valery said. "Do join me for tea? Nora, pour if you would, please."

Nora noted there were two cups available. She did not drink tea herself. The set was the one they used for best, with its pattern of wildflowers and its gilded edges.

Miss Lowrie removed her hat and took the other seat.

"I'm in the dark as to what the doctor requires," she said carefully.

"My husband is a very simple man, very predictable in his wants and foibles. What he requires is never any mystery. A shrewd woman like you can't have failed to notice that about him."

"I'm afraid I'm in the dark," Miss Lowrie repeated quietly. She sipped the tea, and crinkled her nose, as if the taste were unaccustomed. Valery was staring at Miss Lowrie's middle. Miss Lowrie self-consciously placed a hand upon her waist. With new decisiveness, she drained her cup, and followed by saying: "I've recalled another appointment."

Valery, her eyes still trained on the younger woman's abdomen, enquired: "Then we're graced by your presence. I'm sure the doctor will appreciate you making the time for us."

"I should have remembered before. And as the doctor is yet to arrive, perhaps it would be better if I honoured my prior arrangement. I'd be very happy to talk to him if he came to the school with Nora in the morning?"

"I'm sure you would be," Valery said. "But you're here now, aren't you. More tea? These cups are so dainty – one sip and the tea is gone. Part of my trousseau, you know. I expect you have your own such things in the bottom drawer, don't you, Miss Lowrie? Though time is ticking on for you in that regard."

Miss Lowrie's eyes closed. Nora assumed that, as usual, this was a precursor to her speaking.

"I really should go," the teacher said. "I feel quite faint, all of a sudden."

"You were faint in the woods!" Nora interjected, glad of having something to contribute.

"That was different," Miss Lowrie snapped. She picked up the empty teacup and stared into it. "What tea was this?"

"The ordinary tincture," Valery said mildly. Nora noticed, then, that Valery's cup was still full. Miss Lowrie let her head fall back against the chair, and she appeared to sleep.

"She won't be at rest for very long," Valery murmured. "I wish she'd drunk a second cup."

"What was in it?" Nora asked, alarmed.

"Just a potion your father won't miss. Now, I need your help to move her to the kitchen table. Take her feet, I'll grab her under the arms."

"I'm not strong enough, Mother."

"You're useless, is what you are." Valery stood, and left the room, muttering, presumably to fetch whatever resources were needed from the kitchen if she couldn't get Miss Lowrie there.

Miss Lowrie's eyelids fluttered. Nora knew she should fetch her mother, but she no longer trusted Valery's plans for any of them. The teacher rose from her chair and shuffled a few steps. She picked up her hat, which was testimony to the petty norms one observes in dire predicaments. Miss Lowrie didn't say anything to Nora at all, as she half tottered, half lurched her way to the front door and out again. She didn't shut the door behind her and a breeze was admitted which Nora felt even by the hearth.

Valery reappeared with a cleaver.

"For pity's sake, Nora! Can you not be relied upon for the simplest of things?"

"Miss Lowrie is my elder!" Nora protested. "I was too little to stop her."

Valery seemed to think this was a poor excuse but was in too much haste to reprimand Nora for any longer. She, with cleaver in hand, left the house in search of Miss Lowrie. When she returned, half an hour later, with a bloodied bundle wrapped in her own shawl, and the cleaver in her other hand, her expression was grim but satisfied.

She announced: "Miss Lowrie is dead."

"Dead? From the tea?"

"No. From loss of blood."

Nora followed her mother into the kitchen. She watched her unwrap a severed arm, the sleeve still in place upon it until she cut the fabric away. There Nora saw the mottled pattern of skin marked by hokey pokey, and a floral tattoo. She felt nauseous at the arm's heft and flaccidity. It was inert flesh now, instead of a working limb, and that was only underlined by its flopping heaviness as Valery held it this way and that. She cleaned it with cut lemons.

"What are you doing?" Nora asked.

"Exacting a bit of justice," Valery said. "And I don't care who catches me."

She filleted the arm and diced the flesh. She put the meat in a large mixing bowl, the bones in boiling water for stock. With a large frying pan, she melted a block of lard. When the fat was hot she dropped a handful of meat onto the spitting surface, and hummed softly while it browned. When the colour met her satisfaction she spooned the meat into a big pot and browned the next batch.

Once the meat bowl was empty Nora watched her mother pour in the stock. Valery chopped onions while the meat bubbled. Nora's eyes prickled with the scent. It was a relief to feel the tears soothe the sting.

"Don't cry over her," Valery scolded. "What is she to you? A girl no better than she ought to be. And they placed children in her charge! I've served the village well this evening, Nora."

"I'm not crying over her," Nora protested. "It's the onions."

"Good." Valery's own eyes were dry. She mixed the onions into the pot, and tomatoes too. Sugar, salt, seasoning – the caraway seeds Jaroslav so delighted in – everything was stirred together, then covered with the pot lid.

Nora withdrew from the kitchen, out onto the back step, in search of fresh air. Her mother had been neat, for there was no trail of blood leading the way to Miss Lowrie's corpse, but the body could not be far away. Nora couldn't accept Valery was a murderess. And yet – of all the people Nora had met in her short life – it was also true that Valery was the most likely to commit such a crime.

★ ★ ★

The lack of trail notwithstanding, Nora was, with some meandering through the trees, able to find her mother's victim. Miss Lowrie was right at the side of the stream, beyond which Nora had never seen her mother cross. Now Nora crouched down, unable to look at anything other than Miss Lowrie where she lay among the nettles. Between the flushed patches of wheals and welts her skin was bluish-white. Beads of perspiration lined her lips and hairline. Her eyes were closed, as they were so often when she addressed the children. She was trying to address Nora now, or so Nora assumed. Miss Lowrie's breaths wheezed. Her tongue swept over cracked lips. Nora hoped the words that proved so difficult to utter wouldn't be a plea to get help from the village. Without having been told, Nora knew that her mother would be furious if she did such a thing. And now she saw what her mother, in rage, was capable of, Nora had no desire to defy her.

"Edward," Miss Lowrie said, her voice hoarse.

Edward? Mr Markham, Nora realised. He was an odd person to call for. Nora wasn't sure if it were an instruction to her to fetch him, or if Miss Lowrie was confused over who was present. In either case, he was an unsympathetic man, to Nora's recollection of their exchange in the schoolhouse.

"*You must be undetectable*," Nora said in his voice.

This did seem to calm Miss Lowrie – at least, the wheezing diminished, though Nora wondered if that was because she was trying to hold her breath, the better to please Mr Markham, rather than because she was soothed by the knowledge of his presence. Had he ever made a kinder comment, Nora might have repeated that instead.

She speculated if there were some other way to make Miss

Lowrie more comfortable. Moving her from the nettles, if only Nora matched her weight, was the obvious measure to take. But Nora couldn't move her, and the next best thing was applying dock leaves. Nora scampered over the nearest ground, in search of the soothing plants. A clump nestled close to the earth. She tore half a dozen leaves, their edges rubbery against her skin. She walked through the nettles to get close to Miss Lowrie. Her boots and skirts were protection enough from the sting, though she was careful, as she bent closer to her teacher, not to let her arms be in contact with the jutting stems. She dabbed the dock leaves on Miss Lowrie's cheeks as if she were applying a compress. There was no noticeable reduction in the rash and Miss Lowrie still didn't open her eyes but she made a tiny sound, not quite a cry or a sob, a sort of mewl. At this range the smell of the blood was overpowering. It was black and thick on the earth but Miss Lowrie's dress was redly sodden with it, the wet fabric clinging to her skin. Nora wasn't squeamish. She couldn't be, if she was going to be a doctor. She assumed Miss Lowrie would die shortly. Nora didn't know how long such a wound would take to prove fatal, and in that sense, she supposed this was an informative experience. She could see, through the stretched bloody fabric of Miss Lowrie's dress, that something was moving under her stomach again. Nora placed a hand upon the woman's middle to feel whatever was inside beat against her palm. Miss Lowrie must have been very unwell. Maybe she would have died anyway; Valery's actions had hastened an inevitable end, no more. Maybe Valery's actions had been a kindness.

Miss Lowrie was muttering again. Few clear words, to Nora's practised ear. Then:

"Baby," Miss Lowrie said distinctly.

"What baby?" Nora prompted.

Miss Lowrie didn't answer. She was suddenly very still, ceasing even those small shivering twitches of the past few minutes, but Nora could still feel warmth when she placed a hand before Miss Lowrie's mouth. She was still alive. For now, Nora kept dabbing with the dock leaf. Her death should be as comfortable as possible, at least.

She might have remained there till the end, except she heard approaching footfall, and the bright whistling of a man coming closer through the trees. "Come into the Garden, Maud", he was whistling. Nora dropped the dock leaf and sped from the song as quickly as she could while making minimal noise herself. Whoever the man was he would ask questions of her that she didn't want to answer, couldn't answer, unless she was to implicate her mother. It occurred to her, as the cottage loomed finally in her view, that the whistling man would want to fetch a doctor. She wondered if her father had already left the surgery for the day, or if he might still be there if the whistling man ran to get him. It was possible. If her father were called by a third party, and he arrived to help Miss Lowrie, she might yet be saved without any need for Nora to betray her mother's deed. And if Miss Lowrie should name Valery, why, that was Valery's own fault. But Nora couldn't be blamed for it. This thought was very consoling; until Nora saw her father approaching the cottage on a parallel path to her own, and knew that even if the whistling man should run to the surgery at maximum speed, no help would be waiting for him there.

4

"Dinner smells good, doesn't it, Nora?" Jaroslav was jovial in greeting. And the smell was appetising, if you didn't know its provenance. Valery rarely cooked, letting the girl from the village prepare their evening meals to general indifference, but she possessed a talent for it. Nora supposed the girl had been dismissed for the day. Jaroslav would wonder what the special occasion was.

She left her father in the living room and sought out her mother in the kitchen, where she was sipping at the stew she had made, her face flushed with heat from the stove.

"You said it was to be a cure," Nora reminded her mother. "You were going to cure Miss Lowrie of her sickness."

"I did cure her," Valery said with satisfaction.

"You killed her, Mother."

"It is the same thing."

"And will you do the same to Father?"

Valery laughed. "What makes you ask that?"

"You said he had the same sickness."

"I can't do the same to your father." Despite the laughter,

141

Valery's resentment on this point was evident. "He *stole my tooth*, Nora, there is no biting him."

"But why does—"

"I don't know how he came by the knowledge. But he saw what I was the day he arrived in the woods and he knew how to trap me. Now hush. I can punish him in other ways. Jaroslav will learn what we've done soon enough."

"We?"

"You brought her here, didn't you?" Valery said indulgently.

Yes, Nora saw, she was at fault too. Not only by bringing Miss Lowrie to her death, but by setting this strange episode in motion. She had listened in on Miss Lowrie's pain. She had repeated it to her mother. She had lied that her father was present, and though Nora did not fully know why, she saw this detail had angered her mother more than any other.

"Why do you mean to make us eat her, Mother?"

Valery smiled cruelly. "That is your father's punishment for humiliating me."

"But why must I eat her too?"

"You?" Valery said. "You are like me. You will enjoy the taste."

The trio sat at their dining table. Jaroslav was in good spirits; Valery was in good spirits. Only Nora was afflicted with terror and revulsion. She stared at the bowl before her. The stew was stained deeply red. Paprika, and blood, with a sheen of fat glinting on the hot liquid.

Jaroslav spooned the mixture into his mouth with

enthusiasm. "There is nothing like guláš to keep you in good health."

Nora contemplated telling him the truth. *Mother put Miss Lowrie in a stew.* She would be believed, because the evidence was on the forest floor; the body would be silent, but still corroborate Nora's version of events. But the moment to do so had passed, because she watched the tendrils of meat worm their way round her father's teeth. If she told him now, he would know she'd let him eat Miss Lowrie's flesh.

She looked trepidatiously at her own cooling bowl. Jaroslav pointed a knife at her dinner. "Eat," he ordered.

"I'm not hungry," she muttered.

"Eat," he said again.

"Remember Augustus, who wouldn't eat his soup," Valery said warningly.

"Eat or be thrashed," her father added, because he disapproved of waste in any form, and disobedience was scarcely more tolerable to him.

Valery rose from her seat, and knelt before Nora's own. She gripped Nora's face with one hand and turned it towards her.

"Do you ever wonder why your mimicry is so exact, so indistinguishable from the real thing?"

Nora couldn't speak, because Valery's hold was too tight. Her mother continued anyway.

"You're not human, Nora. You're a hyring. That is why you can copy people so well; hyrings imitate. So you can eat your prey then take their place. Now feed."

Valery released her, and Nora saw that she was pretending to be a person, just pretending, nothing more. Nora glanced at her father. He was still, gazing out the cottage window; oblivious to Valery's voice because he was frozen for those few moments in a different reality from theirs. He sighed as the two worlds rejoined.

Nora dipped her spoon into the grease and spice of Miss Lowrie's remains. It was Nora's imagination that made her see a tattoo on the bobbing square of meat. It had gone, when her tears cleared. Raising the spoon to her mouth filled Nora's nostrils with the pungent odour of Miss Lowrie's marinated skin. It passed over her lips, slippery and peppery on her tongue, the meat perceptibly grained, and skidding between her teeth as she ground her jaw on it. She chewed till Miss Lowrie was pulp in her mouth, to postpone the point she must swallow. Eventually she closed her eyes as Miss Lowrie would have done before speaking, before death, and gulped, taking the morsel inside herself. And this was the most terrifying realisation of all: to swallow felt right. Nora had always suspected there was something wrong with her. Now her monstrousness was confirmed, and it was almost relieving to give in. Would she take on Miss Lowrie's qualities too with this irreversible deed? She certainly felt more faint, as Miss Lowrie had been in her final hours. She stood up, her head swimming.

"Is something wrong, Nora?" her father asked.

"*Not a bit of it*," Nora said in Miss Lowrie's voice. "*I'm merely light-headed.*"

She was unconscious before she hit the floor.

5

Nora lay in bed for a week. For much of that time she was unconscious. Periodically Valery roused her to force junket between her clamped lips. When Valery finally succeeded, Nora vomited. And she did so again the next time Valery insisted on feeding her. Reluctantly Valery then limited Nora's diet to water and wine, administered by the spoonful. These episodes were hazy and so unreal to Nora that she wondered if she were finally experiencing what other people called nightmares. Maybe she had dreamt the whole thing: Miss Lowrie bleeding among hokey pokey, the cooked limb, and Valery forcing them to eat her. Sometimes Valery seemed to change shape before Nora's eyes: her teeth lengthened and sharpened, a snout protruded from her face. Sometimes the beast would speak to her: *you ate of me once, in my belly and at my breast, and that is why you are like me.* She would explain the habits of hyrings, their tendencies and weaknesses. Nora's vision would blur. When it returned Valery looked to be her usual self.

Eventually, during an episode of such transformation,

Nora dared to ask a question, her voice croaking: "Was your mother a hyring too?"

"No. When I was eighteen I met an English Lord. He told me the word *hyring*, and what he was, and said I was too pretty to eat. It entertained him to feed me from his wrist."

"How often did you kill?"

"Six or seven or twelve times," Valery said dismissively.

"And you imitated all of them afterwards?"

"Only to make my initial escape. I always returned to the face I was born with... and Valery is the name from my baptism." She sighed with disgust, her sharp teeth glistening. "And now I see no one to imitate. Only the rats, who I run with between the gate and the river. When your father realised, he poisoned them all from spite. The smell of their corpses mocked me."

Valery grew rat-like now, then was her human self once more. The questions were over.

Every time Valery left the bedroom with the empty wine bowl and a silver spoon and a soiled bedpan, Nora lapsed immediately into dead sleep, until she was shaken again. Eventually she woke of her own accord – her mouth was dry and her head pounded, but her sight was crisp and clear, instead of blurrily double-edged. She watched dawn breaking through her window, and when daylight filled her bedroom, she saw that her father was sitting in the corner. He wore his coat and held his hat, in readiness for work.

"What day is it?" she asked, her throat burning with disuse.

"Wednesday," he replied.

"I should wash and dress for school."

"There is no school," he said. "Miss Lowrie is dead, and no decent teacher wishes to replace her."

His voice restored reality after her long sleep, and Nora wished she had remained unconscious.

"Will Mother go to jail?" she whispered.

"What nonsense are you talking?"

"For killing Miss Lowrie."

"Edward Markham killed Miss Lowrie. He has already been apprehended."

The development shocked her. "But Father... It was Mother did it. She cooked her and served her and we ate her."

"Stop saying that!" the doctor roared. "You'll be thrashed if you persist. It's wicked to slander your mother, and a poor reflection on your character to play at such games."

Nora nodded, cowed, yet was inwardly incensed. Her father was staring at the curved brim of his hat. Finally, he said: "I have an aunt in Zurich. Her name is Františka. She can take you, and you will receive tuition there."

"In *Zurich*?"

"Yes, she married a Swiss man, she has been widowed a long time and will welcome the company. The sooner you're gone the better. An incident like this, Nora – it leaves a taint on the community entire. The girls especially. Your prospects could be damaged by association. Every father in the village will be making arrangements for his daughter."

"When will you come to Zurich?"

"We won't."

Nora did not consider protesting. The prospect of escaping Valery was a relief.

"You must eat," Jaroslav instructed Nora. "I won't stand

for you refusing food any more. It is essential you are fit to travel. You will leave by the end of this week, no later."

He stood abruptly and left the room. A few minutes later, she heard the cottage door bang with his departure.

For a while, Nora felt too weak to raise her head from the pillow. The yew trees on the far side of her window were still too, as if they were waiting. No breeze outside today, and no birds to stir the branches. The rats had all been burned.

Unsteadily, Nora got out of bed. Some water remained in the wash stand. She cleaned herself and dressed in a white high-necked blouse and dark skirt. Her father was right; she was wasting from not eating, and felt small in her clothes. Could she bring herself to have breakfast? She thought she could, and hated herself for it. *You're a hyring*, Valery had told her. As a test, Nora pictured the spice-stained flesh, to see if she still wished to eat. To her disgust her stomach growled again with hunger. It was as though her body had betrayed her. She thrust away the thought of the stew.

She clutched the handrail with both hands when she walked downstairs. Valery's chair was empty. Yet the cushion was indented still. Nora sat down there herself. With the fire tongs, she sifted through the ash in the hearth. Yes, there was a single large charred bone, and several smaller ones. They must be fingers.

For now Nora left the remains where they were. She went to the kitchen, and cut herself some bread; there was precious little else in the larder. She ate the bread dry, chewing slowly. Through the window she could see her mother gathering gooseberries. Valery had a crime to answer to. Nora had aided its concealment, because she was terrified of how Valery would react to disloyalty; but could Nora's conscience withstand an innocent man accused? The answer was no. Nora would wrap up the bones and take them to PC McEwan's house on the other side of the woods. They would be the evidence that Valery had killed Miss Lowrie. Nora was not a fool; she knew that monsters were not the business of the police, and yet, in her childish way, the policeman remained the most obvious upholder of justice and the law. Who else could ensure punishment? She reasoned that Valery would be easily cornered, rooted as she was to her lair, and that her weakness and discomfort at being separated from it would limit the damage she could inflict on people from a jail cell. Nora must gather her courage and admit her own part in the crime – the luring of her teacher, and the eating of her. It would be shameful. But afterwards Nora would take comfort from telling the truth.

She wrapped the bones in a small muslin tablecloth, making a bindle of them. She put on her tweed coat and tam o'shanter then carried the bindle by the neck as she left the cottage. The day was bright, though as quiet as she'd observed from the window. Her pace was slow because dry bread for breakfast could only fuel her so far. Every branch and pebble she stepped on was loud in the breezeless air. Nora knew nothing of how arrests proceeded. She assumed she would be incarcerated as soon as she made her confession, and maybe even put to death thereafter. This might be her last chance to walk freely through the world, and believing so made everything uncanny. The comforts of nature – the ordinary benevolence of trees budding, and moss spreading, and ants crawling beneath the rocks – were replaced with a sense that every living substance observed and judged her.

Eventually she came to the glade where Miss Lowrie had died. The hokey pokey was felled in the outline of her body, the stems crushed and criss-crossing each other over the earth. Her blood still stained the leaves. Nora stood there a while, uncertain whether she was imagining a pattern in the red and green. When she looked up, she startled, for she was being watched. James Markham, his back against a tree, was staring at her. His hair was uncombed. He had no coat, and his shirtsleeves were pushed up to the elbows, so that she could see the brown skin of his forearms. She wondered if he was being properly looked after – given that his mother, like hers, was prone to long spells of languor, and his father had been arrested. The sight of James both fed her guilt, and her self-congratulation that she was on her way to report Valery's murderous act. Nora was doing the right thing. She was inhuman; but she need not be immoral.

Nora said, quite boldly, and with the intent to reassure: "I can prove your father is innocent."

"He's as guilty as the devil." James was unequivocal.

Set on explaining, Nora persisted. "My mother killed Miss Lowrie."

"This isn't a woman's crime."

"She isn't ordinary that way," Nora said. "She says she's a monster – called a hyring – who can transform her shape and eat human meat and make me of her kind. My mother *cooked* Miss Lowrie. Part of her. She put her arm in the pot."

The revelation made an impact on James. His mouth fell ajar; she wondered if shock had winded him. Then he laughed, hard and loud.

"The cooking pot! Like something from Grimms' Fairy Tales! What a child you are."

Nora knew her claims were fantastic, and she would need proof to overcome scepticism. But she had expected James to seize on the chance to save his father, not to insist on condemning him. Her hands shook as she untied the knot in the bindle and let the bones spill to the ground. "This is what's left. My mother threw the remains in the fire."

He glanced at the black fragments. "Beef bones."

"They're *not*. Do you *want* to see your father die for something that isn't his fault?"

At this James's eyes turned flinty. "Unlike your mother, my father has a motive. Miss Lowrie was going to have his child."

"A child?" Nora was too old to believe in storks – yet she didn't have an alternative theory for the arrival of babies. Nor did she understand how Mr Markham was the child's father; for surely that role would be fulfilled by Miss Lowrie's husband, if she only had one. "How could Miss Lowrie have his child?"

James sniffed. He picked up the largest bone and with the broken tip rapidly drew a series of diagrams in the loose soil, giving brusque statements of explanation as he went. With each line Nora, reddening, felt the world fall into place, her understanding of many disparate things knitting together. Now she knew the meaning of opaque conversations in her father's office. Now she knew the meaning of Miss Lowrie's nakedness in the loft. Now she knew why her mother was so angry when Nora said her father, not Mr Markham, told Miss Lowrie to be quiet.

"My mother did have a motive," Nora said. "She thought the child was my father's."

"That would do it," James conceded, gathering the rest of the bones into his pockets.

"But she was wrong."

"I know. Miss Lowrie told her sister earlier in the month who was responsible. That's why the police came for him." He met her eye, and asked: "Did your mother really eat Miss Lowrie's arm?"

"We all did." Nora coloured with shame.

"The police won't believe a story like that," James said.

"The bones prove I'm right."

"I have the bones. I'll say my father tried to burn them."

"My mother needs to be punished for what she did." Silently, Nora added: *as do I.*

"I'm telling you to say nothing," James said.

"Don't you have a heart for your own father – he didn't do it—"

"Stop." James looked again at the diagrams on the ground. "Let him hang."

Nora made it as far as PC McEwan's house. It happened as James predicted. She was a little girl, telling a story of a wicked woman in the woods with a cooking pot, and without the bones she had no proof. It was more plausible that she had fallen ill, overheard Valery and Jaroslav discuss the mystery of who killed Miss Lowrie, and merged these fragments into a feverish hallucination where Valery was guilty.

For Nora had been in a delirium all week. Anyone could see she was still weak. The clothes were hanging from her. The policeman sent word to her father: she must be collected. Dr Čapek had to carry her back home, she was so tired. And at the end of the week, he sent her to Zurich.

6

Nora didn't return to England for ten years. The war wasn't long over, and she was just about to commence her medical studies in Switzerland, when she received word her parents had died in a house fire. This ran counter to Nora's expectation Valery would outlive Jaroslav.

So Nora came back to the country of her birth for the nominal purpose of attending the funeral; but when the day arrived, she felt no inclination to travel from London to Alspath. Instead, she diverted to Mayfair. This was where the beauty salons proliferated. She was in search of a very particular treatment, and had identified, in a ladies' journal, an advert for surgical procedures upon the skin. Such a procedure was part of the new wave of services using electricity, which also included hair drying, massaging of the face and removal of hair. Nora wished to avail herself of one particular electrical gadget: a square box of vibrating needles which imparted ink to the body, usually for the purpose of permanent rouge.

The salon was on North Audley Street, in a quiet spot surrounded by townhouses of the affluent. Nora was admitted by a well-spoken receptionist in a nurse's uniform, who took twenty-five guineas from her, then led the way through to the consulting room. A man with a stiff-bosom shirt, a cravat and a stethoscope sat behind an imposing desk ornamented with anatomical mannequins. Eye test charts hung on the wall behind him. As a doctor's daughter who planned one day to be a doctor herself, Nora recognised that these were props to reassure the customer rather than signs of genuine medical expertise. The nurse informed Nora this was Professor Charpentier, passed him a chit with Nora's details upon it, then left the room silently.

"Mademoiselle." He bowed his head courteously. "Let me begin by assuring you of the safety and simplicity of our procedures. The operation is virtually painless, and uses the very safest vegetable matter for colouring the top layer of your skin. We harness the very latest—"

"I have some specific requirements of my tattoo," Nora interrupted.

In a tone of mild reprimand, he replied: "We do not speak of tattoos in Professor Charpentier's salon."

"Very well, I have specific requirements of my procedure. I need the blushing to be imparted to my forearm, not my face; I wish it to have the appearance of a nettle rash. And I would like a small illustration. Will that be possible?"

"Bien sûr," he said with a nod, and Nora cringed inwardly at his ersatz accent. "There will be an additional charge for the illustration. What would you require?"

"A small chrysanthemum, about the size of a postage stamp."

"That would be fifty guineas."

"Can it be done right away?"

"If that is your wish. It is our practice to take a photograph of the finished work; once the procedure is complete you will be shown through into the relevant studio."

He walked her into an adjoining room which seemed at pains to suggest luxurious comfort rather than the medical authority of Professor Charpentier's quarters. The curtains were swagged taffeta, the floors elaborately mosaiced, and pink marble abounded – both in the fireplace and the pedestals that supported palms at the borders of the room. At a black lacquered table, seated in a bamboo chair, was a man of perhaps thirty – balding, bespectacled, braces over his shirt. At his fingertips were a selection of inks in jars, a blade, and the machine which Nora had come for.

"Professor Thomas," said Professor Charpentier. Nora wondered who at the salon was not a seasoned academic. "Mademoiselle has requested some special ornamentation. Might you show her the possibilities?"

Nora took the other bamboo chair as Charpentier left, and explained to Thomas what her requirements were. He provided her with a large bound book, containing a variety of tattoo designs. She turned the pages for some time, newly nervous that the image she had in mind was going to be difficult to replicate exactly. How much variation could there be in a flower? Endless, it seemed. But a third of the way through its pages, her eyes settled upon one that was indistinguishable from Miss Lowrie's. It had not, then, been drawn uniquely for her teacher. It was an image common enough for Nora to find, years later and miles away from the village by the woods.

"This one," she instructed Thomas.

He nodded, and indicated she should roll up her sleeve.

Once the work was under way she grasped that Charpentier had lied about it being painless. But she was glad to endure it. The pain was minor compared to amputation. It was minor compared to lying on a forest floor while your blood nourished the earth.

"You could have paid less if you'd come to me at Mile End," Thomas said quietly, his vowels recognisable as east London. "The society ladies... They don't want to be associated with sailors and the like. But you're not one of those, are you? You're not titled."

"It doesn't matter," she said. "I didn't want to pay less."

Thomas gave his full attention to the artwork, dotting the nettle rash where she indicated she wanted it. The rest of the procedure was conducted without conversation, and Nora departed bearing a permanent reminder of her crime. She had meant the image to be an act of remembrance. It elicited another feeling Nora barely dared own. She enjoyed the resemblance to Miss Lowrie she had created. It was not the result of shifting shape, yet it felt similar, and it tempted her into whispering the words of Miss Lowrie she still remembered. Nora was blessed with a prodigious skill for mimicry. Didn't all prodigies regard their talent as an ambiguous joy?

PART THREE

The Regent Hotel, Birmingham, 1929

I

Carlo Merlini woke in the darkness of his suite. It was glade-like in his bedroom, because of the green suede which covered the walls, and he thought he might have been dreaming of wolves. Cancelled performances often made him sleep fitfully, as though, having anticipated hard work, his body refused to adapt to the new circumstances. But he suspected – this time – *something else* had startled him into wakefulness. A noise? He could hear nothing now; the bedroom was too far from the corridor for him to be troubled by the other guests, and the rain on the window panes was soft.

"Tuono?" he muttered to himself. If there had been thunder, it had ceased. No, it wasn't thunder that would put him on edge like this. He couldn't shake the feeling someone else had been in the room. The bedroom door was open, and the darkness in the gap was pitch. Merlini sat up in bed, with the cautiousness of someone who has read too many cheap ghost stories, trying not to catch the attention of shadows. Berenice had a key, of course, though he was not expecting her.

He cleared his throat. "Vroni?"

The name was loud in the quiet of the suite. No response came. Normally Berenice's perfume preceded her. There was a scent in the room, but it wasn't her. Merlini sniffed: what was that? Decaying leaves? The thaw had made the hotel damp, perhaps. If only he had one of Berenice's stray kreteks to hand. Burnt cloves would have sweetened the atmosphere.

Merlini's wristwatch lay on the carpet next to the bed. He squinted at the faintly reflective figures: two in the morning. The bars and the kitchens would be long closed. A pity. He had no appetite for food as such, but light and conversation would have been welcome. They were the remedy for a tingle in the skin, and an over-fast pulse caused by ghostly visitations. He might prevail upon Berenice for the night instead, except she was displeased with him again. Iva Pacetti had been on the wireless and he made the mistake of praising her singing. Berenice threw a vase at his head. It wasn't enough for her to excel in her own right. It wasn't enough for her to be the best. He mustn't notice any measure of talent in another soprano to avoid offense. But Merlini accepted Berenice's caprice. This was their way; an explosion of temper, a retreat, until one of them flattered the other enough to reconcile. From past experience he knew he should leave her longer to cool. For now he had no alternative to his own company. He would start by drinking a glass of water, and maybe some knock-out drops to send him back to sleep.

The chloral hydrate was in the bathroom. He walked there now, switched on the electric light – a fat white pearl too bright to gaze on directly – and faced his reflection

above the basin. He yawned. Grabbed the tooth mug. Held
it beneath a spluttering tap.

It was halfway to his mouth when he noticed the colour.
Against the mug's white enamel, the water was tinted
pink.

Merlini cursed, tipped the water down the drain, and let
the tap run again for a while. Maybe rust needed clearing
from the pipes. Damp and rust, a fine hotel this was turning
out to be. Once again he filled the mug. Still pink. He wasn't
drinking that.

With a sigh he retrieved the chloral hydrate bottle from
the cabinet. He took it with him to the drawing room,
mixed a few drops in a glass tumbler with a shot of whisky,
and downed it. His clothes from the previous evening
were scattered across the banquette. Once he was passably
attired, he left the suite, to rap on the housekeeper's door.
What was her name – Frye? The matter could have waited
till morning, but if he had to sleep badly, he derived some
satisfaction from waking another person up. The English
said misery loves company. Presumably she was making
herself decent, but his mood wasn't improved by waiting.
He knocked again. When the door opened he reflected
sourly she had a face just like a milk pudding.

"Mr Merlini," she said mildly. "May I be of assistance?"

"Your water isn't clean," he spat, dispensing with niceties.
"I turn on the tap – it's filthy! And there's a bad smell in the
suite."

Frye tried to mollify. She would, naturally, investigate the
problem with the water supply. Her attempt at conciliation
increased his belligerence. After lurid nightmares and the
sense of being watched it was relieving, nay enjoyable, to

shout at this woman about the problems with his room. That was her job, to take his ire.

"Just fix the damn pipes!" Merlini hoped that his orders were loud enough to disturb Berenice, in her room. Curiosity might draw her out, prompting an early peace-offering. He raised his voice further as he demanded of Frye: "Tell Quarrington. Do you hear me? He needs to fix the damn pipes."

He walked away before Frye could reply. The satisfaction his outburst gave him was short lived. Almost as soon as he closed the door, his wariness of shadows returned. He half suspected a curtain or table cloth shielded an assailant. Not an ordinary kind of foe, to be fought with your fists or a broken bottle; but a threat to the soul as much as the body. In such moments, he knew that Berenice's visions were beautiful artifice; sensually charged, compelling as performance, as inspired as her song, and a product of her own exquisite mind. They lacked genuine portent. He'd felt true foreboding only once before, at the Palais Garnier. Merlini knew the opera house in Paris well. He found the building very ugly, and he wasn't alone; amongst singers the Palais was known as the Wedding Cake due to its gaudy ostentation. In the final years of the last century, during a performance of *Helle* one spring, one of the baroque chandeliers – a behemoth of brass and crystal – had crashed from the ceiling. The structural supports had failed. An elderly lady in the top box was killed by the weight and inevitably in the decades that followed performers and patrons alike claimed to have seen her ghost. Merlini made no such claim himself. But his very first night singing there, he had been locked, accidentally, into the trap room below the stage. Before his release he had felt the same tingling of the skin, the same rapid heartbeat, and the same sense of being observed that he felt tonight. He knew the Regent was built over an ancient water source. The Palais had a lake beneath its foundations. Merlini speculated that brick should be planted in solid ground, for superstitious reasons. Maybe water made it harder for the Regent's dead to move to their proper place. Venice must be full of hauntings.

Merlini wished all such experiences could be dismissed as the overactive imagination. He tried again to do so now. His fear should shame him, because it was a child's dread, not that of a grown man. When he was reluctant to undress, thinking he might need to hasten from the suite again, he told himself he was merely too fatigued to disrobe, because the knock-out drops were taking hold and his legs felt leaden. In the bedroom, he took off his shoes but nothing else before lying down. Paper rustled in his pocket. He removed it, puzzled. Ah. Those notes from the mad house that Vroni stole. He settled in to read the reverse side, which he'd ignored last time, hoping the detached language would trick him into thinking more rationally about his own surroundings. The doctor emphatically dismissed such fancies. *Patient MCCLX does possess unusual powers of vocal mimicry; she is typically indistinguishable from the human or animal she is repeating. In her accuracy she is disconcertingly similar to a dictation machine. She attributes her skill, in her delusion, to being a hyring, though she conveniently claims she isn't sure how to physically transform in appearance as her mother did. I suspect she has a defect of the respiratory tract. If we draw a comparison with mimetic birds we might develop a reasonable hypothesis regarding her physiology.*

Birds have a syrinx which is situated low in the chest, with a two-part structure, which enables a wide reproduction of sounds beyond the capabilities of other species. Exploratory surgery upon the throat of Patient MCCLX, should it be compelled, would identify what features of her voicebox and respiratory tract allow her extraordinary powers of imitation. If she can be trusted that she has possessed mimetic abilities since infancy, and her mother had the same trait, the defect is likely congenital.

The words stopped staying in one place. Merlini screwed the note paper into a ball and tossed it to the carpet. Scientific talk had failed to influence his foreboding. That left only prayer. When he extinguished the light the room was glade-like again. Beneath his breath, for as long as he stayed wakeful, he murmured a petition to God. The plea petered and stalled. His sleep was drugged but the dreams didn't abate: more wolves, in the over-bright bathroom, and the stink of rotting foliage. Merlini turned the taps in his dream too. This time, they ran red with blood.

2

A mere month of work remained for Geraldine Frye. She was engaged to be married, to a colonel rather older than her, who had frequented the Regent for years. With her new life in prospect she was less inclined to run herself ragged for guests. She thought them self-important, Merlini included, and her livelihood no longer depended on soothing them. Against a history of diligent service, who could object if Frye's work were merely sufficient in these final few weeks? Her prior standards were so exemplary that relaxing brought her in line with the average. She chose to address Merlini's complaint at a pace comfortable to her. Rather than trouble Quarrington immediately, she first checked whether her own sink were affected. Although she tried very hard to imagine the water was clear, she did have to accept the tap gushed with a suspicious tint.

Her bathroom was downpipe of Merlini's suite. The problem might yet be confined to their rooms. Better for her beauty sleep if it wasn't. She would suffer a trip to the fourth floor, and if they were having the same issues, Harvey could stay awake to sort it out with Quarrington.

The practice would be good for her. Frye held the most prestigious housekeeping position; when Frye was gone, someone would have to step in. A touch more responsibility would put Harvey in good stead for the role. Frye was almost doing Harvey a favour.

Fortunately Merlini's outburst hadn't summoned any of his neighbours. As Frye passed through the corridor all was quiet. The sullen liftman was on duty, not the chatty one who would tell you how to build a clock if you asked him the time. All of which boded well for her fast return to bed, except a distraction arose at the final hurdle. Just before reaching Harvey's room, Frye noticed there might be a problem with number 427.

The door was open. An arc was scratched into the pine floor near the threshold. To her annoyance, Frye sensed something was wrong, something needing further inquiry. She entered reluctantly. The room was moonlit. A boggy, foresty smell mixed with something sharper and more chemical was on the air.

"What a pong," she murmured.

Someone had moved the walnut dressing table from its rightful place; it stood far from the wall and was askew, as if it had been pushed in haste then abandoned. That accounted for the scratched floor. Unfortunately there were also scratches on the top of the dressing table, right underneath the mirror. That could only be intentional. The guest must have vandalised it.

Hotel housekeeping soured you on people's nature. And guests did worse than scratch at the furniture. This had been a source of pessimism for Frye before her engagement: she anticipated never marrying, because men liked an ignorant

bride, and hotel women saw too much to be truly ignorant.
The work made you worldly. When you looked at old
housekeepers you could see in the lines of their face and the
wariness of their posture that they were jaded. They were
up at all hours, at dawn, at noon, at two in the morning;
they inhaled, drank and ate the hotel. Frye had joined the
Regent in 1919; she'd been given her start in the laundry. At
any English hotel you might expect, in the course of the year,
one or two guests to die; often of natural causes, sometimes
from mishaps. Excesses of drugs could lead to deaths on the
premises. Many people plotting self-slaughter were drawn
to the anonymity of hotels. Laundries saw the results of
the clean up. The Regent workers did clean everything up,
scrupulously; they were discreet for the sake of the guests'
reputations and their own. At least they'd never had to
report a murder. Yet they did have a peculiar, inexplicable
secret, which Quarrington discouraged them in the strongest
terms from discussing. From 1922 onwards, the number of
suicides at the Regent had increased to four or five a year.
Still stranger, the overdoses and hangings they were used
to became a minority of cases: the increase was in bloody
deaths, savage cuttings in the bath or on the bed sheets or
what-have-you. Over the same seven years the Regent saw
an increase in unpaid bills from guests on midnight flits,
who resisted subsequent attempts to trace them. It made
no odds that the Regent was a hotel of standing, the first
choice for the very wealthiest visitors to the city. Rich guests
had demons and vices and unpaid debts. And they got up
to other things too; dirty business. Adultery for one thing –
like that Miss Oxbow and Mr Merlini carrying on. He had
a key to her room. Quarrington bent the rules for guests

in the suites and Frye had to stay tight lipped. But they probably did it the normal way, unlike some. Frye didn't like to think of the guests' peccadilloes and very soon she wouldn't have to.

Money was no guarantee of decency, though Frye still had faith in breeding. She ran her fingers over the spoilt dressing table. Had someone taken a chisel to it? Those marks looked like claw damage. Once she had a landlady whose cat used to go at the cupboards.

But could a cat scratch as deeply as this? The grooves were unusually wide.

Over on the bed the sheets were in disarray, as if someone's rest had been interrupted. The scene suggested a disturbance, possibly an altercation. Belatedly, she thought of the missing Mrs Reid. Hadn't the old lady's room been on this corridor? And wasn't there that *other* problem on the fourth floor a few nights before? Harvey raised the business about an intruder, didn't she, and intimated it was Westall before he made himself scarce. Had to be him, because who else with a big dog had a key. It was funny; Frye had never thought Westall was that sort. He was so polite. But quietness could hide all kinds of sinister inclinations. Might he have come back, to finish... whatever he'd had in mind? A theft? Taking liberties? Surely not. He knew he was suspected among the workers even if they'd hushed it up. He'd have to be mad to risk being seen.

In the adjoining bathroom someone sobbed. Frye jerked, noticing for the first time the illumination beneath the door. A shadow passed over it, though whoever was inside must have the quietest footfall, as weightless as a ghost. Not the intruder – an intruder wouldn't cry. The guest, then. Such a spectral guest... That sob was low pitched and echoey. People did talk of ghosts at the hotel. They were bound to – with the cemetery over the way and the killer who worked round the corner, that horrible man with the axe – even if Quarrington ensured his staff's silence on the suicides.

The handle turned. How slowly it seemed to revolve.

Frye jumped. No ghost stood in the frame; only Harvey.

Her expression was – guarded? Guilty? She hadn't expected to see someone waiting in Frye's spot, at any rate.

With an outbreath, Frye spoke first. "You did give me a scare. There's a funny feeling in this room, gives me the heebie jeebies. What made this mess?"

Harvey turned her attention to the bed, straightening the pillows and blankets. "The lady doctor was sleeping here. You know, the same guest who complained about the dog... She's been odd ever since. Very jumpy, nervous about staying in the same room although I did offer to change it. Miss Oxbow fetched me. She said Dr Dickinson wasn't herself and had left the room in a bit of a state. Now the doctor's staying with Miss Oxbow in *her* suite for the night."

Marvellous. Any further trouble with her would be on Frye's own floor.

Harvey looked at the dressing table critically. "She was probably trying to bar the door. I need to move it back into place. Will you give me a hand?"

"Wait," Frye said. "I came down to say – there's a plumbing problem upstairs."

"Bits in the tap water?"

"It's happening down here too?"

"I noticed, just a moment ago." Harvey nodded her head towards the bathroom.

"May I leave that with you, then? To tell Quarrington? Doesn't need both of us."

Harvey chewed her lip before replying. Frye wondered if she was going to shirk.

"Yes, all right," Harvey said. She picked up one end of the dressing table, and looked expectant. "With your help I can get this straight in a jiffy. I don't want to leave more tracks by dragging it back."

Frye gripped the table's underside. She still wasn't quite at ease. "You seemed upset in the bathroom."

They took small sideways steps like crabs.

"Hm?"

"You sounded tearful?"

They settled the dressing table in its proper place.

"You must have misheard," Harvey said. "I'm quite all right. As you can see."

Frye didn't believe she'd misheard. Harvey just didn't want to say. Probably a matter of the heart. Or more dirty business; not all housekeepers were averse.

"I half expected to see a ghost before you walked out," Frye commented. "That would be splendid, wouldn't it... to finally see a hotel ghost in my last month. This room had such a creepy old feeling to it when I arrived, enough to give Miss Oxbow one of her visions."

"I don't believe in ghosts." Harvey gave the dressing table a final nudge to make it flush against the wall. For a few seconds her fingers slid into the deeply scratched grooves. Frye realised that the gaps between the scratches matched the span of a human hand, Harvey's hand, quite closely; as if the wood had been scratched *by* a human, or a creature of similar size.

Not Harvey, though. Frye noted her fellow housekeeper's nails were filed short in accordance with hotel regulations, and even a floozy's talons couldn't cut through walnut wood like butter. Heaven knows what Dr Dickinson had scratched it with. The polisher would need to fix it after the storm, before the room was given to a new guest. The cost would be added to Dr Dickinson's bill.

Harvey slid open one of the drawers, removed a pastille burner and some matches, and held a flame to the incense. The sandalwood scent hit Frye's nostrils, though the room's mysterious, dank odour could still be detected.

"You can go to bed now, Geraldine," Harvey said, in an absent-minded dismissal that made Frye bristle. Harvey didn't have her job *yet*. "I'll see to things with Quarrington."

3

Harvey alerted Quarrington to the discolouration from the taps. He was relieved the problem had come to light in the small hours, when the majority of guests wouldn't notice. Barnsley, who had responsibility for maintaining such issues, was summoned. He theorised that, as the problem affected more than one floor, the source of the problem would be in a shared tank, or else the well serving the whole hotel. If the well had been disturbed in some way, sediment may have clouded the water.

"What do you mean, disturbed?" Quarrington asked.

"Likeliest explanation is the frost broke a pipe." Barnsley shrugged. "Or maybe somebody lifted the cover on the spring and was larking about in there."

"The problem still needs to be isolated properly. Check the tanks on each floor to start with," Quarrington ordered.

"That'll take about an hour," Barnsley said.

"Then you need to start immediately."

Barnsley took his leave, and Quarrington ruminated. A frost-damaged pipe would be an expense and an inconvenience. But Barnsley's second, offhand suggestion bothered Quarrington more. Tampering with the water supply, in jest or no, was nefarious. He decided he'd take a preliminary look at the well himself. He would also take Harvey – he privately considered her the most reliable of his housekeepers – in case he needed to delegate without leaving the wellside.

Equipped with torches, they took the back stairs, each step creaking as they descended. Harvey walked ahead. They didn't speak, and he wondered if she, too, were anticipating trouble. Too much had gone wrong in the hotel these past few days; it primed one, irrationally, for further calamity. Quarrington recognised this feeling from heavy snowfalls in prior years. He theorised that hotels should be for pleasure, or business, but never an emergency in a storm. As soon as people were confined to them, things went wrong. So many people in proximity, none of whom belonged there, and who had been deprived of their exit, were bound to start acting strangely. Because of this, no building, cut off, could rival a hotel for claustrophobia.

They were below ground now. Quarrington had managed the hotel for decades. He knew every inch of that dark lower floor. Any departure from the norm would be clear to him. He and Harvey turned on their torches, illuminating bricks in the cross of their lightbeams. On initial inspection the spring appeared untouched. The well cap was in place as usual. It was heavy, but one strong man would be capable of sliding it out of position, if he stood on the step to the side. Quarrington passed his torch to Harvey. He jostled the cap over the edge of the well. He peered down the shaft, tongue trapped between his teeth.

Harvey stepped forward, directing both torches into the

depths. They now had a clear view of the artesian spring that fed, by upward pressure, every pipe in the hotel. Mrs Reid's head floated upon the water.

Quarrington looked at Harvey. Her face was illuminated from below and her expression was impassive given the horror in the well. Harvey made a better housekeeper than she would a wife, Quarrington speculated; for he, no doubt unfairly, saw a lack of sentiment as both invaluable to a hotelier, and rather revolting in a woman. He took back one of the torches, and in the adjusted light Harvey's expression seemed to change again. Not to the distress he would have preferred, but a flash in her eyes of – satisfaction? Triumph, as she took in the old woman's bloody decapitation?

Quarrington scolded himself. Harvey was a serious woman, amongst the best of his workers. What possible reason could she have for taking pleasure in Mrs Reid's fate? It was so improbable he must have misunderstood. He focused on the immediate practicalities.

"Place a barrier at the stairs," he instructed. "Say nothing yet of the reason. Invent a flood or a leak if anyone enquires. That'll be in keeping with the plumbing problems. You'll need to bring back with you blankets, or towels at a pinch. Whatever you can salvage unnoticed from the laundry. A bucket, mopping bucket or fire bucket, it doesn't matter."

"And the police?" Harvey pressed.

"The lines are still down." Quarrington left unsaid the possibility of sending a note.

After a few seconds of silence, Harvey nodded. "It would be indecent to leave Mrs Reid in that state until the police can arrive."

She returned the way they had come. Quarrington looked again at the head in the water. Parts were – missing. Gnawed. He could see several bloody puncture marks. Quarrington recalled being bitten by a dog as a child – these marks were similar. Mrs Reid had been attacked by an animal, then. But an animal couldn't lift a cast iron well cover or neatly replace it to store a human head. And where was the rest of the body?

He redirected his torchlight, trying to discern a limb or a torso beneath the surface of the water. Nothing. As he moved the beam upwards, he saw two fingers protruding from the end of the overflow pipe. The other remnants must have passed into the drains.

Quarrington assumed the attack had happened here in the bowels of the building, because it wasn't such an ideal hiding place to risk lugging body parts through the hotel. He circled the spring, keeping his eyes on the ground. Knowing what to do was his job. And he was a calm man by nature. Still, he could see no good outcome from this affair. A hotel worker might have committed the crime – the Regent was unlikely to recover from *that*. Alternatively they had admitted a murderer among their clientele, which was scarcely preferable. Hotels thrived or failed upon the calibre of their guests.

Quarrington strode through the empty cavern that lay beyond the spring. The torch revealed a trail across the brick floor – a path of dried blood – culminating fifty yards away in a dark crescent. He looked at it in silence for some time. The scene of the attack, surely. Mrs Reid had been lured down here somehow. Possibly the prospect of seeing the spring was lure enough. Quarrington couldn't deny that they encouraged that myth of the spring bestowing forgiveness. It lent the hotel additional mystique.

He heard footsteps behind him, and turned to see another point of light in the dark. Harvey's return.

"I've cordoned the stairs. Nobody was around to ask why." Her voice was low. She looked at the blood on the ground dispassionately. In barely a whisper, she continued: "When you do contact the police... what will you say about Westall?"

"Westall?" Quarrington repeated.

"Yes."

"Why would Westall do this? What motive could he have?" Quarrington asked.

"I can't tell you." Harvey's eyes met his. They were clear, and steady; her view untainted by emotion. "What I can say is there are dog bites in the body. Westall's been missing almost exactly as long as Mrs Reid. He'd already trespassed in another guest's room."

"We didn't establish that."

"Glennard..." Harvey didn't ordinarily use his first name; for a housekeeper to do so was an impertinence. But they were no longer abiding by normal rules. "You must see that, in the balance of likelihoods, he will be of interest to the police."

"We found no evidence Westall trespassed," Quarrington repeated. He spread his hands. "We shouldn't volunteer mere gossip. I think we should be as conservative as possible in any claims we make."

"The police will speak to the guests, who'll happily volunteer gossip. What if Dr Dickinson says her room was invaded? It sounds very bad, such a short time before the murder of another guest. The police will ask you why no invader was identified."

"I shall say truthfully: my impression was the lady dreamt the dog."

"Yes. So it was."

The rebuke was mild, in deference to his seniority. Were they equals, she might throw back, in his face, their prior disagreement. Harvey had consistently said Westall was the likely invader and should be dismissed; Quarrington ordered her to say no such thing publicly. He didn't rue his choice. Dr Dickinson was an overwrought bluestocking, and if she were indulged, her panic might have spread throughout the guests to the Regent's detriment. Even now, the very best thing for the Regent – regrettably for the family of Mrs Reid – would be if the police could identify no culprit at all. What if the police never knew there was a corpse? Wouldn't that be the simplest development? She couldn't be brought back, no matter how many livelihoods were lost along with the Regent's reputation.

As if she sensed the direction of his thoughts, Harvey noted: "Most of the remains are already missing."

The rest of the old woman's body must have been pulp and smithereens to pass through the pipe. The hideousness of whatever had happened to her torso, her hips, her ribcage to enable such a fate infiltrated Quarrington's thoughts. Could he, and Harvey, also crush the head somehow? Distasteful. His stomach turned.

Incineration, then?

"There's the furnace," he mused. "But how long would that take?"

"Three hours," Harvey said firmly. "And it isn't hot

enough to burn bone. Even if it were, there'd be fragments we'd have to grind."

His mouth parted in dismay at how specifically she'd answered. She continued.

"It would smell, anyway. People would ask questions."

What options were left? Burial? The nearest soft ground – they could hardly go far, given the state of the roads – was the graveyard. That was too overlooked, especially with dawn coming. As Quarrington cogitated, Harvey placed her lamp upon the well rim. She stood upon the plinth. Rolling up her sleeve – revealing a set of pink lines in the whiteness of her forearm, which Quarrington could not recall seeing before – Harvey reached into the well. Grimly she fished the head from the water by the hair, and lowered it into the bucket.

"The... in the pipe, there," Quarrington gestured.

Harvey retrieved Mrs Reid's fingers, which joined the head in the bucket. She carefully felt in the overflow pipe for any other concealed remains. Finding none, she shook the water from her hand.

"Where to?" she asked Quarrington, as she knelt to tuck a dirty towel into the bucket. He was reminded, incongruously, of packing picnic hampers. *Pull yourself together*, he instructed himself. Time was moving apace and he must resume control. He was no criminal schemer, versed in the destruction of bodies. It would be sufficient, it must be sufficient, to relocate the pieces. Mrs Reid's head would be found, but away from the hotel. A short physical remove would make all the difference in protecting the hotel's reputation, not least because it left room for the possibility of a villain wholly unconnected to the Regent, while the illusion of being safe inside the hotel's walls remained intact. Yes. With some distance likelihoods might be fashioned; a story in which the attack was random – the work of a vagrant, perhaps.

He told Harvey: "Go anywhere as long as the damned thing's off the premises."

"Needless Alley?" A dark, abandoned street, where there would be no witnesses. "The snow is thawing... she might have lain there and only been revealed now. We can let it be discovered."

"Yes, yes. Needless Alley is fine. Quickly. We can take the exit by the bins, while it's still dark. That way we stand least chance of being seen."

"Good. But Glennard – if this isn't enough, and the police guess the crime happened here despite our best efforts – you must name Westall as the most likely. You *must*. If it's better for us to protect him now, it will ill serve us then."

"Yes, yes." Barnsley must have few tanks left to check. He'd be coming to inspect the well soon.

They departed, passing no one on the stairs. On ground level the cleaning ladies were at work. Their eyes were always to the floor, but Quarrington reasoned they would notice buckets, and dirty towels, if anyone would. *They won't assume there's a head inside*, he told himself, but he was still relieved once they had passed. The bin exit was by the kitchens. On arrival he held the door open for Harvey to pass through. Neither of them had stopped for coats in their haste.

The snow was liquefying and translucent, from the rise in temperature. Rain was still falling. Quarrington realised the floors below ground were in danger of flooding. Ordinarily he wouldn't welcome the ensuing chaos. But it occurred to him the blood below stairs would at least be washed away.

"I can go on my own from here," Harvey said. "Your absence will be more obvious than mine."

"It shouldn't take you more than a few minutes."

She nodded. She had taken a few steps when he called her, in a stage whisper, and she half turned.

"I saw the marks on your arm," he said. "How long have they been there?"

"A long time." She smiled. "I'll always keep them covered when I'm around guests. You mustn't worry."

She resumed walking. Harvey had a job for life. It didn't matter what Quarrington knew about her now – the marks on her arms or anything else – because she could ruin him in a sentence. *Quarrington found the head in the well.*

At the end of the gully, Harvey turned up the edges of the towel on the bucket, as if checking her baby under a blanket. But in the moonlight her face showed none of a mother's tenderness. The triumph had returned, and Quarrington watched her spit upon Mrs Reid's remains.

4

Enid woke to the sound of lapping water. The sun was yet to rise, but she knew, as she tentatively sat up in bed, that the lino would be submerged. She tested the floor with one stockinged foot and the threadbare wool was instantly sodden.

The boarding house stood at the bottom of the hill, and Enid's room was on the ground floor. Before the morning was out the flooding would surely get worse. She didn't want to wait till she was marooned in her bed. Her boots were just in reach by the kitchen door. They'd have to go on first. With her feet more protected – the boots didn't form a failsafe seal but they'd do – she set about dressing the rest of her person. The emptiness of her stomach and the stiffness in her joints made her slow. She kept in mind the cathedral as a shelter. It would be dry there.

Outside the world was turning to water. She drew her scarf around her face. With one hand on the railings, she inched up the slickening path until the cathedral was visible on the brow. Small islands of snow remained, those that had been hardest packed, and over the white streak of one she saw the unmistakeable dark silhouette of Markham's dog. He stood at the narrow entrance to Needless Alley. Enid stopped short, breathing heavily, and let her head fall when the dog turned in her direction. She didn't want him to know he was seen. Unsettling enough to be watched by the dead, never mind meeting eye to eye. Odd that he should come back lately. There had been several sightings after an absence of years. Something had disturbed his rest.

She dared look up again when she heard him moving, his paws wet upon the cobbles. He was walking towards the cathedral now. She saw him weave through the gravestones, his tongue unfolding redly from his jaw. At the doors he butted his large head against the wood until it opened, and widened enough to admit him.

Enid didn't want to share the church with him. Normally he vanished of his own accord quite quickly. She would wait a few minutes before checking. For now her eyes wandered back to the darkness of Needless Alley. Not one of the dog's usual haunts. She resumed shuffling through the slush, to the spot where she'd first caught sight of him. All feeling in her toes was lost. She squinted down into Needless Alley: no living creature was visible, man nor beast. A single fresh footprint was still clear in the mire, though. Too dainty for a man – Enid guessed a woman or a growing child. She rubbed her eyes, and let them adjust to the poor light ahead of her. Then she saw, perhaps three yards away, clawed fingers, palm up and disembodied on the ground. And behind that, a battered head.

Enid stepped back. Her first thought was: *Here's a bad penny*. She knew who that head belonged to. She'd told the police, when they came asking, that Mrs Reid had been nosing round the cathedral, asking about Markham's ghost. That was all, Enid said nothing else, not how highly Reid considered herself or the nasty look she gave Enid's coat. Mrs Reid was a wrong'un. She'd been loitering by the crypt door. It was always locked, but she wanted to poke round the other side, that much was clear. Everything about her said trouble, for her and whoever was unlucky enough to cross her. True in life, true in death, Enid felt, looking at what was left of her.

She shouldn't be lying in bits down Needless Alley.

The rain wearied Enid. She made for the cathedral. From the narthex she tried to see the dog. She gasped. He was up on the altar, looking down on his reflection in a silver plate. He pushed his forelegs into it as if it were a pool. His head, body, hind legs, tail followed, and he was gone.

Enid walked to the votive candles. She took a fresh one from the box. It took her a minute to find the box of matches. It had fallen to the quarry floor. The first match wouldn't light, the rain on her hands had left it too damp to catch, but the next one burned well enough as she held it to the wick. The little flame on the candle jumped and shivered. A fire that small couldn't warm you.

She crept to the pew, genuflected as well as her knee would let her, and sat down to pray. Soon she'd have to walk to the police station. If anyone had seen her leave Needless Alley, they'd wonder why she didn't report it. She was the last one they knew of to see Mrs Reid alive, too. *A bad penny*, Enid repeated. As soon as she'd said her prayers she'd go. As soon as she stopped feeling so cold.

PART FOUR

1920s ZURICH

I

During Nora's six years of medical studies, she assisted the psychiatrists at the Holzberg lunatic asylum. Psychiatry and psychoanalysis were closely aligned in Zurich and once she was ready to practise she remained in this field. That same hospital had a role for her: her days would be long, up to fourteen hours from seven in the morning; or from six in the evening for night shifts.

The hospital was far quieter and cleaner than the traditional stereotypes of such an institution would lead you to expect. It lay two miles from town, close to the mountains, on the site of a former monastery. Three low buildings accommodated predominantly acute cases, who were favoured for admission over the chronically insane. Dr Claus Kruger, the Medical Superintendent, was proud they had neither locked doors nor perimeter walls. In other cities the treatment roster included hydrotherapy, the diathermic use of electromagnetic current, barbiturate-induced sleep therapy and insulin. These were all thrust aside at the Holzberg in favour of psychological and occupational approaches. The aim was to attend to everything the patients said, no matter how delusional or nonsensical, as a source of potential meaning. Accordingly each patient was seen in the morning and afternoon for psychoanalysis and detailed written transcripts of their comments were submitted to the Superintendent at close of day.

Patients laboured for the hospital as part of their recovery; women carried out domestic work, including knitting, sewing and laundry, while the men did farm work, gardening and assorted trade duties. Not unlike the monks they'd supplanted, all patients bound books. They had a chapel for their souls, food grown on the premises to nourish their bodies, and when they were capable, they were encouraged to stage plays or hold a dance in the amusement hall. Nora and the other doctors ate alongside their patients. The wardens lived in; they slept in the corridors. To live communally, the Holzberg reasoned, was healing. Certainly the hospital felt like a place of industry and clear rules, despite the expected outbursts of violence and excitability from patients in distress. And yet Nora knew it was not a community of equals. Privacy was a privilege of the twenty-five wealthiest patients; the remaining three hundred lacked solitude, for supervision rather than locked doors was the means by which they were contained. Sometimes Nora stood quietly on the first floor, to look at the grounds from the hall window. It was true there were no garden walls. There were no obstructed sightlines anywhere; the flowers the patients walked among were ground cover. No trees or hedges were cultivated. On the horizon the mountains met the sky. God and the Holzberg had a clear view. The only place to hide, Nora thought, was a moonless night, because the darkness was total and enveloping outside the city.

At this stage of Nora's life she rarely demonstrated her mimicry. There was no one, any more, to demand Nora's faithful recordings of life around her, partly because she swerved from close relationships of all kinds. She refused two proposals of marriage from the mathematician who had prepared her for university. They were, however, sexually involved, through a combination of curiosity and isolation rather than true desire on her part.

Though she still occasionally impersonated Miss Lowrie, she did so secretly, in acts of shameful compulsion. She would disavow the horror of what happened in the woods while still enacting what Valery had made her: a mimic, a recorder of truth. She might have been tempted to close her eyes and utter a line of her old teacher's if serendipity made it appropriate, but all those lines were English, and would not have passed as her own in a hospital where everyone spoke German.

Leo Cadieux's mother tongue was French, but he used High German at the Holzberg. Nora heard him speak before she first saw him. She was approaching one of the patient's private rooms; these incurred the highest price, while the dormitories were somewhat cheaper. The door was cracked enough to let Leo's words travel from within. His voice was soft – Nora could hear a smile in it, as he teased the invalid for disobeying the nurses. Then Nora saw the back of his head, his hair straight and fair as wheat. Silently she collected the written information from the patient's notes that the Superintendent required; they were clipped to the file by the bed. Nora was good at being unseen, when she was being herself, and the patient – some rich Swiss man's daughter – ignored her. But Leo glanced over his shoulder, and paused in his teasing, to direct that smile at Nora. She guessed he was older than her, though he was wide-eyed enough to seem boyish. His left earlobe was missing. A childhood injury, maybe, or something that happened at war. Or both.

He turned back to the rich Swiss girl. Nora left as quietly as she'd entered. Their paths didn't cross for another three weeks. This second time, she heard his shout for assistance, again from a patient's room. The urgency in his call sped her arrival. He was trying to revive, on the bed, a male patient who Nora recognised as a recently admitted Romanian artist with dementia praecox. The patient had shaved his head before his arrival and a warm dark layer of fuzz covered his scalp. His neck was freshly bruised. The artist's eyes were open but one pupil had expanded and wouldn't return to normal. His breathing was much too rapid. They made him as comfortable as they were able. He had repeated fits over a two hour period before his heart gave out.

"He leaves a widow," Leo said. "I don't think she'll be surprised. This wasn't the first time he'd tried."

"The same way?"

"No." He drew the sheet over the patient, and unbuckled the contraband belt from the bed rails. "I don't imagine he knew the rate of failure."

"Don't tell her how bad it was," Nora blurted. "His wife."

Leo paused, then nodded. "Of course. I'll send word to her and inform Claus."

Claus. That showed a degree of familiarity with the Super-intendent that Nora, and her other colleagues, refrained from. She wondered if it was a permitted familiarity;

perhaps Leo took liberties, or perhaps he had charmed their mentor. She could believe the latter. In the Superintendent's office, they learnt that the artist's wife could be spoken to by telephone. Leo sat in the Superintendent's Windsor chair and inked a fish upon the patient's records as he waited for the operator to connect him. Nora listened to his soft explanation when the time came.

"The death was instant," he said. "I can assure you your husband didn't suffer."

The lie was smooth, and it was kind. Nora had witnessed the death – knew it was prolonged! – yet she believed Leo's words. She repeated his lie in her thoughts as she stood before him. When she walked home that night, she mouthed the lie silently, her lips forming the same shapes his had done. Before she went to sleep, she repeated his words, in his gentle, French-accented German. How familiar it was, the sensation of slipping into another person; even though it had been years since she tried to be anyone besides herself, and Miss Lowrie. To replicate Leo felt almost like a homecoming.

For the next few months, Nora mimicked Leo's four words – *the death was instant* – every day; but only when she was in the privacy of her own bedroom. Then she grew careless. As long as she knew she was alone, she reasoned, what did it matter where she was? And then she started thinking: what did it matter who overheard her, as long as they didn't know how she really spoke, or who she was imitating?

It was summer, and as she left the Holzberg in the warmth of the morning after being there all night, the patients were hanging their bedclothes from the windows, to benefit from the summer air. Half a dozen patients were already dressed and outdoors, to work in the kitchen gardens: they would be picking vegetables ready for use in that day's meals. They were out of earshot but Nora could see them with their spades and shovels. One of them was manoeuvring a wheelbarrow. Nora walked in the opposite direction across the grass, with her eyes closed against the sun. *The death was instant*, she said in his voice, and then she walked into him.

She stepped back, fazed. He had arrived for his own working day. Although he smiled at their collision (why, she wondered, had he not stepped aside from her path? *His* eyes hadn't been closed), Nora read nervousness in his expression.

"What did you say?" he asked.

"Nothing," she claimed, futilely, because everything in her own words was fated to be dismissed.

"You were possessed." He was teasing, but the nervousness wasn't gone.

"I have to go home. And they'll be expecting you—"

"Say it again."

Now that he had ordered her, she obeyed, as she'd once obeyed Valery. Because now, as then, she wanted to.

"The death was instant."

A few seconds later, Leo replied: "Are you mocking me?"

Nora shook her head.

"Why did you do it, then? You must have practised, to sound so much like me."

"I don't need to practise." Nora felt the tattoo on her arm prickle. "It's just... something I can do, without trying."

"But—"

"You'll be late for work," she reminded him, and ran across the grass towards home.

That day, as whenever she worked overnight, she sank fast into a dreamless sleep, and rose to eat her evening meal. Shortly afterwards, Leo knocked on the front door. Nora's great aunt Františka was long bedridden, so there was no one to object to gentlemen visitors. All the same, Nora did not invite him in.

"Why did you copy *those* words?" he demanded.

She shrugged.

"They possessed you," he said.

"If you like."

"I'd like the truth."

Nora leant against the door frame, weary. She had only ever received one explanation for her uncanny mimicry. It was Valery's explanation, and Nora believed it, because it spoke to her fear she was not normal. More than that: she was monstrous.

"I'm not human."

"No?"

"I'm a predator who copies humans well."

"What do you do with your victims?"

"Eat them." She paused, wondering if he would take her tale for metaphor, remembering that the police had thought her delusional. "When I was a little girl I lived in an English wood. An important thing happened when I was eleven. My mother killed my school teacher, because I said my father seduced her. We ate my teacher's arm for dinner, because my mother thought I would enjoy the taste. An innocent man hanged for the crime. And now it is years later, but I still remember every word my teacher said to me before she died, and I can replicate her manner exactly. What do you think of that? Don't you have a theory, for my elaborate cannibal fantasy?"

"No."

"Why not?"

"It isn't fantasy, is it? Fantasy is not the domain of lions, or snakes, or any other creature that would enjoy feeding on me. They just want to eat."

As he spoke he touched his maimed ear – a habitual, unthinking gesture that she had seen him make before. He never mentioned the cause of his injury. Something had happened to him, she thought, that accounted for his calmness now, in the face of her deep uncanniness. If he believed her she must scare him. But he did not preserve himself from danger as other people might.

From the floor above, Františka called Nora's name.

"You're needed," Leo said, their watchfulness of each other broken.

He nodded goodbye, and Nora let him go.

2

Nora and Leo continued to work alongside each other without mentioning her confession. He had not accused her of delusion nor deceit, and his acceptance of her story helped soothe the old injustice of James Markham, the police, and her father denying what had happened. She hoped Leo would raise the topic again; as the time passed, she eventually came to think he never would.

But then, the following year, Leo said: "I have a patient I need your help with."

"Who?" They were in the lab, at the close of Friday, writing up interminable daily reports.

"A patient I see privately, she's not at the hospital."

This wasn't unusual, where the family required more discretion, or where the patient had maintained a sufficient appearance of normality to conduct much of her life independently. Not unlike Nora herself.

"I'd like you to attend some of her appointments," Leo continued. "She's an opera singer. Quite a famous one. A White Russian – her family were killed, but she escaped as a child and trained in America and now she performs here.

Or did. She came to me because she can't sing any more. There isn't any physical reason – she's very healthy, with no problems affecting the throat or lungs. But she opens her mouth, and nothing emerges. Unless..."

"Yes?"

"Unless she can't hear herself. When her ears are covered, or her hearing is otherwise blocked, then she's able to sing. So it seems to be neurotic."

"I see."

"We have old gramophone recordings of her operas. She is able to sing as they play, I assume because the recorded voice masks her own and her self-consciousness is lowered. I've tried using progressively softer needles, so the record is quieter each time we play it. Because I think – if she can be tricked into singing independently – it will trigger some kind of memory she is currently suppressing. That's how we'll learn the cause of the neurosis. I wanted to ask, can you mimic singing?"

So much time had passed since they discussed her mimicry, the question took her by surprise. Unsure of his purpose, she said: "I can mimic all voices and gestures. Including song."

"But surely you'd need training to mimic an opera singer? She's a performer of many years' standing."

"I don't need training." No more than the gramophone did. "Why do you want me to mimic her?"

"*You* could mask her voice as she sings. I've discovered the difference between the needles isn't quite gradual enough – she can hear the drop in volume too distinctly, her self-consciousness returns, and she doesn't sing. But you could duet with her, and lower your voice much more slowly."

"She'll have questions," Nora pointed out, "about why I'm so good at imitation."

"I'm not sure about that. Miss Oxbow's not interested in other people; she's self-absorbed to an astonishing degree. An astonishing woman all told. She claims to have visions of the future, very vividly described, and she deflects any attempt to test her on that point extraordinarily well."

Despite the outward criticism, Nora detected Leo's admiration, as if he thought the singer's vanity were understandable. Nora disliked it. She didn't really know much about opera – she didn't recognise the name *Miss Oxbow*, despite Leo saying she was famous – and Nora realised she had been picturing a middle aged, perhaps matronly singer, in the mould of Nellie Melba perhaps. Leo's fondness suggested quite a different sort of woman. A younger one. A prettier one.

Nora asked: "You're willing to put her in a room with a snake, or a lion?"

"Certainly. She bites back. She's escaped murderers in the past, though she hasn't broached those memories yet in analysis. Will you help as I ask?"

She wished to please him. But Leo wasn't looking Nora in the eye. Something was driving his request beyond the belief she could restore Miss Oxbow's singing. She couldn't grasp his true intent.

"Let me listen to the records," Nora stalled. "I'll let you know if I'm willing to go ahead after that."

She signed the last report, and passed it to Leo to file with his share.

★ ★ ★

Nora had a gramophone in her bedroom, a pale green Nirona that pre-dated her arrival. That evening she blew the dust from it. The only time she'd ever used it was to conceal her maths tutor's presence, and that was years ago. With coral light hitting the faded flowers on the walls, Nora examined the record she had collected from Leo's apartment. He'd said until recently he'd preferred jazz, but opera had got its claws into him since Miss Oxbow's arrival. He hadn't expected to be so transported.

Nora slid the record from its brown paper sleeve – the torn label said *Orfeo ed Euridice*; she knew the story of Orpheus, though not the Italian this version was related in. She fumbled the record into position on the Nirona.

The needle on the record's surface produced crackling and whining at a greater volume than discernible song. But Nora knew the soprano was clear enough to imitate accurately – no, to imitate uncannily. Nora sat on the bed, and as the sun dropped low enough to warm her fingers in her lap, she let the record play to completion.

In the quiet that followed, she watched the sky turn the colour of larkspurs. She broke the silence singing the words she didn't understand:

> *Che farò senza Euridice?*
> *Dove andrò senza il mio ben?*
> *Euridice, o Dio, risponde!*
> *Io son pure il tuo fedele,*
> *Euridice!*
> *Ah non m'avvanza*
> *più soccorso più speranza*
> *ne dal mondo ne dal ciel.*

Her chest expanded and her head swam. This mimicry was different from copying Leo's smooth, kind lie that a botched hánging was quick and painless. And different again from repeating the words of the villagers she knew in childhood: their reports of petty ailments and underplayings of slow tumours in the surgery, the snivelling of a philanderer in a school loft, a young school teacher's mind breaking down as she bled in a glade of nettles. For once, Nora was a record of something beautiful. She envied Miss Oxbow for being the origin of such beauty, and despised her for the affectation of no longer being able to sing.

Nora hadn't asked Leo when Miss Oxbow stopped singing. Presumably she'd been previously ensconced at the Zurich Opera House. The building stood down on Sechseläutenplatz. Years ago Nora had been inside – she'd accompanied Františka to some charitable musical. Nora recalled the posters of past performers that adorned the walls of the foyer. Maybe those pictures now included Miss Oxbow. It was tempting to check, because Nora wanted to know what Miss Oxbow looked like, to see if she was as beautiful as her voice. Leo's attitude implied she was.

So Nora decided to go there. She walked through the darkening streets, one hand deep in her coat pocket, the other warmed by a cigarette, past shuttered cafés, the cigar shop, the papeterie. Trams clanged and jangled by, near-empty but for the conductors with their flat service caps and their Lenker Schnurrbärte. The opera house was a great square stone building; the roof was busy with angels, holding horns aloft in the moonlight. That night there was a late performance, indicated by the crowds amassing.

She joined them, climbing the steps and passing with

them through the doors; the women smelt of lily of the valley, the men of cologne. The foyer floor was marble and the walls ornately plastered. As she had guessed, the alcoves displayed posters of previous operas. None of them featured Miss Oxbow's name. What an irritation. It was possible Nora should have been looking for a different name altogether. It wasn't unusual for singers to have stage names. Nor was it unheard of for psychoanalysis patients to use an alias. The torn label on the record meant she had no idea if Miss Oxbow was credited as such there.

All the opera lovers had been seated now, and the doors to the auditorium were closing. An usher was looking askance at Nora, prompting her to take her leave, in some annoyance at a wasted trip. It was when she approached the main entrance again that she saw what she was looking for. Quite a large poster, missing a corner, to the immediate right. It was for *La Traviata* – and *Berenice Oxbow* was printed in larger text below. The patient was photographed from the shoulders up, allowing Nora to examine the monochrome image in fine detail. It was clear Berenice Oxbow was wearing a wig. A preposterous, theatrical wig, woven through with pale flowers. But the woman's face; oh, God. Nora had anticipated as much, but it was still shocking to see Miss Oxbow's beauty confirmed. Such large eyes and such luminous skin: an Icon, sombre, ready to be worshipped. Nora hoped neuroses had taken a toll on the singer's looks. Didn't photographs lie anyway? Sometimes they flattered and sometimes the subject was poorly served but they weren't to be relied upon.

Nora irritated herself by clutching at straws. The real information had been the way Leo spoke of her. He had discussed Berenice Oxbow warmly. Lingeringly. Of course she was as beautiful as the picture.

One consolation remained. Berenice Oxbow might be lovely to look at. She might, in that portrait, bewitchingly suggest both vulnerability and the intent to seduce. She might be begging to be kissed.

But Nora had her voice.

Nora reached out to stroke the paper. She mouthed the record's Italian words, watching Berenice's lips, knowing they would have formed the same shapes. In this act of impersonation, Nora's self receded behind Berenice's, like one image overlaid by another in a double exposure. She was hungry to hear more of Berenice: because then she could copy her, and feel what it was like to be her for longer than a single song. Nora decided to take a detour on the way home; she would call by Leo's apartment and agree to his request. She glanced over her shoulder before departing. The usher still had his eye on her. A pity. She would have stolen the poster.

3

The light was on in Leo's apartment window and, seized with whimsy, Nora pelted the pane with pebbles to get his attention. She saw him approach the glass – in the same work suit he had worn that day, except without his jacket, and this made him seem strangely naked to her. He lifted the sash.

"Whatever are you doing down there? Use the bell like a normal person! I can barely see you in the dark."

"No, I'm not staying. I only came by to tell you that I will help, with your patient." She paused. "I listened to the record."

"You can sing it, like she can?"

"Yes."

"Come up." It was an instruction, and an urgent one, not an invitation. But the moon burst from behind a cloud and fell on her like a spotlight, making her laugh. She lifted her arms and sang, at full volume, Berenice Oxbow's aria. When she had finished she laughed again, giddy.

"I don't think you're supposed to laugh," Leo said, but he was teasing, and she knew he was happy.

"Why? What do the words mean?"

"Orfeo has just turned to look at his wife leaving Hades, only to see her die."

"Oh… *That* part of the story."

"You sounded like Berenice." He paused. "You sounded the same. Wait. If you won't come up, I'll come down."

He disappeared from the window. For the next few minutes she felt alone in the silence. Then the door to the building swung wide. Leo strode towards her. He placed a hand over her eyes to hold them closed and then he kissed her in the darkness. She uttered a single surprised cry into his mouth. He let go and she could see again.

"I'm sorry," he said. "I forgot myself."

"It's all right. I—" She stopped, unsure whether to say: *I liked it*. Or whether she was being dismissed.

He ran a hand over the back of his head. He was not, at any rate, going back inside.

"When is Miss Oxbow's appointment?" she checked.

"Monday, here, at three o'clock – so you should be here at a quarter to – and the same each week thereafter. Can you make that? Or are you expected at the hospital then?"

"This Monday is fine. I'll speak to the Superintendent; I can make sure that afternoon is protected until further notice."

"I think—" he said, then stopped. "I think it would be best if for the first appointment, you just observe."

"Oh?"

"Yes, get a sense of, well, *her*, because she's quite – you just need to get a sense of her before I introduce you. And that will allow me to plan… how I'm going to tell her about you. It will be best if you can watch a full session without her knowing."

The suggestion surprised Nora, because she had assumed, if Leo had invited her to take part at all, he would be reasonably sure of Berenice's agreement. But she was getting the impression Berenice might resist. She still couldn't tell Leo's true intent, though she cared less now. She remembered the poster in the opera house, and how beautiful Berenice was; and how good it felt to have her voice. To create beauty while she replicated it. Watching unknown would still let her do that. She would have more words to repeat, and better, the gestures and stance and expressions to accompany them.

Leo was looking up at his window.

"It's late to be on the streets," Nora said, so he might ask again for her to enter.

He nodded at her but did not repeat his invitation to come upstairs; she wished now she had accepted the first offer. All that he said was: "Of course. I should never have kept you."

"Till Monday," she said. He waited in the street while she walked away.

Nora returned there at the expected time the following week. Leo admitted her to the apartment with an air of distraction, a hand upon her lower back to usher her through, as he glanced behind them into the shared corridor.

Inside, a fringed red curtain served as a room divider. Nora could see that this, a triumvirate of mirrors, and a punitive-looking wooden chair in a dark corner were to be the means by which she watched Berenice.

"If I can see her, won't she see me?"

"No. You'll be in the shade while she is in the light. She lies on the couch and tends to look at the ceiling. Just don't do anything to draw her attention – no sudden moves or sounds."

Nora draped her coat over the back of the wooden chair. She took her position. For twenty-five minutes she heard Leo pacing and humming. She had never known him so agitated. It crossed her mind to wonder how, if Berenice usually lay on the couch, the singer was well positioned to accompany the gramophone. The raised end of the couch was visible in the mirror, awaiting the patient's arrival; to the side of the couch was a low table with an ashtray.

Finally the bell sounded. Berenice was ten minutes late. This was the first time Nora had heard Berenice speak, rather than sing.

"What's the matter with your neighbours?" she asked in high, rapid, American English speech. "That old man with the trident who stares and stares at me whenever I come. He hears me on the stairs and opens his apartment door and watches me. Has he never seen a woman before? I know it's barbaric but I crossed my eyes. He went back inside and closed the door then I saw the spyhole dim afterwards. He was still looking at me, I know it."

Maybe she was paranoid. It was unlikely the neighbour brandished a trident. If she were suspicious of people, that might be why Leo thought she'd take badly to a newcomer's involvement in her analysis. So far Leo seemed content to let Berenice talk without greeting. Nora heard him take his chair. In the mirror, she watched Berenice lie down on the couch. Her head was in profile. Nora breathed in. What an exquisitely pointed nose. As Berenice lay, she took her lighter from the clutch bag on her stomach and lit a cigarette. She smoked for a short while in silence, the room growing heavy with the scent of cloves. Nora mouthed: *Has he never seen a woman before?* She wished she could lie down too, in imitation, rather than be confined to a small, hard wooden chair.

"Isn't this comfy," Berenice mused. "Everything's jake."

Nora was just wondering whether Leo understood these Americanisms when he startled her by saying, in English: "We'll begin with word association."

Obviously English was their lingua franca. Presumably Berenice didn't think and feel as well in German, if they'd dismissed it for conversation. But English from Leo's lips felt odd and unfamiliar to Nora. Now he was proposing an analytic technique: he'd say a word, and Berenice must reply with the first association that came to mind. The intent was to reveal hidden traumas by letting the unconscious mind drive the response.

"Must we?" Berenice asked. "I hate that game."

"Would you rather the gramophone, Miss Oxbow?"

"No." Berenice blew a cloud of smoke prettily above her. "Aren't we intimates by now? You should call me Nika."

"Word association, Miss Oxbow?"

"Very well, *Doctor*. Let's get it over with then."

"Head," Leo began.

"Fake."

"Green?"

"Peasant."

"Water?"

"Gossip."

"Voyage?"

"Disguise."

"Dead?"

Berenice paused, then said again: "Fake."

Each utterance, each gesture, each expression imprinted upon Nora as she watched. Berenice dropped her spent cigarette in the ashtray and Nora jumped, lest Berenice look up and see her, but the singer resumed her previous position without breaking the rhythm of the game. The word association continued for some time with Berenice in a state of relaxation. Almost bored.

"Salt?" Leo said.

"Lot."

"Ink?"

At this Berenice convulsed, curving her spine and contorting her face. When the convulsions subsided, she said: "I dreamt of a bottle shattering. The ink splattered everywhere. It was seeping through my shoes. When I ran away they squelched."

"Who broke the bottle?"

"I did." Berenice sounded surprised. "But someone else got the blame."

"Who?"

"The man at the opera house – I saw him, the night I couldn't sing on stage. He was in the audience."

"Who was he?"

"I don't know." She shook her head, and it was as though the dream and all the puzzlement connected to it fell out entirely. The recent convulsions might never

have happened. Berenice began to relate some tawdry
dalliances she'd had with various singers and film stars –
men and women, Nora noted. Nora's aim was to replicate
this gossip as she would the rest of Berenice's speech. The
deflation of tension suggested Berenice had successfully
distracted herself from the dream that had disturbed her.
She kept distracting herself thusly until the hour was over,
and she leapt from Nora's view. An awkward fumbling
with cash followed. She said goodbye to Leo quite
cheerfully.

"You didn't ask her about me." Nora pulled back the
curtain.

"No."

"Why am I here?"

"Lie on the couch."

"I—"

"Lie on the couch." The agitation she had seen before
the session had gone. He was purposeful. "Lie there as *she*
did."

Nora took Berenice's place as instructed, relaxing into
the leather that Berenice had touched minutes before. She
stared at the ceiling. She did not hear Leo return to his chair,
or even stir from that spot by her feet.

She began: "*What's the matter with your neighbours…*"

Leo said nothing as she went on. She imagined the
responses in between her own, replayed words. Berenice's
phrases tasted good to her. When she reached the point of
convulsing, she felt Leo's hand upon the front buttons of
her dress. He unfastened them smoothly, pushed up the
satin of her slip, and she felt the air on her skin. She didn't
break in her replication of Berenice, though she heard the

rearrangement of Leo's own clothing and his breathing quicken. Her words *I dreamt of a bottle shattering* brought on the crisis. He placed a hand over her face. She felt him wipe a cloth across her stomach. When he let her go she continued to speak as Berenice had done right until Berenice's words ran out. Only then, in her own voice, did she ask:

"Did you mean it at all, when you said I would be singing with her?"

"At first. I think."

She remembered the kiss outside the apartment, after her mimicry of Berenice singing. It was not Nora he'd meant to kiss.

"I love her," he said, looking at the damp folded cloth in his hands.

"Don't be silly. It's countertransference."

"Oh, what's the difference!"

"*Leo*—"

"You're angry with me."

Her fingernails were deep in her palms. Heat swept from her neck up: yes, she was angry, and it was mingled with desire for being Berenice.

She stood up from the couch, feeling sullied and in need of a wash. Being herself again was uncomfortable. The beauty was gone and her buttons were still undone. With shaking hands she fastened them. She retrieved her coat from behind the curtain. When she left, as she walked the streets home, she thought Berenice must be a witch, to ensnare the obsession of Leo and Nora both. But everything would be all right if Nora saw enough of her to replicate her completely. That would satiate her; there would be no need for the real Berenice at all once Nora knew enough to mimic her all the time. Alone in her room she sang the aria again and again to feel less herself. She sang until her throat was raw.

4

Of course Nora returned the following week. She heard more word associations, and dreams, and witnessed further convulsions and accounts of multiple affairs. When Berenice left and Nora was replaying everything she had said and done, Leo rolled her over face down on the couch, tore her skirt in the act of shoving it to her waist, then was inside her. Over a year this became the normal sequence of events each Monday afternoon. All the time Nora was accumulating Berenice's words and gestures. Replicating her so thoroughly meant she came to know the Icon's internal drives and fears as well as she knew her tics of speech.

The pattern broke the week that Leo suggested testing Berenice with inkblots. Nora had used them before and was familiar with the range of interpretations. Every one of them resembled a bone, as far as Nora was concerned; a pelvis, a finger, a spine. Put them all together and you were half way to a skeleton.

For the session, as was usual, Nora watched the reflection of Berenice's pretty head upon the couch. She listened as Leo gave Berenice instructions: he explained he would pass her the image, and she must say what she saw within it. She would be free to rotate it as she wished.

"Here's the first," he announced. Nora couldn't see what he passed Berenice, but she knew which image came when on the cards – the order was always the same – and she could visualise the first easily.

"That's a headless woman," Berenice said immediately. "She's pinned down at either side by men in thick coats and hats. And she doesn't have any feet either."

Nora noticed, for the purposes of imitation, that Berenice was smiling as if the image gave her pleasure.

"Who is the woman?" Leo asked.

Berenice's head lifted from the couch with laughter. "I don't know, Doctor; she doesn't have a head, does she?"

"The men, then?"

She stopped laughing. "*Cheka*. Soldiers."

After a silence, Leo said: "Let's look at the next one."

"Girls playing pattycake," Berenice said.

"Pattycake?" Leo must not recognise the English word.

Berenice shrugged. "The Russian name is *Ladushki*. I don't know what you call it. It's a clapping game, little children clap their hands and sing."

"Ah. *Jeux de mains*." Leo had a smile in his voice.

"They must be sisters," Berenice said slowly. "Because they look the same."

"Do you have any particular sisters in mind, Berenice?"

Nora noted his use of her first name.

"My sister was too old to play clapping games with me."

"Remind me – you were the youngest?"

"Yes, of eight, the others were boys. My mother died in childbirth."

"And they called you – do I have this right? – they called you Nika?"

"My father called me that."

There was a pause as Leo held up the next one.

"Two women with cocks," Berenice said, which was a fairly common answer for the third image, but Nora thought it merited more probing in Berenice's case. Leo didn't say anything. Nora could hear the scratch of his pen in his notebook, before he introduced the next image.

"A bearskin rug?" Berenice sounded unsure. "A man seen from below... as if I'm a child. Or lying on the floor."

"A moth, or my sister's hair clip," she said.

"Tut tut, Doctor," Berenice said. She gave a sly little glance at Leo.

Leo waited for her to continue.

"Showing me pictures of pussies now." Berenice put her

thumbnail between her teeth, dropping her head so that she was gazing at Leo through her fringe. "You can't shock me in the least. I've seen plenty."

"I think it is you who enjoys the idea of shocking people."

"If they know I want to shock them, it shows I don't care about exposure – so they can't threaten me."

"Has that ever happened?"

"Oh yes, when I was much younger, and stood to lose more."

"Who threatened you?"

"My sister. Sisters are meant to be equals but she was my father's ally. Especially with my mother gone. He was probably fucking her." A strange agitation was engulfing Berenice. Her shoulders and arms vibrated. Her face smiled, her teeth on show. "When I was thirteen she interfered in some of my friendships. Put a stop to them. Said if I disobeyed her she would involve my father."

Leo produced the next image.

"A bootprint in the snow." Berenice paused. "It's familiar to me, I have that image in my head already. I don't know if it's a memory or a vision."

"Is it normally hard to tell?"

"No," Berenice said gaily. "My visions are more vivid, almost like I'm living them, but also the details change more than in a memory."

"What was your first vision?"

"I knew my sister was going to be murdered."

"Tell me more about that."

"What's to tell? I saw her in my head, being killed – the details kept changing, every time the vision came – and then the details were different again when it happened. But one important thing never changed. I saw her dying painfully, and she did."

Nora wanted to ask: *Did you warn her?*

But Leo couldn't hear Nora's thoughts. He moved on.

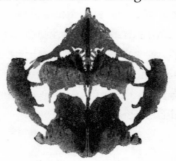

"It's the imperial tricolour," Berenice said. "Or – a crown?"

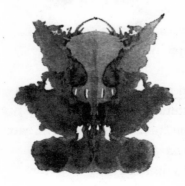

"It's the auditorium of the opera house, with the aisle running down the centre." Berenice was vibrating again. "I don't like this one."

She momentarily passed from Nora's view, as she handed the image back to Leo and took the next.

"This is a mess," Berenice said, letting the image rest on her chest. "It isn't a picture of anything."

"Look longer."

She re-examined it.

"It's the woman from the first image," Berenice said. "But she's fallen to bits. All those fragments are pieces of her dress."

"Our time is up for today," Leo replied.

As Nora adjusted her skirt later to leave Leo's apartment, she raised the topic of Berenice's lost voice to him.

"When will you tell her what's wrong?" she asked.

"What do you mean?"

He didn't listen to a word Berenice said, either the first time or in Nora's repetition, except as beautiful sound – like *Orfeo ed Euridice* was to Nora because she didn't know the language. She would have to explicate as herself, the doctor who'd trained in the workings of the mind.

"Berenice hated her sister, and wanted her dead. Those *visions* were fantasies of what she wanted to happen. When she saw that soldier killing her sister, she was glad, and guilty about being glad. That's why she keeps dreaming of breaking the ink bottle and someone else getting the blame. The ink she's walking through is her sister's blood. If you ask Berenice if that man she saw in the theatre was the soldier, or a man who looked very like him, I think she will realise it was. And if you ask her the method of killing her sister, I think you will find it's something involving the neck – that's why it triggered her inability to sing. It won't be strangulation, because of the blood in the dream. I'd expect her to say her sister's throat was cut."

Leo took a seat at his desk, and made a note.

"All right. I'll ask her those two questions." He rubbed his hands then, vitalised by the prospect. "It's a typical Electra complex, no? The sister standing in for the mother figure of course – but allied with the father – and Berenice wishing her dead to take that role herself. It makes sense of the vengeful gynaecophilia. And her transference in session too – she asked me, once, to call her Niko, do you remember? Her father's name for her, as she revealed today."

Nika, Nora corrected silently. She disliked his interpretation. It seemed clear, from Berenice's responses, that her anger arose from her sister's blackmail. It seemed equally clear that Leo wanted to see an Electra complex in which Berenice was transferring her desire for her father to *him*. But she did not argue with him, for an end to this strange triangle was in sight. The possibility of Berenice being cured was unspoken between them. If she ended her analysis, Berenice would be gone and Nora could indefinitely replicate what she had witnessed. She would keep being Berenice, as long as Leo played his part; Nora's believing audience.

"I'll see you at the hospital," Nora said.

But she didn't, that week. It was fate that decided things against her. She developed a fever and cough, necessitating three days in bed. In her semi-hallucinatory state she took comfort that the illness made her an even better likeness for Berenice. For now, she couldn't sing.

As she recovered she hoped that Leo – if he hadn't cancelled the appointment with Berenice outright – would have delayed the critical questions, to allow Nora to watch how Berenice answered them. She went to his apartment on Wednesday evening, while she was still overwarm, to check what had occurred. There was no response when she rang and rang the bell. She looked at his apartment window, trying to discern if he were truly – and uncharacteristically – out for the evening. The blind was half down. All beyond was darkness.

The old man with the trident – Nora was chagrined to see he did, in fact, carry such a thing – was just climbing the front steps. He looked Nora up from her shoes to her hat, disconcerting her.

"Everyone's been here on the wrong day," he informed her, and let himself in.

"Wait – what do you mean?" Nora called before the door closed.

The old man looked back through. She saw the hand that held the trident had close-cut fingernails, surrounded at all edges by swelling flesh. He shrugged. "You weren't here on Monday; his other one was, but left after twenty minutes. Then she was back again yesterday, for the whole evening."

"Has that happened before?" Nora checked. "Her coming on a Tuesday?"

The old man shook his head. "She usually arrives just after you do."

"You're sure?"

"Oh yes. She's much louder than you on the stairs."

She gave up on the bell. The following morning she returned to work, and shared a ward round with Leo, though in the business of attending to patients there was no opportunity for a private conversation. At the round's completion, just as she was about to ask what had happened with Berenice to require a change in schedule, Leo said: "Best not come next Monday."

His words were casual, and he was about to start a conversation with one of the nurses. Nora forgot to appear polite. She pulled him back by the arm.

"Why is it best I don't come?" she whispered.

"You shouldn't be distracting me. Not when she's at a critical point of analysis. She's reckoning with a feeling she has repressed for years. I couldn't forgive myself for a catastrophic deterioration."

Deterioration was one outcome. Another was improvement. Once the shameful secret was finally voiced and recognised, patients were often restored with astonishing rapidity. How odd that Leo should remember, now, he was Berenice's psychoanalyst, rather than the orchestrator of an odd sexual game. Nora realised she had done something irretrievably stupid. She should never have told Leo why Berenice couldn't sing. He was not content for them to be alone, each week, without the Icon. If the sessions should end he would seek to maintain his connection to her in some other way. It was very common for male psychoanalysts to keep former patients as mistresses. Or less commonly, to take patients as a wife. This had surely entered Leo's head many times in the past, even if Berenice's interest were more recent. Nora should have realised that effecting a change in their weekly routine might not work in her favour.

"I must continue to observe," she insisted. "I gathered the cause of her guilt, after I listened to her more closely in months than you did. You relied on me for that discovery, Leo."

"You shouldn't be distracting me," he repeated. Her hand was still on his arm. He let it fall away, then walked back to the nurse.

For hours she went through her duties mechanically. Another opportunity to speak didn't arise until the afternoon. She found him in the kitchen garden, talking about carrots with a patient. He was carefully ignoring her presence on the side path. When the patient resumed digging, Leo finally approached her.

The breeze made her teeth chatter and she hoped this would not be read as nervousness. Nora did not mention the conversation with Leo's neighbour, to preserve her dignity. There was something humiliating in the thought of her waiting on the step, when she had a suspicion he had left the apartment to see Berenice.

She confined her comments to: "If I'm not to come again, you should at least tell me whether my theory was correct."

He looked at the earth dusting the path, his downward gaze sheepish.

"It was," he owned. "And she took it valiantly. Not initially. She fled, actually, when I broached her memory of her sister's death. I thought I'd made an irreversible mistake. Then she returned – quite unannounced – the following day. She was much more prepared to confront who the man in the audience is. She disclosed that the premonition of her sister's death was fantasy. In fact she confessed, Nora, that her visions are a pretence, something she might have grown out of if they hadn't been rewarded with such attention."

Of course they were.

Leo spoke again, his tone absurdly bashful. "At the end of the session – she was able to sing."

"So fast?" Nora said.

"Yes. Not at her usual level, of course. But she demonstrated for me she could produce a note, without her ears being covered, or the masking of a gramophone."

"I see."

"It was quite joyful to watch her emerge." He was looking into the mid-distance, as if he were talking to himself as he pictured Berenice, and Nora's presence was irrelevant. "I feel a connection between us has been made."

Nora worried what he meant by connection. Without her as a safe duplication he might have made some overture

towards the Icon; the Icon may have accepted it. All things
were possible. He was handsome. Which was of secondary
benefit to Nora – he could have worshipped her mimicry as
an ugly man – but would have eased his path with Berenice.
Worse, Berenice had sung again; Leo's ability to cure her
– *Nora's* ability to cure her – would surely enhance him in
Berenice's eyes.

"Leo," she cautioned, "the connection isn't an ordinary
connection. You're describing transference, and countertransference."

"No," he said. "I don't think I am."

"You've heard her talk about everyone she sleeps with.
Don't forget what a slut she is. If she's flirting with you,
that's because she flirts with everyone. She's just brought
that into analysis with her."

"You're hardly a virgin," Leo said mildly.

"My point is she isn't true – she can barely keep them all
straight in the telling of it."

"She's still capable of love. She's human."

"Can you hear what you're saying, Leo?"

"Why wouldn't she fall in love with me?"

"If she does, it's because I know how to be her – and like
a fool that meant I taught you how to be with her."

"I didn't need to be taught." Leo looked at his wristwatch.
"You're jealous, Nora. It's ugly."

"I don't need to be jealous. I'm the same as her."

He met her eyes properly, and he sighed. "You replicated
everything you'd *watched*."

She felt sick, and small, as she inferred his meaning.

"You look very pale, Nora. Your voice has been hoarse
all day. Are you sure you're better? Don't you need more

rest? I can talk to the Superintendent, if he's being difficult. I'm sure I can make him see sense if he's driving you sooner than he should."

Beneath the surface concern he wished her out of the way: it was clear she was inconvenient to him. To stay calm she focused on the severed line of his ear. She remembered when he had compared her to a lion. No one would treat a lion as small and embarrassing. In the space of a few days he had forgotten how to see her. He didn't believe her as Berenice. Yet he looked through Nora too. The bewitching was complete now. Berenice had made him forget. Nora realised with a jolt that when they were alone Leo always addressed her in English now. She couldn't remember their last private conversation in German. He spoke English *now*, in the kitchen garden where everyone spoke German, when it would seem odd to any passer-by, with its suggestion they were protecting secrets. He was still talking, talking, talking about how he would ensure things ran smoothly without her, the Superintendent would accept it, Leo was privy to all the Superintendent's plans, for the hospital, for him. A patient, one of the ones who never spoke, approached them and pressed an earthworm into Nora's hand. It gave her an opportunity to walk away, and return the still living creature to the black soil.

5

Nora did not oblige Leo by taking her leave. The Superintendent did not wish to see her go, either for convalescence, as Leo attempted to argue was in her interest, or more permanently, which she believed Leo would have pushed for when she'd been away for a while. Instead they continued to work, with a new coldness, exchanging only the information that was necessary – and sometimes, in his case, not even that, perhaps with the intent of causing her professional embarrassment. She worked steadily regardless. Her days were mostly colourless. She continued to replicate Berenice in privacy at home. At those times she came alive, but without anyone to confirm the accuracy of her mimicry she felt lonely. Often she went to the opera to hear Berenice perform, now that the Icon was able to sing again. Sometimes Nora bought tickets on consecutive nights. Seeing Berenice repeat the same actions, near identically, every time reminded Nora of her own careful mimicry, as if there were no real Berenice – just a performance with nothing underneath. Nora saw only a set of actions that could unfold as well through her as through the Icon.

Six months after she last watched Berenice in analysis, Nora was in the small whitewashed room of the hospital toilets. She missed the plumbing of her youth in England: Zurich's toilets were typically a shaft with a plank of wood over them, even in the hospital. As she washed her hands she was joined by one of the nurses, Sister Idda, who remarked on the changing schedules for the doctor's honeymoon.

"Which doctor?" Nora asked.

The sister looked at her sharply, her surprise swiftly giving way to pity. It was Nora's first indication that their colleagues intuited what had passed between her and Leo – the gist, of a connection gone wrong.

"He's to marry Miss Oxbow." Sister Idda's voice was neutral, as she rinsed away the soap.

Nora dried her own hands on a bleached towel. She rolled down her sleeves again, covering the tattoo on her arm. She didn't let the patients see it, if she could help it. In fact people rarely knew it was there because she deliberately favoured long sleeves. Her old tutor knew, of course; and Leo. The tattoo had always been a private reminder of a particular shame, and to that end she'd never been inclined to show it. But that evening she searched through the drawers of her bureau, for the photograph from the tattooists' studio. They had provided her with a copy, keeping one of their own as they did with all their procedures. It took her some time to locate. At one time she had considered throwing it away. She preferred to think of *herself* as the photograph. But she had kept it, and eventually prised it from the join in the wood where it had lodged itself.

The photograph was technically modest. It showed only the square of skin with the flower upon it. Yet the closeness of the image, with the cleft of the arm just in the frame, was provocative. On the photo's reverse, a tiny printed line read: LE SALON DE PROFESSEUR CHARPENTIER, MAYFAIR, LONDON. Above it, Nora poised to pen a note. It bothered her to choose English, but she wanted to be sure Berenice would understand the words. Nora wrote: *L – fantasies are not the domain of lions.* She quaked before the next sentence, but it was essential to cause marital strife. *I love you.* She did not sign or initial it because to write an N would be a lie.

As a plan it was futile. It counted first on her having the opportunity to plant the photograph, and second on Berenice being with Leo when he found it, to ask questions. She could have stopped Berenice at the side door of the opera house, and said: *I watched your analysis for months, then slept with your husband moments after you vacated the couch, while I pretended to be you.* That way she could be more sure of her impact. But Nora had a history of being disbelieved. Better to plant a seed of doubt, subtly, if only fate would allow Berenice to be there when Leo discovered the picture.

Nora carried the photograph with her at all times so that it was on hand whenever she would eventually need it. The wait was longer than she originally anticipated. Leo had been consistent in locking his office. She never saw him leave his belongings unattended elsewhere in the hospital. So the wedding came, and went; though Nora was not party to the celebrations. She saw the wedding portrait in the *Neue Zürcher Nachrichten*. His face was turned so you couldn't

see his injured ear. He wore a white carnation. It was
Berenice Nora studied more carefully; the white dress was
slender and minutely embroidered, the veil floor length and
gauzy. She should have looked demure. Instead she looked
smug in her good fortune. Nora imitated the expression,
just once, and threw the paper in the bin. Leo took Berenice
to Paris. Then they returned – and Berenice met Leo daily
at the hospital as his shift ended. Nora sometimes watched,
through the window, as Berenice walked the path to the
hospital. She wondered what would happen if they stood
before each other, looking eye to eye. It would augur a
death like the meeting of doppelgängers in any gothic story.
Then the victor would eat the remains.

Patience won out. The habitual trying of Leo's door
every time Nora passed by finally paid off. She was quick
to work. His dark coat hung on the hatstand. She found
his wallet in the inner pocket; a lovely worn leather thing,
old-fashioned, with an art nouveau swirl embossed on the
front. The kind of thing inherited from a father, perhaps.
Nora tucked the picture of her tattoo inside the folds. She
replaced the wallet in his pocket. The coat smelt of him,
and of Berenice. Nora recognised the Shalimar from the
impregnated couch. Her eyes brimmed, and she left the
office before she could be caught.

She followed him when he left that evening, maintaining
a safe distance behind the couple in the dark. The nearest
tram was a quarter of an hour away on foot. But it was
a clear evening and they seemed determined to enjoy it,
because they didn't catch the tram at all. Nora trailed them

down Kreuzbühlstrasse and Zollikerstrasse, under the trees and past the grand grounds of the Bleuler family. She had no idea of their intended destination – or even if they knew where they meant to end up. They turned finally on Lenggstrasse and entered one of the city's restaurants, the Kronenhalle. Nora hung back until they were safely through the doors. After a decent interval she walked casually to the building front. The windows were etched decoratively, which afforded her some protection from being seen, but she was able to look through the clear narrow spaces between the grooves in the glass. Berenice was seated with her back to Nora. Leo's face was clearly visible. For the full meal, Nora watched them eat, drink, talk – although, Leo appeared to mainly listen, rapt. Nora wondered if he still ignored the content of Berenice's speech. The heat of the restaurant condensed upon the windows and Nora pushed her face closer to follow Leo's movements. Through the tiny remaining gap, she saw him open his wallet. He withdrew a bank note. Paused. Tugged at the other contents. Nora's mouth parted. He smiled broadly, shook his head, and passed the picture to Berenice.

Nora reared back. It hadn't occurred to her that he would react so lightly. Why wasn't he afraid of discovery? Had he already told Berenice who she was, or the nature of their relationship? She had assumed it was a secret; for why would a woman of Berenice's vanity accept such a thing had occurred? Unless, she found the setup flattering – that Leo's former lover was an ersatz version of herself? This hardly reflected well on Berenice. Nora enjoyed the feeding of her hate this allowed, not least because it distracted her from Leo's betrayal. He had instigated their strange game, and discarded her, only to laugh at her now. She didn't wait to watch any further. Her calves ached. She had worked all day, and walked for half an hour, then watched, in the cool air, this endless meal from a hard pavement. Planting the photo had already taken months of patience. It was time to go home.

She sank into a heavy sleep on her return, and was woken at two in the morning by the bell that hung next to the front door. Františka wailed for Nora to see who was disturbing them. Wrapping her dressing gown around herself, Nora went to investigate, and the bell continued to ring with her every step. It was Leo causing the noise, and when she opened the door, he entered at once without being invited in.

"Why are you here?" she asked, her head full of the smile as he pushed the photograph across the table. It was surprising to her Berenice hadn't insisted on accompanying him.

"You know why," he said.

She rubbed her eyes, and called up to Františka: "It's no one, Aunty; silly boys on a dare."

Leo was pushing open doors off the hallway. He entered the dining room, where he might sit at the table, and he unfolded a piece of paper there. Nora joined him.

"Despite your efforts," he said, "Berenice doesn't know who you are, or what we did."

Nora's head shot up, attentive.

"I told her *that* photograph belonged to a delusional patient. And she will not discover otherwise."

"I can tell her the truth," Nora said, although without conviction. Her aim had been to replace Berenice, and be loved by Leo as such – destroying his marriage was incidental, rather than the aim of her plan.

"If you do I promise to discredit you," he said, firmly. "I have told Berenice that my patient is obsessed with me. For now she doesn't know your name or profession. Reveal yourself to her, and I'll have no choice but to publish the following as a case study. I've protected your identity in my notes, but rest assured I *will* remove your anonymity if you threaten my marriage."

He held his paper before him. She waited as he cleared his throat, her fingers twitching.

"Patient MCCLX suffered a cold, uncaring mother, and as a result had an extremely fragile sense of self. The patient frequently questioned whether she had any real self at all; she compared herself to machines like phonographs or Dictaphones; she doubted she was human. During adolescence this disturbance of the self had progressed to full-blown delusion. In a perversion of the nurturing bond she craved, the patient imagined that she led her mother to a homicidal act of violence, and that her mother served the body to her as sustenance. The patient fantasised she was a supernatural entity who enjoys human flesh and assumes the identity of its prey; she had intermittently adopted the mannerisms and speech of her mother's supposed victim. The attraction of this fantasy was that the patient could split off her true, fragile self and disavow it. Desiring this split is a sign of pathology."

Were even his notes in English now?

"I'm not your patient," Nora said.

"You have lain on my couch weekly for a year; what am I if not your analyst? The neighbours have seen you come and go. If you deny, publicly, you were my patient, which of us is more credible?"

Her profession was no shield. Psychoanalysts treated each other all the time. And when a man treated a woman, people trusted his word over hers. That her friend should put her in such a position appalled her.

"Stop being absurd!" she said. "You know I'm not deluded. I told you the truth."

"I know you *believed* it and I misguidedly humoured you. You might have noticed patients believe all sorts of things. Take, for instance, your claim to be a predator of people – that you are psychologically capable of eating human flesh. One can challenge that belief straightforwardly enough."

"Are you going to prepare me a stew of human meat?" she asked witheringly.

He took a small pair of golden scissors from his pocket.

"I don't feel pain," he explained to her. "I haven't since the war. They told me it was beriberi. They were wrong; I just forgot how to hurt."

Nora wanted to stay his hands. But she also knew she must see what would happen. She watched the golden blade draw closer to his perfect ear, all the time his eyes fixed on hers. With two clean cuts the lobe was severed. It fell to the table, and on the high gloss of the shellac, created a crisp reflection below. Blood ran down Leo's neck to his collar.

"Eat it," he said.

She looked at the crescent of flesh. It was curled in on itself, like a dead maggot. She grabbed the lobe and crammed it into her mouth, attempting to swallow without sensing it on her tongue. She succeeded and vomited as quickly, her head dropping between her knees as her stomach emptied upon the rug.

"There," said Leo. "Let's hear no more nonsense about killing people and eating them. You're a fantasist, and I feel sorry for you. Leave the hospital, Dr Čapek. Don't approach me, or my wife, again."

She had no reply. For the police to contradict her was one thing; for Leo to do so was another; but her body had rebelled, and it was that which threatened her memory of the murder. She recollected, when swallowing Miss Lowrie's flesh, a sense of relief and rightness: if that memory were false, she didn't know how to trust the rest. While her eyes were closed she heard Leo shove his seat away from the table. The front door slammed moments later.

6

This time, Nora did give up her duties at the hospital. Františka's health took a plunge for the worse, and her aunt would need constant care. Never mind that nurse maids could be hired; Nora seized on her aunt's changed circumstance as a reason to take her leave. If Nora's shame and shock at Leo's attitude made her continued presence at the Holzberg untenable, there was no reason to mention it.

Nora was scrupulous in giving bed baths, changing linens and administering medication. These days the dowager's hair was fully white, and she suffered a cataract over her right eye which halved her field of vision. She assumed Nora was dutiful to ingratiate herself: come the old woman's death, Nora might lose a roof over her head.

"I'm of age, Aunty. I have my father's money," Nora pointed out, in the Czech the two women always used to address each other. Soon she would have no one to understand her Czech. She was replacing her aunt's blankets, smoothing the edge down at the top to the sound of wheezing.

Grudgingly, Františka replied: "I suppose his death was useful too."

Jaroslav had been much on Nora's mind. Since Leo had shattered her certainty of those last days in the woods, she had reassessed her father's decision to send her away. He had claimed to fear the taint of scandal, and its effect upon her prospects. If this were true, he could have relocated all three of them, as a family; or at least visited his daughter, which he never had, not once before his death. She had often hoped he was being protective in a different way: by silencing her attempts to tell the truth, and despatching her, he was placing her beyond the influence of her monstrous mother. Nora was his child, and thus he must have had hope she contained enough humanity to turn out differently. This made sense if Valery was a hyring, caged by her father for everyone's safety. But if Nora had fantasised the entire episode in the woods – Valery's murder of Miss Lowrie, her transformation and claim to being a hyring – her mother was innocent. What then was Jaroslav's motive for banishing her? Nora suspected that Jaroslav was ashamed of and disgusted with his daughter's mental frailty. With Nora's mimicry, her fainting fit and inexplicable illness, he started to fear his daughter would be a burden. She must have made it worse by going to the police, where she was heard to rave, in public, as if she had lost her faculties. So Jaroslav had washed his hands of her.

"Why do you suppose he sent me here?" she asked now.

Františka grunted. "He liked the idea of being a father more than he liked children."

"I didn't realise you disliked him, Aunty."

"I'm dying, how do you expect me to talk? Might I have a cigar?" she cajoled.

"No. Listen to your breath."

"It will relax my lungs."

Nora relented. She fetched one from the box in the drawing room. On the way, Františka's description of Jaroslav needled her. What was a father, if he didn't care for his child, and why would he be worth missing? For she did miss him, she realised, or the recently lost possibility that he may have tried to do right by her. And a father was someone who knew where you came from, in the most material way. Nora didn't *know* herself. For all her self-sufficiency, she feared whenever she couldn't sleep at night that beneath her mimicries she was nothing but a hollow space. It didn't seem to matter as much, when, for that period, she might have fully replicated Berenice so truly, and had Leo affirm her accuracy with his attention. Now it did matter.

She brought back the cigar, ready to light it for the old woman. Predictably it triggered a coughing fit and yet Františka persisted. Her breath settled back into that laboured wheeze. Cigars always smelt dirty to Nora, almost faecal, compared to the clean smell of her cigarettes. She felt cheered by remembering a preference that was wholly her own, and not a replication of another person's. The smoke was pretty in the pink evening light, too.

"Here is a secret. I *have* arranged to leave my house to you," Františka said magnanimously. "You seem determined to be an old maid, and Jaroslav's money won't last forever, so I must make provision."

Resigned, Nora said: "I've earnt my way well enough. Didn't you wish to marry, either? Marry again, I mean."

"Once was enough."

Nora laughed. She couldn't help it. In her mother's voice, she said: "*Men like to put wives in their place, and remind them of their failures.*"

Františka turned to face her, shocked. Had she recognised Valery's voice? It seemed unlikely – if they had ever met, it must have been over thirty years ago. But it must be confusing, when she was half in this world, half the next, to hear Nora use a voice not her own. Nora must stop doing that.

"What is your favourite colour?" Františka's good eye focused on Nora.

The question was a non-sequitur, and child-like. Her mind must be wandering. Nora was gentle.

"I don't know, Aunty."

"Humour me."

Nora shrugged. "Lilac."

"That is *my* favourite colour."

Two people could like the same colour. It meant nothing. *I have a self*, Nora thought. *I am not fragments of other people*. With forced cheer, she returned: "What's your favourite scent, Aunty?"

"Anisbrötli," Františka said promptly, naming a variety of anise-flavoured biscuit, as Nora had known she would.

"Mine is apple blossom," Nora said with satisfaction.

"Your old tutor," Františka said. "The one you opened your legs for. His fiancée loved apple blossom. Do you remember? She doused herself in it."

Nora coloured, and not at her aunt's deathbed crudeness, but because she had failed to give an answer of her own.

"My favourite poet," Nora announced, "is Coleridge."

Františka shrugged. "I never cared for poetry."

It was a poor effort anyway. Nora knew Coleridge was Miss Lowrie's favourite poet. They sat in silence for a while, then Nora took the burning cigar from Františka's hand, as her breathing worsened. The wheezing culminated in a death rattle. Nora closed the old woman's eyes. She rationalised to herself: *Favourite colours and favourite poets don't matter. Who cares! What matters is whether you can think of any occasion when you have done the right thing. That is what makes a person.* Except Nora couldn't trust that she had ever done that: she believed she had done the right thing the morning she went to PC McEwan. But she was deluded. By any measure, she suspected, she failed to be a person. She was nothing but a void.

Over the following days Nora was efficient in arranging the removal of the body and the execution of the estate, all the time ruminating that her stated reason for avoiding the Holzberg was at an end. She was unable to sleep, less from grief for Františka, and more from agitation at how she should occupy herself next. When she checked the local newspaper for the death announcement she had placed, she saw on an earlier page that Berenice Oxbow was soon to embark on a world tour, accompanied by her husband. They would depart after Berenice's final performance in *Hipermestra* at the Zurich Opera House. That was a week away; the same night as Františka's funeral. Nora wondered at Leo's speed in removing her from the hospital if he planned to travel so soon himself. Maybe he had been taken by surprise by Berenice's schedule, and had not realised he would be abroad this quickly. In theory, Nora might ask the Superintendent if she could resume her duties. The idea did not appeal. Leo would return in time and might be vindictive. For all she knew, he had already poisoned the well. Better to start afresh. Nora would travel herself for a while – to Berlin, and Vienna, where she might sharpen her knowledge – and then, taking possession of Františka's house, she would commence a private practice. Seamlessly she moved from administration of the dead to that of her own future: the purchase of train tickets and the telephoning of hotels.

In an echo of her parents' funeral, when the day came to bury Františka, Nora did not go to the church. She told herself she was going; she dressed for it. But she delayed her departure from the house, distracting herself by packing the items she would need for her trip, until the afternoon had passed and she knew her aunt would be below earth. She could still pay her respects at the graveside, she reasoned, and finally left, a dark coat and gloves to keep her warm and her vision filtered through a black veil. The mourning garb felt like a disguise, which may have been why – despite Leo's warning to never approach him, or Berenice, again – she dared turn off the path long before the church, and walked up the busier road to the opera house. That evening's performance of *Hipermestra* was just about to begin.

Nora requested a ticket. She removed her gloves as she fumbled with coins. The grief of the day left her struggling to count. How naked her hands looked. The man gave her the billet, and she took a seat as the curtain rose. She dared not lift her veil, but she wanted to hear, not see, the results of her work once more. She was the one who had allowed the return of Berenice's voice.

Nora knew the old Greek story upon the stage; fifty princesses must marry their cousins and kill them at their father's behest. From the darkness Nora watched the wedding banquet unfold. Berenice was in the title role. She entered like the bride she was, a white posy in her hands, white gauze framing her face, wide white skirts. When she sang, Nora gripped the arm rests, her nails forming crescents in the cloth. She envied the Icon the beauty of her voice. She, Nora, had achieved its return, and she still had the skill to replicate it perfectly. But she had lost her best audience – and worse – he had revealed she had no substantial core of her own. She was no snake or lion. She was a sad deluded neurotic.

Berenice's voice trailed mid-aria, halting Nora's train of thought. Even at this distance Nora recognised the expression Berenice assumed before she faked a vision. The rest of the audience were less prepared, but they could read alarm in the other performers' faces. People shifted in their seats.

The wedding table banquet was laden with wax food, including a roast boar. Berenice raised one white arm, pointing a shaking hand at the audience.

"A tragedy's coming! A woman here is in terrible danger. I see her! I see her in my mind's eye! She has a tattoo!"

Nora leant forward in her seat.

"Find the lady with flowers tattooed on her forearm," Berenice said more loudly, with greater urgency. "A horrific fate awaits her! Where is she? Can you see her?"

The emergency curtain fell. A second later the audience

broke into confused noise. Nora was thankful for her veil, aware again that Leo might be here somewhere watching, and see her. Berenice had stolen the only detail she possessed of Nora, and implored the rest of the audience to look for it. She couldn't know Nora was there; but was that the point? Did she do this every night? Invoke her anonymous rival, before a crowd of hundreds, from the mere hope she'd be watching? From hope it would draw her to the light? A round tuxedoed man scurried past the footlights to announce the performance would begin again very shortly. Nora had seen all she wanted to. She abandoned her seat.

In Germany she attended a few events held by the Psychoanalytic Society where yet again she was outnumbered by men – oh there were women around, especially the wives and mistresses and patients who informally did a great deal of psychoanalytic work, but they were used to being excluded from the herrenzimmers in their own homes, where the men entertained each other and smoked. Nora repeatedly found herself in the company of a square-faced, dark-haired analyst named Bruna Wenig, who was the only other woman there with her own practice; she was in an ambiguous position, lacking even a bachelor's degree, but had benefited from the patronage of a man in the Society. Bruna increasingly took a seat by Nora during lectures, solely on the basis of their similar positions at the margins. Unfortunately Nora didn't like her. In their discussions of child development – the specialism where female psychoanalysts' insight was most tolerated – this stranger got under Nora's skin. She argued that patients' accounts of their childhood, including transgressive descriptions of incest and molestation, should be trusted rather than regarded by default as fantasy.

"Deep down," Bruna said once, as they settled themselves in the lecture hall, "no psychoanalyst disbelieves such accounts. We believe, but it is more comfortable to deny the truth."

Nora fidgeted with a lorgnette. She didn't want to reply, and fortunately didn't have to, because Ernst Simmel was approaching the lectern with his paper. Bruna's opinions on belief touched a nerve. They disturbed Nora's perception of her own experiences, at this point in her life. The inability to eat the flesh Leo laid before her had been an effective challenge. It had persuaded Nora that her memories were unreliable. Which meant the police were right: it was a fevered hallucination. James Markham had vacillated, but his instinct had been to call the remains *beef bones*. To surrender was a relief. She slowly acknowledged she would rather be wrong, than right and disbelieved. If she were to accept Bruna's observation, and they *had* all believed her but denied it from convenience, she would be lonely enough to break reality.

7

Nora was calm on her return to Zurich. She refurnished
the house to accommodate the seeing of patients, especially
children. Thereafter she worked, if not contentedly,
without emotional turmoil: patients came in the morning,
and she spent each afternoon to evening writing up
personal research with a detached attitude. Everything
felt flat and unchanging. Only the seasons progressed as
normal, which seemed inconsiderate of her mood. As 1928
drew to a close, the weather dropped below freezing: in
the evenings she took to the lake with her skates, amongst
the children sledding or even, trepidatious, the courting
couples walking over the ice. Nora felt like an ice sculpture
herself, cold and sharp edged, cutting through the air at
speed. No matter how hard she pushed herself, to the
point her limbs ached and there was no air in her lungs,
she could not warm through.

One such evening as she readied herself to leave the
house, she saw, through the window pane of the door, Leo
standing in the street, his hat held against his chest despite
the cold. She knew he had seen her looking, so she left the

house to speak to him, burying her hands in the fur muff that hung from her neck.

"Am I breaking your rules by coming out here?" she asked tartly in German. "I realise I'm to keep my distance."

"I'd appreciate you letting me in," he replied in English.

She wouldn't switch languages. To do so would be a step closer to her imitations of Berenice. "You're not welcome inside. I don't know what you'd cut off with scissors."

"Very well." He scowled, still steadfast in using English, so that he and Nora must sound as if they spoke to themselves rather than each other. "Berenice is having an affair."

She ignored the disclosure. "The last time you were here, you left with blood all over your shirt and two incomplete ears. How did you explain that to your wife?"

"I said I'd been attacked by a patient. Please, Nora – I need your help."

"I *told* you that she would be unfaithful!"

"Aren't you the clever one," he said, though he sounded more tired than spiteful.

"Not clever." She shook her head. "You broke me."

He scratched his temple, uncomfortable at the word.

"Don't worry," she added. "I healed."

"Then there's no reason why you can't help," he rushed in. "I have hunches – suspicions – but Nora, I don't have *proof*. And I think she realises I'm looking for evidence. She won't take me with her on the rest of the tour. She is in France now, and shortly she leaves for England. The thoughts of what she might be doing are driving me mad."

"What of *your* behaviour?" Nora asked quietly. "She's shown her colours. Have you been unfaithful too?"

"No. The very suggestion is despicable."

Hyperbole was often a sure sign of dishonesty; but Nora hadn't any heart in believing that particular sin of him. He was constitutionally monogamous. Nora had fulfilled a particular role for him, then Berenice assumed it next; there had been no question of overlap.

"I need you to follow her," he asserted again.

"Why should *I* do that work for you? There are investigators who specialise in this sort of thing. Hire one of those."

"*No.*" For the first time in the conversation he sounded angry. "Employ a man, an outsider, to witness my humiliation?"

"This is nothing to do with me." She took a step backwards into the road.

With the hat still gripped in his fist he reached towards her. If he wished to grasp her, he didn't dare touch.

"You can overhear her in company," he pleaded. "And repeat it all back to me."

"A fine plan." His suggestion awakened the longing to watch Berenice but she did not think he could be serious. "Will you arrange a curtain and mirrors in all her hotel rooms?"

"There are bars. Dining rooms. Gardens! You can watch her in all those places, to see who she meets."

In all these months alone with the unchanging flatness of her thoughts, she had thought her lack of self was insoluble. She still thought so. Here was the prospect of watching Berenice at close range again, gaining material with which to inhabit her, and yet she did not trust the plan was in earnest.

"You showed me I was insane," she hissed. "Why are you sending a mad woman after your wife?"

"Because I don't care if you're mad," he cried. "You know how to watch her. You say it yourself – you saw this coming. You *know* her, on the inside. I said you were deluded to think yourself a hyring. That doesn't change how accurately you record the behaviour of others."

She paused, then shook her head. "Go away, Leo."

Her skates were still in the house, she realised; and when she went to fetch them, the desire to exhaust herself under the evening sky was gone. She was already tired. Half an hour later she checked through the window. In the gathering darkness she could no longer tell if Leo was there.

Nora's refusal was punitive. She wanted the satisfaction of Leo begging, and not getting what he wanted. And she wanted him to come back, to ask again. When the punishing was done she would agree. She savoured the prospect. Between seeing patients she stayed in her leather armchair, her hands interlocked over her knee, imagining the trailing of Berenice in England. The Icon would be outside, rather than upon Leo's couch, living her public life, all under Nora's eye. They might even talk. Nora could watch, and copy, and when she had the evidence she needed of Berenice's infidelity, she would return to Leo, and he would validate the copy was better than the original. That was why, when the punishing was done, she would comply.

Two days later Leo had still not returned. Nora began to feel uneasy. Twice she placed her hand on the telephone to contact him, and stopped. The third time she did this, it rang, making her jump.

"Please, Nora," Leo said when she answered. "I don't trust anyone else. I trust you to do this. I want you to."

"Speak German."

"Very well," he said, doing as she asked.

"And I have another condition."

She could hear the wariness in the pause that followed.

"What condition?"

"An apology."

"Oh – is that all! I'm sorry, Nora – I'm sorry."

"For what?" she pressed. "For threatening to slander me? For using me for months until you got what you really wanted? For ignoring my warnings about that disgusting little imbecile? For assuming I would do what you wanted again as soon as you clicked your fingers?"

"Yes – all of it. I am more sorry than I can say. Is that enough, Nora? Do you forgive me?"

"No I don't," Nora said. "And I never will. But I will follow your wife, Leo, and I will report back every squalid thing that she does."

She spent the following fortnight making arrangements for her departure. Her patients were moved on. The timing of Leo's request meant that joining Berenice at her last calling point in Birmingham was the most practical plan. With travel, Nora must pack for three weeks. During her preparations she spoke and walked and reclined as Berenice. In the mirror, she admired her exquisite mimicry of the Icon, which hadn't dulled with the passing of time. She allowed herself to listen to *Orfeo ed Euridice*. She sang with the record, and she sang without it, in every room of the house. Imagine if anything happened to Berenice between performances. Nora could step up in her place, and no one would hear the difference. Of course Nora wasn't as vain as Berenice. She didn't want adoring applause from faceless crowds. That took a particular personality, one concerned with artifice and flattery, rather than any interest in what made an individual *them*. Still – to experience it just for one night – wouldn't that validate her mimicry was as beautiful as the real thing?

The day that she left for the railway station, she was optimistic of finding the evidence Leo so desired. Nora never doubted that Berenice would conduct affairs. A related, but separate fear nagged at Nora, regarding her fate afterwards. When Leo last abandoned her, he had said she could only copy what she had witnessed of Berenice. He meant that Nora knew nothing of Berenice as a lover. Maybe, when Nora returned, Berenice would be tainted enough in Leo's mind that the differences between the women in that regard would be a point in Nora's favour. But it could never be an advantage in Nora's own mind. She *wanted* the mimicry to be complete, in every respect where Leo was able to judge it. The solution wasn't obvious to her; even though, again and again, her thoughts turned to the problem.

PART FIVE

THE REGENT HOTEL, BIRMINGHAM, 1929

I

In the pineapple suite Berenice was the first to rise. Nora woke to see her standing by the rain-spattered window, fully clothed in navy bloomers and a buttoned blouse. She was beautiful in the peculiar silver sunlight; and Nora could enjoy her beauty without any past hatred.

"How much do you know about me?" Nora asked.

"Leo told me very little," Berenice said. "We went to dinner. He pulled a photo of your tattoo from his wallet, as if he didn't expect it to be there – and he gave this phoney fakeloo laugh. Then he told me you were a delusional patient. He said you were obsessed with him, that you'd put the photo there without his knowledge to seduce him. As if I hadn't been his patient once, and knew how easily he could be seduced! He's never looked so shifty in his life."

"I did put the photo there, to make you suspicious. But I was never his patient."

"Sorry, angel. That's how *he* saw you, whatever you thought."

This was surely true. Nora recollected: "He did say he would write a paper about me."

"Sometimes he's threatened to publish one about me. If he did, everyone would know I'm not clairvoyant. All the love people give me for it – the adulation – would be gone."

This was the first time Berenice had admitted to Nora the clairvoyance wasn't real. The confession was made with so little fanfare. Either Berenice trusted completely that Nora's adulation would remain; or Berenice valued Nora's opinion so little she didn't count her among *people*. Nora realised she wanted Berenice's trust – not to make subterfuge easier, as on her arrival, but from a true desire for alliance.

"Leo said nothing else about me?" Nora checked.

"Nothing. No name, no other details. The conversation in the restaurant lasted less than a minute and took root in my head. It became unbearable, whenever we were in public, to think you could be there and I had no way to single you out. At the opera house I told the ticket seller, if ever a woman with a chrysanthemum tattoo came to a performance, he should alert me. And one night, he did, just before the curtain rose."

"*Hipermestra*, your last night in Zurich," Nora murmured.

"The ticket seller was a dunderhead. I should have told him to keep you waiting by the booth while someone fetched me. Instead, by the time he came backstage you were already seated. I looked out at the audience and still had no way to know which face was yours. My vision was meant to cause a showdown."

"You underestimated my restraint."

"Hardly restrained to follow me across a continent."

"How did you guess you'd been followed to England?"

"When I arrived at the hotel," Berenice said, "telegrams were waiting from the Zurich Opera House. The opera secretary queried an extra receipt Meiss had sent her."

H. Meiss was the general agent for booking travel from Zurich.

"All the payments for my travel come from Leo's account," Berenice went on. "After Leo paid for *your* tickets, Meiss must have accidentally included the receipt with my paperwork. The secretary said the receipt had no name associated with it but Leo's. I knew his lover had been watching me at the opera house. It stood to reason she was the one spying on me now."

"So you faked another vision, in the Pinfold Dining Room, still hoping to provoke a confrontation?"

Berenice shrugged. "Maybe. I wanted to say: I know I'm being watched. It felt less pathetic than doing nothing. I hoped you might leave, because it's harder to spy on someone with suspicions."

"So... when I first came to speak to you, did you guess I was the woman in the photograph?"

"Whenever a strange woman comes up to me, wanting to talk, it crosses my mind that maybe *she's* his lover. I considered it pretty briefly with you. Your tattoo was disguised – and you were English, Leo never said you were English." Berenice wrote НИКА in the condensation on the window, before immediately wiping the Russian name away. "But then you made that comment in the graveyard about phoning Leo, that he wouldn't be able to tell us apart. It sounded personal, Nora. That's when I guessed you *are* his mistress."

"I'm not. I might have been once, before you were married. I'm not any more."

"Then why act on his orders to follow me?"

"To learn everything I could about you," Nora said. "I was obsessed with you. Not in the manner of a mistress for her rival, not really. I wanted to own every little detail about you, to make those details mine and live in them. I wanted to devour you—"

Nora halted herself at the thought of devouring Berenice.

"What?" the Icon asked.

"The monster I saw in my room," Nora said. "I think I'm one of them – or something very like."

Berenice was as eager as a racehorse at the gate. "What do you mean, angel?"

Nora recounted her childhood in the wood – the murder of Miss Lowrie and her mother's transformation; the roots of her own mimicry. She detailed hyrings' dangers and vulnerabilities, including the constraints on their travel by mirrors. The explanation took some time. She concluded: "There is another hyring in this hotel, I saw it with my own eyes, and it must be responsible for these disappearances."

"That's *much* more thrilling than an ordinary murderer!"

Nora wondered if Berenice's titillated reaction was because she continued to think Nora's tale was as fraudulent as her own visions. If hyrings weren't real, they weren't frightening. "Do you believe what I'm telling you?"

"D'you know – I think I do!" Berenice said. "Although I have some questions. If the hyring exists, why didn't it follow you to my room? The mirror was uncovered, so it had a means to enter."

"Maybe it wants to be alone with me," Nora faltered.

Berenice clapped her hands. This was a game she would enjoy playing. "Maybe it will be jealous of me, now I've seduced you. I might be in danger."

Nora considered the death drive. "I feel like you want to get yourself killed."

"No, you silly girl. But I do enjoy the idea of a hyring that *wants* to kill me – then I'll wrap it round my finger. They'll eat everyone else. I'll be the exception."

Like a lion tamer; or a snake charmer. She seemed not to understand that for hyrings, love didn't win against the pleasure of a feast. Not in the end. You could only contain a hyring, as Valery was once contained. You couldn't change its nature through human feeling.

Berenice looked out through the window again. "You need to see this."

Nora cloaked herself in the bedspread and joined her. Bright rays in the sky shot through dark grey cloud. As the hotel was on high ground, the thaw had seen most of the snow run off to the city's lower streets. But deep kerbs bordering the road and rain which fell faster than the water could drain had led to the spontaneous formation of a canal below. It appeared quite filthy, compared to the picturesque snow that had preceded it. The cellars here must be in trouble, Nora realised. Would there be food served? What contingencies did the Regent have in place for such catastrophes?

"You're not paying attention," Berenice said. "Look, further down the street!"

Nora saw boats in v-formation, advancing down Temple Row. At the front was a helmeted policeman: upright of back, and moving the oars with vigour as the sun flashed off his coat buttons. A swaddled box lay at his feet – presumably destined for the nearest station.

"Too small for a body," Berenice speculated.

Thinking of Miss Lowrie's arm, Nora said: "It might be part of one."

"Westall? Or Mrs Reid? Or some other victim?"

"I know someone who might find out for us." Crouch would glean any relevant tittle-tattle from the hotel workers.

"You're a real secret agent."

Nora grimaced, anticipating the final disclosure. "There's a last thing I haven't told you; about me, and Leo."

"What?"

"Every week you went to his apartment, Berenice, he had me observe."

"Why?" Berenice turned her head back to the rowing policeman, but Nora didn't think she was seeing him at all.

Nora considered saying: *to treat me as his consolation prize.* But she was no longer sure that was true.

"He liked that I wanted to eat you. If I had, he would have kept me, I think." Nora paused. "I helped you, instead. I told him the meaning of the ink bottle in your dreams."

"Then you're to blame for the marriage," Berenice said. "I thought he'd given me my voice back. He told me how much, deep down, I'd wanted my sister dead, and I couldn't sing for the guilt. When he'd finished, he asked: 'But Véro – didn't your sister deserve it?' That freed me. I liked what he was saying. I liked hearing that my sister had it coming and I stopped feeling guilty. I knew Leo was a monster with those words. But I thought he was a monster on my side."

The flourish was Leo's own. He'd taken Nora's insight, one he was incapable of reaching by himself, and turned it to his advantage. She abetted his monstrousness, and he hers. Maybe that was how most monsters were made: through accomplices.

"Leo's on your side when it suits him," Nora said.

Berenice walked away, out of the bedroom, closing the door behind her. A stifled scream followed. It was fury, not fear; Nora was not alarmed. And all the time, the policeman was rowing, and rowing, and rowing.

Eventually, when the boats had passed out of view, Nora dressed and left the bedroom too. From the hallway she could hear Berenice talking with someone, though she couldn't make out the words, and Berenice was just closing the apartment door as Nora reached the drawing room.

"That was Mr Quarrington," Berenice explained. "The communal rooms are closed, so we better get used to these four walls. I explained that you'd come up here as my guest. For now the lift's out of order. Some kind of water damage, I don't know. He said all meals would still be cooked, but they'll be brought to our door, and we can request any other services we need from the floor housekeeper."

"Did Quarrington say who the body belonged to?"

"Obviously I asked but if he knows, angel, I don't think he'd say. A guest or an employee would be bad for business. Bet he's hoping it's some other rube besides Reid or Westall. Someone without an immediate connection to the hotel, who the guests won't care about."

Someone like Enid. Nora wondered, with a pang, how Enid was faring in that small room as the snow turned to flood. Then she wondered how Crouch would gather

intelligence if confined to his quarters. From the relevant
floor housekeeper, supposedly. He still seemed like the best
chance of learning what the police had discovered. Without
knowing his room number the easiest way to get in touch
was to write him a note and ask their own housekeeper to
make sure it reached him.

She asked Berenice for pen and paper, and kept it short
and cryptic lest the note be read en route. *I think I saw one
of our friends abroad this morning? If you want to clue me
in I'm in the pineapple suite with Miss Oxbow, or suggest
another waterproof spot.* She wasn't sure he'd talk in front
of Berenice, given his previous aversion to her, though he
would probably be wildly curious as to why Nora suddenly
occupied the same rooms. She signed the note *N. Dickinson*
and took a few minutes to drop it off with the woman
stationed at the end of the corridor.

On her return, Berenice was stretched out upon the pink
carpet with a fan of magazines, admiring the fashions and
ignoring the words, while one of her own recordings played
on the gramophone.

"I don't know how soon that message will reach him,"
Nora said. "And he may want to dig around before
responding. He'll certainly want to have a theory ready to
present."

Berenice nodded. "He doesn't like to admit to ignorance?"

"Quite. Let's wait and see." Nora sighed. "In the
meantime we should obey our curfew and make ourselves
comfortable; there isn't anything else to be done."

"My magazines are your magazines," Berenice replied.
"The suite's at your disposal."

As the day slipped by, the thunder and rain lessened then

stopped. A meal, as promised, arrived at the door beneath a silver dome. Berenice ran herself a bath, and Nora was quite alone when Crouch finally knocked. His expression was downcast. He looked over Nora's shoulder, searching for the hostess.

"The woman's practically amphibian," Nora explained. "By her own account she might be gone for three hours. Do you want to come in?"

"No, I won't stop. I'm only here to say I don't have any information for you. Sorry to disappoint. The workers had their hands to the pump. No time for them to chat."

It was a reasonable explanation. But his unwillingness to speculate, the curtness of his words, made her feel she was being punished for something; though she couldn't tell what.

"Never mind," she said uncertainly. "No educated guesses, either?"

"It will be Reid," he said.

"Why do you say that?"

"Do you think *any* of the staff would be working as hard today if it had been Westall?" Crouch was just turning to leave, but he looked back. "I have to ask, about your new room. Have you befriended Oxbow? To give a better report to your chap?"

Nora was disinclined to explain to him when he was so hostile. It was simplest to say: "Yes. That's right."

"OK then." He nodded. "Good luck."

She watched his back as he walked away, and caught his face as he turned the corner. Not angry. Unhappy.

★ ★ ★

The floors below the waterline had flooded. The laundry rooms were the worst affected. As soon as the rain ceased, the strongest men from every department of the hotel had been diverted to help. They waded through standing water, clearing what they could with pails. Porters sweated as they carried waterlogged laundry upstairs for disposal: the bed sheets, the table linen, articles of the guests' own clothing had been torn and saturated with grime. The wine cellars and the well room weren't much better. Once the water level dropped sufficiently, thick mud remained. Night fell and the storekeepers, the book keepers, the waiters and sommeliers – even the violin quintet – scraped shovel after shovel through the dirt. Any old floor stains round the artesian spring lost their significance; you couldn't tell them from the marks left by the sludge. Eventually the men downed their shovels, and the cleaning women, including girls from fourteen years of age upwards, began to scrub and rinse the walls with disinfectant, as their heads ached from bleach fumes. Above them the ground floor was unsettlingly silent for the hour. The Pinfold Dining Room, the Hagley Tea Rooms, the Reading Room, and the Narcissus Bar were deserted. Restricted to their own quarters, the guests sought diversion or oblivion. A pair of New York stockbrokers made short work of a whisky bottle. The cinema king and his wife played gin rummy while the Pomeranians watched. Three honourables and a marquess drank a surfeit of champagne, and what they didn't drink they sprayed upon the walls. With relish they cracked the wood panelling, vandalised the paintings and pull down the curtain rails. Other guests, like Nora and Berenice, looked to sex as a distraction.

Afterwards, while they lay in the midnight blue bedroom, Nora asked: "When did you last see Merlini?"

She knew she was breaching Leo's instruction not to confront his wife. This no longer concerned her. How enjoyable, not to care what Leo thought.

"My husband picked a real spy," Berenice said. "Merlini's in his room. He did something unspeakably rude and I told him not to bother me for a while. You have to keep a guy in line."

Berenice's eyes closed. Within minutes she was deeply asleep; no one would know people were mysteriously dying, from her contented expression at rest. It was Nora who lay awake for hours, and because of this she realised, at dawn, that they were being watched.

The hyring stood alert with its back to the wall.

Did that mean it had, indeed, been drawn to her? Was it jealous? Might it be roused to eat Berenice? Nora knew she was seeing the hyring's true nature. When it was in human form, who would she know it as the rest of the time?

"What's your name?" she addressed it.

The beast's breath was suddenly hot on her cheek.

"Markham," it said, in the accent from the woods she had known as a little girl.

The answer was senseless. Edward Markham was a weak man who wanted his mistress to keep her mouth shut, but he was no hyring. Nothing had ever led Nora to suppose he was of the same kind as her mother. So this beast was doing what it did best: assuming another's name and voice. Maybe it had once fed on the hanged man's remains.

Now the beast walked the periphery of the bed, back and forth, three times. It lowered its head between its shoulders as it stretched. Taking these movements for the prelude to an attack, Nora feared it was stalking. Instead the beast wrenched itself together with a crack, turned, and stood upon its hind legs before the mirror on the dressing table. It brought its head to the glass, close enough for its breath to mist the surface, and slid through as though the mirror were air, its ungainly limbs pulled after it. They looked dislocated.

She assumed that the beast had emerged through a mirror in another room of the hotel. The room of a third victim, perhaps. She didn't know why it had left without attempting to feed. And then she realised, with certainty: *because it thinks Berenice is my kill.*

2

At breakfast, Nora didn't mention seeing the hyring, though she thought of nothing else and was thus rather subdued. Berenice was happy to talk enough for two, toast in hand, first about the water levels – which the view told them had fallen somewhat in the night – and then about the body, but she did notice eventually that Nora was quiet.

"Are you still brooding on your Mr Crouch?" Berenice asked.

"No," Nora said.

"He was probably just hungover, angel."

"Very likely. He had a lot to drink the night before."

"We don't need his help, he isn't the only one who can make enquiries. Didn't you say Mrs Reid has a niece?"

"Yes." Nora sliced through a poached egg and watched the yolk spill thickly across the plate. "I think she may have been staying in the room opposite mine, actually."

"Why, that's perfect! We can ask *her* what she knows, as soon as we've eaten. If the police found the old woman's body then her niece will surely know by now."

"She might not be amenable to two strangers interrogating her on her missing relative."

"Not interrogating; expressing concern."

"I suppose I could pass for a concerned acquaintance. Mrs Reid ate dinner with me; that might be enough to enquire if there's any news."

"Yes! You're just being a kind new friend," Berenice said winningly.

Nora nodded. If they learnt who had died, and how, it might say something about the identity of the hyring too. *And then what?* she asked herself. The beast was killing people, but there was no higher authority she could appeal to which would keep it contained. She knew Berenice's fantasies of trying to tame a beast were naive. The one reassurance was that it had made no move to harm Nora, nor Berenice in Nora's presence. That meant the best course of action was to humour Berenice until the floods had cleared and then leave, as planned, once the trains were running. As a child Nora had tried to see justice done once before. She knew now that was futile.

Berenice accompanied Nora, arms linked, to room 426. They knocked, and as soon as the door opened, Nora saw she had guessed right about Mrs Reid's niece staying there; for though the woman was thirty years younger than Mrs Reid, and a clear foot taller, they shared a strong resemblance in the face. They sported the same dated chignon, too. As Nora explained the purpose of their call the woman never took her eyes from Berenice, who remained charmingly poised.

"Oh – please do come in," said the woman at the door, as tears gathered in her eyelashes. "My name is Miss Block – you must call me Pretoria. My aunt would have been so delighted to receive you as a guest, Miss Oxbow."

The past tense. Nora felt Berenice's hold on her arm tighten. They entered a room which was the exact inversion of Nora's own, where Pretoria Block gestured to the easy chair for Berenice, and took the desk chair herself. Nora stood behind Berenice, awkwardly.

"My aunt Jemima was hoping to meet you during your stay, Miss Oxbow. She was intrigued by you – especially your visions. Was that what brought you here? Did you *have* a vision?" Pretoria's voice dropped to a whisper. "Has she spoken to you from the other side?"

Berenice was about to respond, but Nora cut in.

"No, Miss Block, it's as I say; several nights ago, I became acquainted with your aunt at dinner, and I've grown terribly concerned by her disappearance. We wished to know if there was any news?"

Pretoria looked at Nora properly for the first time, then responded dazedly: "Jemima is dead."

"We're very sorry," Berenice said.

Pretoria's lower lip trembled. "I was almost put out when Jemima asked me to travel with her. It implied that I might as well be on the shelf. But I saw the sense of it. She a dowager, I unmarried. We both needed company, in our own ways. I agreed, then as soon as we arrived I fell ill and she was left to her own devices regardless! A fine companion I turned out to be."

"What was your business here, Pretoria?" Berenice asked.

"This was the first stop on a short tour. Jemima planned

the journey herself." Pretoria swallowed, and coughed for a minute; she seemed yet to recover from bronchitis. "You could say she has always had an appetite for the darker side of life. We were to visit the sites of known hauntings. She wished to hear about Edward Markham, the axe murderer – the one who hanged for killing his mistress. He worked just around the corner, you know, as an accountant. The last morning I saw Jemima, she announced she was going to the cathedral, because his spirit was sometimes sighted there."

"What happened then?" Berenice said.

"It is very strange and sad. The police tell me – she was found on Needless Alley, when the snow melted. It's one of the side streets, not five minutes from here."

"Did she fall?" Nora asked quietly. "I was worried about hypothermia, if she were trapped somewhere."

"Hypothermia would have been far preferable." Pretoria raised a handkerchief to her mouth. "We won't be able to have an open casket."

Nora asked: "Did someone hurt her?"

"Very badly. I can't imagine her last moments. It isn't delicate to speak of it – I won't speak of it. The police will have a difficult task to understand all that was done to her. You see, it seems afterwards, a dog, a stray I suppose..." Pretoria's voice trailed.

"She was bitten?" Berenice seized.

"Yes. And carried from the scene of her attack. Miss Oxbow, will you contact me again if you hear anything, anything at all, from Jemima?"

"Is there a particular message you're waiting for?"

"I've discovered she left many unsettled bills. While I

was ill, it seems she took all the money I'd brought with me. I don't wish to think ill of her – we shouldn't of the dead, should we? It would help so to hear an explanation. Perhaps she merely moved it for safekeeping, and will speak through you, to tell me the location!"

"I'll let you know," said Berenice. "Would you like an autograph, too?"

The suggestion was bizarre to Nora, but it did seem to console Pretoria for some reason. Berenice suggested writing it out to Jemima, but Pretoria preferred it to be addressed to herself; and once this was done, with further condolences offered, they left.

In the corridor, Nora said: "It's a good thing you were there. She was smitten. I doubt she would have said half as much to me on my own."

"She seemed quite sure about the dog. How do the police decide that, do you think? The pattern of the bite?"

"Depends how much of a mess was made, surely," said Nora. "A brutal enough attack might make it hard to tell."

"I don't believe it *was* a dog for one second. It was the hyring."

"Yes. It would be quite a coincidence for her to be partially eaten by another creature."

"A hyring would have a motive, wouldn't it?" Berenice speculated. "A dog would need nothing but hunger."

Once, Leo had told Nora that predators just want to eat. But he hadn't proved a reliable authority. So Nora said now: "Yes, I think we might find a motive if we keep looking."

★ ★ ★

At Berenice's suggestion, they put on boots, with the intention of visiting Needless Alley. Hopefully they'd find something relevant to the hyring's identity.

They asked, at reception, which of the surrounding streets were flooded. The receptionist said that on the southern side one still had to wade.

"But if you only wait until tomorrow all the water will be gone," he added, implying he thought they were – what was the expression people used when Nora was a child? – *gadding about.*

"The roads are draining that fast?" Nora asked.

"Yes, and we've been informed the railway bridges are already being checked. If they find damage, that will incur a further delay, but there's a good chance trains will resume tomorrow."

"So soon?"

"Nora," Berenice interrupted. "Come on."

Another guest caught the receptionist's attention. Nora let Berenice lead her away; there was no point obtaining directions, as they'd doubtless be discouraged from visiting the site of a recent death. The escapade might even look suspicious. Berenice's plan seemed to be that they would stumble upon Needless Alley; hadn't Pretoria said the street was very close?

The sun was out but there was a pervasive unpleasant smell – probably drains that had overflowed. For some time they sloshed about, the water lapping their ankles, as they checked one street sign here, another there. The splashing seemed to put Berenice in a frivolous mood. Her giggling would have looked very inappropriate had anyone known what they were trying to find.

"Don't," Nora kept telling her. "Please, do behave yourself."

They had checked all the turnings on the same street as the hotel, and cut across to the opposite side of the cathedral. The very first entry was the one they were looking for: the words Needless Alley were high on the wall. They peered into a narrow passage which admitted little daylight and provided back doors to small shops and businesses. A sliver of New Street was visible at the other end. Berenice stepped fearlessly into the shadows.

"There's nothing very much down here to have interested Mrs Reid," Berenice said. "She might have been cutting through to New Street. I wonder where that man worked – what was his name, Edward Markham? Pretoria said it was near. Do you think Reid was looking for that?"

"He worked for Parkes and Son. That's on one of the other side streets, I think."

"We should go there too. Maybe she didn't plan to come down this alley – but something fleeting caught her attention? Maybe she was lured! I wonder if we can tell where she was found."

Nora looked for marks on the ground, but saw nothing resembling bloody shoe prints or paws; the snow would have taken the impression, only to melt.

"She must have screamed," Nora murmured. "But no one heard it happen."

Berenice's brow furrowed. "I'm not sure these shops are occupied. They look dusty."

She peered through one peeling gridded frame after another, then paused outside one. Something had caught her attention; Nora didn't have the vantage to see.

"What is it?" Nora asked.

"Did Pretoria say when the police were last here?"

"No."

"Come look."

Nora joined her. Just behind the window, in what looked to be an abandoned store room, a hanged man was suspended from a ceiling hook. He wore a flat cap and a dog's leash was half stuck in his coat pocket. The body swayed in a draught. Nora remembered Františka's grandfather clock which would slow down without intervention until the pendulum barely moved back and forth inside it.

A handwritten note, in broken sentences, was pasted to the other side of the glass.

Jemima Reid tried to blackmail me. I killed her and thought I could feed the remains to my dog but he could not finish her. She knew I was guilty of indecency with the guests I let myself in with a key of a night and she saw me do it. It is no good can not live with the guilt. Roderick Westall.

"Isn't this hotsy-totsy," Berenice said drily.

"Who wears a hat to hang himself?" Nora asked.

"Maybe he wanted dignity."

Except it seemed the opposite of dignified. Something in the angle resembled mockery.

"Crouch said Harvey, the housekeeper, thought Westall was invading women's rooms," Nora said. Still she felt sick, because his dog was the wrong dog. It had never been in her room, and so it stood to reason he hadn't been either.

"I have a bad feeling, Berenice. I don't think that note is genuine."

"The police can get a sample of his writing, to compare, can't they?"

"Hyrings can forge handwriting as easily as they can mimic a voice. Likely it used some of Westall's real phrases too, taken from a different context. I think the hyring ate Mrs Reid then framed Westall for it."

"So if the housekeeper, and Crouch, accused him before, could one of them be the hyring?"

"Yes, I think we need to consider that. We can probably assume Westall died today, or in the small hours at the earliest. No matter how harried the police were in a flood I'm sure they would have noticed a second corpse a few feet away." Nora covered her face. "This isn't our problem. Let's report the finding of the body at the hotel, they can contact the police, send some boy round to the station if the lines are still down or what have you, but we don't need to give any theories. I mean it, Berenice. The trains are running tomorrow, most likely, that's what the man in reception said. We can just *leave* the city, return to Zurich."

"Return to Zurich?" Berenice echoed. "Where Leo is?"

"Or you can... go to wherever you want to, but the main thing is we won't be *here* with all this mess."

"I'd prefer the hyring to Leo," Berenice said.

"For the love of God." Without Nora around, the hyring might well decide Berenice was fair game again. "Will you stop throwing yourself in the way of danger for one minute?"

"You *have* changed, Nora. When you got here I think you

would have happily seen me dead." Berenice shuddered and looked back at the corpse. "What do you think happened to his dog?"

3

As soon as Nora and Berenice notified him, Quarrington sent an under-manager to the police station; they could expect him to take ten minutes there, and another ten minutes back. Quarrington's typist, who was secretly promised to Westall and among the first to overhear the news, politely excused herself to the cloakrooms. Her stomach was in revolt at Westall's alleged confession. The thought of suicide, too, could be contagious; as she stood with her back to the lavatory door, her eyes fell on the bottle of Jeyes Fluid beneath the cistern. She wondered if to swallow it would be fatal. In her absence Quarrington instructed another under-manager to fetch Harvey. The young man took a circuitous route, whispering details of Westall's death to the administrative workers by Quarrington's office, which travelled soon enough to the kitchen staff, the cleaners, the porters and the housekeepers, floor by floor. Harvey was preparing the chambermaids' rota when the under-manager knocked on her door with the news. She put down her pen to better conceal the tremor in her hand, though she thanked him for letting her know calmly enough.

The police arrived. Berenice and Nora were questioned in turn about the discovery of the corpse. Nora was additionally of interest because she had reported the dog in her room. She told the police, truthfully, that she had met Westall during a snowball fight in Victoria Square, but couldn't confirm either way whether he'd ever intruded upon her at night, because she had never seen a man at all, just a large dog in the darkness. Her one aim was to be done with the sorry affair as soon as she could. To her alarm an imminent departure was threatened.

"We may need to talk to you again, depending on what we learn over the next few days," the policeman said. "You weren't leaving the country soon, were you?"

"Yes, as it happens."

"How unfortunate. Don't act on any plans without informing us."

If she left, they would not be able to trace her easily, because she had given her name to them as Dickinson. But they might well ask the hotel to notify them if anyone on a given list departed before they had permission. She would then have to exit the hotel, with her belongings, and take a train to the port, before she boarded the steamer under her true name. The risk of interception seemed high. When the police questions were finished she returned gratefully to the pineapple suite with Berenice.

Nora dropped onto the curved sofa. "What an officious little man, telling me what to do. But with any luck they'll see the confession as open and shut and we can still leave when the trains are running."

She tried to forget that Westall had parents, for whom the supposed confession would be life-changing.

"There's no rush to get away," Berenice said soothingly. "Why run before the mystery's solved?"

She unlaced and pulled the boots from Nora's feet. Her hands were on Nora's sole, as she pushed her thumbs into the ball of the foot. Berenice sang, under her breath, words that Nora couldn't catch.

"The night you sang in the bar," Nora said. "Your Russian song. I never knew what it meant."

"That," Berenice laughed. "It's a song about chasing."

"Tell me the words in English?"

"I can't make them fit the tune," Berenice warned.

"I don't mind. Just say them."

"*The girl pretended to be the grass. She pretended to be the weeds. She pretended to be the fields. I pretended to be a scythe. I have to tell you, I'm thousands of years old, and this is the pretence of love. The girl pretended to be a story. She pretended to be a page. She pretended to be a book. I pretended to be a storyteller. I have to tell you, I'm thousands of years old, and this is the pretence of love. The girl pretended to be bread. She pretended to be milk. She pretended to be meat. I pretended to be teeth. I have to tell you, I'm thousands of years old, and this is the pretence of love.* Are you asleep, baby?"

"No."

"It's a love song."

"Oh... I thought it was a parent and child."

"I probably gave a bad translation."

"No, I think your words are correct." Nora curled foetally on the sofa now.

Berenice walked to the window that overlooked the street. "The police are still going in and out of Needless

Alley... but I can't see much of what they are doing over there."

"Making extra sure there are no other bodies," Nora said without stirring. "Do come away. I've had enough of the police for one day. And dead people."

"But don't you think it's likely the hyring is down there too? Watching what's happening?"

"As long as it stays away from us I don't care."

"Don't be such a flat tyre," Berenice said teasingly. Then, with over-brightness, she added: "I'm going to see Merlini."

"Merlini? Why?" Nora sat up again.

"I'm all out of gaspers, baby."

"But we shouldn't split up, not while the hyring is roaming. I have cigarettes, take one of mine, or the housekeeper will send downstairs for some."

"They don't sell kreteks in the lobby. I need to find Merl; he'll have my brand."

Nora tried to retrieve her boots from under the sofa. "I'll come with you."

Berenice raised an eyebrow. "Whatever do you think I'll get up to?"

Naturally that's what Berenice would assume: Nora feared usurpation, despite having no right to resentment. Annoyingly Nora didn't know how to refute this impression. All she could do was say, feebly, *it's dangerous*, when Berenice wanted danger.

"It's cute you're jealous, angel." Berenice was halfway out the lounge. She'd never even taken her coat off. "I'll be back in no time."

Nora finished relacing the boots but didn't run after her. How long did it take to collect cigarettes? Ten minutes? Less, if Merlini turned out not to be in his room, and Berenice had to come straight back? Except where would he have to go, while the city was waterlogged? When should Nora start to worry? It would probably be all right. Whatever territory the hyring thought she'd staked, it was unlikely to lapse while Berenice went downstairs.

A few minutes before, fatigue had her prostrate. Now she was agitated again. She took Berenice's place by the window, looking down on the suspects she would have searched for the hyring. Crouch was down there. He had already come up on the list of potentials. He *did* appear to be interested in the activities of the police, motionless and staring as he was on the pavement. But he could just be showing customary nosiness. The doormen were outside, but that obviously didn't mean much, they were working... A few other people were milling about, who possibly lived on the streets nearby, or were even hotel workers in mufti. There was Merlini, too. Berenice must have seen him down there, and that was where she was headed, not his room.

Still. At least Nora could keep them in view here. Berenice wouldn't get eaten out there in front of everyone.

If these were the suspects, how to narrow them down? Berenice thought the hyring had lured Mrs Reid into Needless Alley. That would be easy, for anyone who knew she was looking for ghosts. All the hyring would need to do is imitate Edward Markham, and she would follow them of her own accord. Nora mentally listed who might know Reid was ghost hunting. Pretoria, obviously. Nora herself; she was in the lounge when Reid told Harvey she hoped to see some ghosts in the cathedral. Which meant Harvey knew too. And Harvey told Crouch it was probably Westall in Nora's room; that could be groundwork for eating Reid and framing Westall. Nora surveyed the crowd for Harvey, until she was distracted by a woman with platinum hair sauntering down the hotel steps. Berenice pecked Merlini on each cheek. They spoke, Berenice taking her box of kreteks from her pocket, and offering him one.

"You little liar," Nora murmured, though not with genuine anger.

Over by the cathedral, a small stooped figure walked through the graves towards the great wooden doors. Enid. When they last met, Enid had mentioned a snob of a woman who asked about Edward Markham's ghost. At the time Nora had been sure it was Mrs Reid. So Enid knew Reid was ghost hunting too.

Nora sighed heavily. The fact was Mrs Reid could have told any number of people she was looking for ghosts. Even on her first night she was going on about—

"Lord God," Nora said in Czech, raising her hands to her mouth.

That dinner. Nora had tried *very hard* to ignore the conversation between Mrs Reid and Arthur Crouch. They had been distracting her from Berenice, and the words kept breaking through, irritating her: talk of the dead lying beneath the road; talk of sinners staying at the hotel; talk of murder. Crouch had said: *When I was young I knew a schoolgirl who confessed to murder. She was a mere slip of a thing.*

Nora had taken it for painful coincidence. No, not even that, she had barely allowed herself to acknowledge why the topic disturbed her. She had seen Crouch's face – known it was familiar – and immediately told herself: *he is so blandly interchangeable he could be any man.* Now she made herself think of Edward Markham. Did Crouch look like him? Did they share the same nose, the same eyes, the same mouth? She thought of Edward's son James, at twelve years of age with his sleeves rolled up in the forest, condemning his father to death. Nora pictured James's face and aged it, in her mind, by twenty years. Did Crouch look as James would do, fully grown?

She tried to find him among the people. In the past minute he had disappeared. She searched again. Yes, there he was, right next to Berenice, tapping her on the shoulder. She was turning to him now. What could Crouch have to say to her? They began walking back up the hotel steps, rather close to each other, leaving Merlini as gooseberry; he can't have liked that, but he wasn't Nora's concern. It was the departing couple she was interested in. As if Crouch sensed her watching, he upturned his face, right in the direction of Nora's window, while he led Berenice towards the doors.

Nora asked herself again, now his face was in her view: *is that James Markham?*

Yes. That was exactly who Crouch was.

4

Nora ran. She ran from the suite, down three floors to reception, to intercept Crouch and his prey. They were gone, inevitably, by the time she arrived. Merlini wasn't there either, or she would have asked him what Crouch had said. Instead she asked one of the doormen, when she could get more than three words out, if he'd seen what direction Crouch had taken.

"They both went straight into the lift." He pointed.

It must be back in order. Blast it; had she known, she would have already met them on her way down.

Nora ran for the lift herself, and when it arrived, she adjusted her question for the attendant: which floor had Mr Crouch and Miss Oxbow disembarked? He couldn't recall. Nora was wavering, unsure whether to return to Berenice's suite or locate Crouch's room, or whether they would have gone someplace else altogether. More guests crowded in on the first floor. She had just decided to work her way down from the top when the doors opened on the second floor. Only one man waiting to enter this time: Crouch was standing there, smoking. Alone.

She stepped into the corridor, pushing him back with a hand on his chest.

"Where's Berenice?" she demanded as the doors closed behind her.

"Good day to you, too," he said. "I have no idea where Berenice is."

"Don't play games." She peered down the corridor, looking vainly for the singer. "You know I saw you. The doormen saw you too."

"That hardly makes me her keeper. We did speak. I'd overheard her expounding on her visions of Mrs Reid's fate, and I couldn't resist a few questions."

Nora sniffed the air. Cloves. "That's one of Berenice's cigarettes you're smoking."

"Steady on, Tuppence. What, exactly, are you worried about?"

Two dead bodies at his hand, and Berenice as the third. She stared at him, finding in his face the boy from the woods. Was there a mirror anywhere on this floor, she wondered? He might have used it to transport Berenice away from here, to harm her in greater privacy. There was bound to be one hanging somewhere in these halls, or even in his own room, if it were nearby and he had compelled her to enter. She walked down the corridor, in search of a looking glass. He kept pace behind her.

"I know who you are, James," she said. "I didn't, until today."

"Ah," he said, with a nod. "I changed too much for you to know me."

"I realised eventually. I know *what* you are, too. Although

I don't understand it. You weren't a hyring when we were children."

"No, I was human. Then."

The corridor branched in a y-formation. The routes looked identical: in each stretched ahead one smooth aquamarine door after another, all of them bearing a glinting brass number. Nora hesitated before continuing right. No mirrors so far. Some framed pictures of local scenes, was all.

"What did Berenice say about Mrs Reid?" she asked.

"She knew she'd been ghost hunting Edward Markham... Miss Oxbow wanted directions to Parkes."

She'd asked the worst possible person. Markham's son; Mrs Reid's murderer.

"And what did you say?"

"What do you think? Heavens above." He was scathing. "People come here looking for Markham's ghost all the time. If it bothered me I should never have set up residence here. I told her Parkes and Son was on Cherry Street, and it's impassable because the road's flooded. She seemed to accept that. I said, if she wanted me to point out the correct building, there are some photographs of Cherry Street hanging on the walls up here." He gestured at the sepia prints suspended from the rails. "I showed her the right one. She took it straight off the wall and tucked it under her arm. Then she ran off giggling, like a half-wit playing *chase me*. I wasn't going to join in. I'm not one of her janissaries."

He said it with authentic petulance. But Nora couldn't trust him. Berenice knew he'd been on the list of possible hyrings; she may have thought she could trick him into revealing himself. She would have thought she was in control, and realised too late she wasn't.

"I don't believe you." Nora wished these corridors were easier to tell apart. She had the sensation, once more, they were playing a trick on her – that she was only imagining she was getting somewhere, while they folded around themselves like a Piranesi illustration.

"Then here's a practical consideration. You arrived on the second floor mere minutes after we did. She's hardly likely to come a cropper in that time, is she?" Casually, he added: "More to the point, Nora, I wouldn't rob you of a feast."

She had guessed correctly when he passed through the mirror: the beast thought she had prior rights to Berenice. *Let him think that*, Nora thought. It was safer to let him. And it was, from one perspective, true.

"Thank you, James." She'd hit a dead end, and a mirror hung upon it. She touched the glass, realising the futility of her search. If Berenice had been taken somewhere, how would she have followed? Valery had never shown her the use of mirrors – she couldn't when Jaroslav had banned them. Nora didn't know how to get through.

Crouch said, from behind her: "I'm your brother, in a way."

Creatures like them were rare enough for him to say so. To his reflection she replied: "All God's children, I suppose, even us."

"I don't mean that. I mean your mother made me what I am."

She asked: "Whatever are you on about?"

"Find Miss Oxbow," he said. "Seeing as that's so urgent. I promise she was hale and hearty when she ran away from me. Then we should have a talk. I'll be in my room when you're finished; it's 324."

★ ★ ★

Nora checked the rest of the corridors on that floor, without success. Finding her way back to the lift involved several wrong turnings and finding herself on the same spot. Eventually she escaped. She returned to the pineapple suite. Her hope was that Berenice would already be there; but the suite was also quite empty. Nora paced from one room to another, and stood in Berenice's bedroom, cursing that woman's death wish. Nothing had altered since their departure earlier – there was the same unmade bed, and clothes littered upon the carpet. Leo's photo, absurdly, still had a prominent position upon the bedside cabinet.

Think, Nora ordered herself. *Think.*

If Berenice *had* left Crouch freely, where would she have gone next? She couldn't get to Parkes and Son. She hadn't provoked Crouch into exposing his true nature. She would seek out the next person of interest on her list, perhaps. Harvey, the housekeeper, was the only other suspect for the hyring they had discussed. Nora felt relieved that there was one more place she could check. She made her way to the fourth floor, and Harvey answered at Nora's knock.

"Miss Oxbow did come by," Harvey confirmed. "She asked if I'd let her into your room, to collect some of your belongings. I explained that would be against the hotel's rules, without advance permission from you. She did try her hardest to be persuasive."

What was Berenice trying to do there? Nora guessed that,

by forcing Harvey into tracing the hyring's steps, Berenice hoped to elicit something from the housekeeper, a sign that she was the guilty party.

"Did Miss Oxbow say where she was going afterwards?" Nora asked.

Harvey shook her head. At least, though, Berenice hadn't been eaten by Crouch. Nora felt sufficiently reassured to go down another flight, to the third floor, where Crouch said he would be. He had made overtures of kinship, and to her dismay, they felt potent. She had never successfully conveyed to another person how terrifying her mother had been. But Crouch would know, if his claim of a bond with Valery was true. Nora needed him to say exactly what kind of brother he thought he was.

Crouch's room had a different atmosphere from the others Nora had seen in the hotel so far. It was smaller than the pineapple suite by some distance, and closer to the proportions of Nora's own bedroom, but he had incorporated furnishings of his choosing, reflecting his longer residence there. The armchair, for instance, was not of the hotel's style; it was a striking thing, with a black square upholstered seat, and polished wooden arms that swept up from below like the crawler belts of a military tank. Two expressionist paintings hung on the wall: a dizzying landscape of city buildings and a brightly coloured portrayal of St George on a rearing horse, with a dragon at his feet. The fire was lit, and as it was just beginning to get dark outside and none of the lamps were burning, Crouch's face was eerily illuminated from below. He indicated she should take the chair and then sat upon the rug. *Like a dog, before the hearth*, she thought.

"I'm glad you came." Crouch's eyes were fervent. "Did you feel, when we met at the hotel, how different we were from everybody else? I kept waiting for you to acknowledge it. Do you feel how separate we are?"

Nora had always felt separate from everyone else: the way a talkie was separate from the real people who performed in it. She suspected Crouch meant something different, but nodded, in the expectation he would reveal more.

"Take Reid," he said. "She broke rules too, but my my, she was grubby. I can't abide grubbiness. She was fascinated with my father's supposed crime. She knew he had a wife and child who had adopted new names, and that the son must be a man now. Her perspicacity with public records allowed her to work out my alias before tracking me here. She assumed I must be living in shame and would pay to protect my identity. None of this was revealed immediately. The night we met at dinner – she said she was very keen to explore the passage from the cathedral crypt, the one Quarrington keeps under lock and key. I thought there was something admirably rebellious in her disregard for safety, and said I'd see how I could help. It shouldn't surprise you I can get any key I want. We arranged, in a clandestine fashion, that she would sneak into the crypt the next morning, and I would admit her from the other side. This all proceeded smoothly – she arrived without the bodies of Birmingham falling in on her head; I let her into the cellar; and I locked the door again behind her. I started telling her more about the history of the well, only for her to interrupt me with threats of blackmail. I laughed in her face. Then I ate her."

"Pretoria Block said she stole money," Nora reflected.

"When I checked her room by mirror later, I removed a notebook with all the details of her victims. She'd already squeezed Harvey, told her she'd be dismissed, that she'd never work in another hotel unless she coughed up. You see the girl suffers from morphinism – I help her from time to time; mirrors make it easy for me to lift that sort of thing, and it's useful to have someone here who owes me favours."

Nora remembered, on her first night, how she'd overheard Harvey, in the back corridors, talking heatedly to a man named *James*. It was odd he should want favours, given the extent of his powers. *He's rooted here*, Nora realised, remembering how her mother had been unable to pass the river. Nora knew he could travel as far as Victoria Square. If that were his limit without mirrors, a beholden housekeeper would certainly come in useful. She wondered when, exactly, he'd understood he was stuck.

Crouch pulled a loose strand from the rug and tossed it in the flames. "The irony was, I'd been expecting threats of exposure, just not from Reid. I thought they might come from Miss Oxbow's quarter."

"What?" Nora asked, surprised.

"Come now. Her fake vision? She described the very tattoo borne by Miss Lowrie, while I was just a few feet away? I knew *your* face as soon as you sat down, so I assumed you were the source of her information, and that you were pretending not to recognise me. That was why I took the form of my father's dog, in your room, to try tricking an acknowledgement from you. Except you didn't seem to make the connection then, either. Things made more sense once you explained about your chap. I saw then that Miss Oxbow had obtained her information through him, not you, and that you truly hadn't realised who I was. Except I don't understand why you haven't killed Miss Oxbow yet; it's in your nature. I can see you've had the desire."

"I wanted more time to record her ways."

The words were true, and as long as Crouch thought Berenice was Nora's kill, he would leave Berenice alone. But she realised, as she spoke, that since sleeping with Berenice she hadn't imitated the singer once. What was more, she hadn't noticed that she'd stopped. How strange, to no longer want to be someone else.

"I see," Crouch said. "It crossed my mind, many times – when you didn't acknowledge me, or my father's dog – that you'd forgotten who *you* were, or at least grown confused. A hyring can lose its stomach for blood if it goes long enough without feeding. That would account for you procrastinating with Miss Oxbow too."

Thinking of Leo's ear, Nora asked: "Might one be sick, in the attempt?"

"Certainly. Imagine eating a rich piece of chocolate after a monk's diet."

Nora shook her head. "That can't be right. My mother said I was a hyring because she breastfed me; but between then and Miss Lowrie, I never fed on a human. Why did eating her still taste good to me?"

Crouch smirked. "Are you sure you didn't feed in between? Did Valery have access to your food?"

"Of course she did – but – she couldn't leave our land. Who would she have fed me on?"

"Herself. It wouldn't take very much, a few drops of blood in every meal would suffice to prime you."

Nora thought of the marks on Valery's hands, and the way she'd jab Jaroslav with a needle.

Crouch's smirk persisted. "You won't find feeding difficult next time."

"Why not?"

"I hid Reid's remains in the well, so that she'd get into the water supply. You were consuming her for days. As I say... a few drops at a time. Just to bring you back to yourself."

His manipulation revolted her. She wasn't sure whether to trust it. "Reid was found in Needless Alley."

"Yes, that development was out of my hands. The man who found the body wanted to distance himself from the crime. Fortunately I'm adaptable. I moved Westall's body there to make the suicide note more convincing. But I guarantee you this, the well was where I left Reid."

"It was a disgusting thing to do to me," Nora said. "And you'll be punished for it one day. If you're always as reckless, you'll get caught."

He shrugged. "No, I won't. I've too many means of evasion. I can't easily stray far – I've been rooted here for a while now – but I've made my victims look like suicides for years. Even if the police worked out I was responsible, I can always become someone else. That's the beauty of hotels. They're full of people. People to mimic. People to frame."

"Why Westall?"

"Oh, I had nothing personal against him. After I'd been in your room, and you made a fuss about intruders, Harvey suggested we frame him for it because he had a dog. Then when I needed a scapegoat for killing Reid he came naturally to mind – her room was close to yours; she could have seen his shenanigans, and blackmailed him as she tried to blackmail me. That gave him a motive for murdering her. The self-same dog could have left the bite marks in her body. So, I killed her; I killed him; and I framed him with that note." He grinned. "I did try to bolster the story by pressuring you into saying the dog was Glennard. It was annoying you wouldn't comply."

"I've never wanted to be compliant," Nora said. She had always wanted to be true, instead; though she had failed at that.

"Which is admirable," Crouch said with more gravity. "Albeit inconvenient for me. I did forgive you for it – yes, I see that look on your face, I see you think there was nothing to forgive, but I forgave you anyway – and I tried again to visit you. You might have forgotten my father's dog but you couldn't mistake the form of a hyring. I even told you my name, in the suite. And the next day – you knew me. At last."

"Yes. Though a few other things had to dawn on me in between."

"Now we are united. Brother, and sister."

"You said that before," Nora pointed out. "But I don't know what it means."

"Put some more coal on." Crouch nodded towards the tongs at her side. "This requires a longer conversation."

When Nora had built up the fire, and Crouch had obtained some tea from the housekeeper – which he added whisky to – he described the months following his father's execution.

"My mother and I moved to London shortly after your departure. Although her family never wanted to see us again, they did provide for us financially. Crouch was her mother's maiden name, and I chose Arthur for myself."

"So long ago?" Nora asked.

"You assumed it was recent?"

She shrugged. "I thought Arthur Crouch may have been a guest here. And that you'd... succeeded him."

"No. I'm of my own invention," he said. "Even if I didn't immediately credit it, the idea of hyrings intrigued me. When the scandal hit, to be such a creature – to feed on the contemptible; then transform – would have been an enviable asset. I had to settle for pseudonymity. In London, I completed a grammar school education. I enlisted, and at the end of the war began my architecture apprenticeship. I thought, often, of the woods, but not from any maudlin sentiment for my childhood. It was *your* family I dwelt on; your mother, and the audacity of her crime. When I was twenty-three I made my first return to Alspath, and I kept returning. I'd walk through the woods, to watch your mother. Her favourite spot was a seat in the bay window. She would sit there for hours. At first I'd go by night, because she would be illuminated while I was concealed by the darkness. Eventually I saw her change shape; she heard a fox cry in the woods, and her face morphed to a fox's and back. The change was so swift I might have dreamt it, but I knew then she truly was the monster you claimed. Even in her womanly form she had the same inhuman quality as a perfectly crafted mannequin. It was her choice to appear thus; the illusion of warmth and caring was in her ability, and she rejected it in defiance of the world. I began travelling to Alspath at haphazard times to see how she spent her days, but she barely stirred. There she would be, just staring straight out. Her hands were scarlet."

"Did she sew?" Nora asked, wondering if the marks were new wounds or old scars.

"Not while I was watching. She sometimes had sewing in her lap, but she didn't work upon it. Eventually I decided I would speak to her. I chose the anniversary of my father's death, the tenth anniversary in fact. That morning, when I'd already seen Dr Čapek leave, I stood directly before the window. There were warps in the glass and her hair and yellow dress looked spotted. I'd already aged too much for her to recognise me. When I told her my name through the glass, I added: *my father hanged for murder.* Then she laughed on the other side of the window. The door to the house was unlocked, so I let myself in and joined her."

"Was she beautiful?" Nora asked.

"No. Why?"

"I thought she had been," Nora said. "I suppose everyone says their mother was beautiful, when she was young."

"She looked powerful."

"Even though she was leashed?" Nora thought of the missing tooth. She thought of never leaving the house.

Crouch's expression was bewildered at the question.

"She had something I wanted," he said, which may have been all *powerful* meant to him, when people rarely had the means to deny him.

That day, Crouch, not Valery, had spoken most.

"My father was weak," Crouch told her. "He had to be, if he couldn't evade hanging for another person's crime. There is no question of me seeking to clear his name."

Valery didn't reply. She may have thought Crouch was entrapping her, or she may not have cared, but she made no admission of guilt. That was praiseworthy, in his view: to say nothing. To refrain even from asking why he had come. He waited for her to ask but she didn't.

"I want to know how hyrings are made," he said.

"Why?" Valery was insolent.

"So I might become one. Is it impossible?"

She shook her head very slowly. He was uncertain whether she was answering his question, or disparaging it.

"Is there anything I can offer you in exchange?"

"Bring me back my missing tooth," Valery said. "I lost it biting my engagement ring. Jaroslav stole it and has owned me ever since."

Crouch took her left hand. "This ring?"

"Yes."

He slid it from her finger, and stared at the substantial diamond. The setting had grown delicate with age. He placed it on the floor and ground it beneath his heel, before scooping up the loosened diamond.

"Open your mouth," he said.

He thought she might disobey. She glared; her irises were as pale as sea glass. The scrutiny made him think he'd erred. Then she let her jaw fall, to offer her mouth. He held her by the chin, saw the gap near the back, and pressed the diamond between two molars, hard enough to draw blood from the gum below. It glinted in her mouth as he let go.

Valery probed the diamond with her tongue before laughing long and loudly. Her lips were smeared with blood, and so was Crouch's fingertip.

"I could obtain your real tooth more easily," Crouch pointed out, "if you transformed me. Is such a thing possible?"

"Yes," Valery avowed. "Hyrings are made, not born. Our young feed of us in the womb and at the breast. But anyone can feed of me, if I let them. Would you be willing to make Jaroslav your first victim?"

"I'd do so gratefully."

"How can I trust you to keep your word?"

"You can't. But isn't it likely that, in coming to you, I have the disposition to eat?"

Valery looked away, through the window. Crouch waited, wondering if he should call her back to herself. Finally, she said: "You may feed of me. You may feel sick at first; the pleasure will come the next time. Take flesh where there is flesh to spare."

Crouch contemplated her. She was a slender woman. He knelt before her, and raised the verdigris skirt to see the white thigh. He took one bite – the blood ran down his chin, sticky as the juice from a peach, and he wiped it upon the cotton. Valery sobbed.

"That is enough." She pushed him away. "You will be like us now; you will have our powers of mimicry, and pass through mirrors, and take the form of a beast, but you will live no longer than any man."

The blood audibly dripped to the floor. The warned nausea was tolerable, for what he'd gained. Fatigue crept over him.

"You may sleep upstairs," she told him, as he tried to keep his eyes open. "When you wake, Jaroslav will be home. I'll expect you to fulfil your bargain."

Crouch slept on Nora's old bed, deeply, and woke after nightfall with an alertness that was wholly new to him. He could hear Jaroslav's voice downstairs, commenting on the acidity of his wine. The clink of silver on ceramic suggested they were at dinner.

Silently Crouch arose, and keeping close to the wall, walked downstairs again. Through the dining room door he could see Jaroslav, with his back to the hallway, seated and head down over his meal. The firelight in the room flickered.

Crouch walked past him, to pick up a poker from the hearth. Jaroslav's fork clattered to his plate at the sight of an intruder.

"Who the devil—"

Crouch swung the poker at his head, felling the old man, who took his chair with him. Valery stood, her face unchanging, the jewelled cross at her neck reflecting the dance of the flames. She watched Jaroslav paw at the flagstones. He could not right himself. Crouch sat nearby on the floor. He lowered his face to the expanding pool of blood and licked it from the cool floor. Valery had been right; the second meal was delicious.

Jaroslav mumbled in Czech. Insults, or a curse, from his tone, and aimed at Valery, who could enjoy his downfall but still – without her tooth – not partake in it. Her husband raised one shaking arm. He yanked at her skirts. The injury to her leg meant this was enough to unbalance her. Emboldened by his success, Jaroslav pressed his advantage – he half slithered, half dragged himself towards the fire, pulling his wife with him by the hair, and Valery could not fight back against him. She was reliant on Crouch, who still lapped at the blood on the floor, too drunk upon it to stop.

"Where is my *tooth*?" Valery shrieked at her husband. "Thief! Bastard!"

Jaroslav ignored her insults, his crown pouring blood, his breath laboured, as he yanked her by the neck into the hearth, and held her head to the fire. She screamed again as her scalp burned. Still Crouch couldn't tear himself from his feast. Valery shifted shape, to a rat, and Jaroslav finally released her. She ran aflame across the room to the open window, attempted to scale the curtains, and the cloth caught alight.

At last Jaroslav was still. Crouch looked up sharply, sensing the loss of life, and leapt upon the man's neck, biting through the skin and muscle. He ate until the smoke drove him from the room.

"You made no attempt to save her," Nora said.

"That wasn't the bargain," Crouch said. "I'd upheld my promise. Jaroslav was my first victim. With or without my help, she didn't go quietly. She spat in death's eye."

"Yes, she used to spit at my father, although she couldn't bite him. He never admitted what he'd done with the tooth."

"That theft wasn't enough to break her," he said. "Which was the measure of the woman. You were lucky to be her child. I wish I'd been born to her. My parents were despicable."

"But you pretend to be Edward, don't you?" Nora pointed out, thinking of Enid's sightings, her own sightings, the ghost hunters who came on holiday. "Why? Is it just a cloak for harming people?"

"If someone claims to have seen a man trespassing, or in any nefarious activity, the credibility of their whole account is undermined if they also claim the trespasser was a ghost. That can be useful. As to why I chose my *father's* ghost…" Arthur jabbed his index finger into the arm of his chair three times; an irritated gesture. "When I left Alspath for the second time, I had no one to encourage me in my mimicry as Valery did you from birth. I had to learn from first principles. No one's words linger in the memory like those of a hated father. I made good use of that to practise mimicry. I first came here, the streets he used to walk, feigning man and dog together, to see who recognised me. Every horrified reaction convinced me of my growing skill. But eventually I had less need of him; there were new models for me to imitate. Until you came, and I wished to shock you into honesty."

The dog, as Arthur imitated him, was bigger than the original. A boy's memory of the beast, perhaps. Despite Arthur's profession to honing his skills on Edward, Nora thought his mimicry of Valery was truer and more instinctive. Arthur's habitual arrogance was unmistakably hers.

Nora said: "Valery wished I had been a boy. I think she would be happy to call you her son."

Elated, he said: "Think of the joy we can share with each other."

"I'm not staying in this city," she said, meaning: *I don't want to stay with anyone who mimics my mother.* Except part of her did want to stay. They had lived the same horrors, and though he had embraced it while she fled, that still created a bond. "As soon as the police let me, I'm catching the train out of here."

"The train?" Crouch laughed. "Why would either of us ever need a train? The police can't hold you anywhere. And I can find you, whichever city you're in."

The hairs across her arms prickled. She had kept telling herself she could leave; she had waited for the snow to melt, and then for the floods to drain, and now for Westall to be ruled Reid's murderer. But there was no leaving, as long as any room contained a looking glass. Crouch would be able to find her until the day either he, or she, died.

"Mirrors are simple, though I only discovered so accidentally," he said, standing up. "I had to learn their ways on my own. If you don't know, I will show you. Where would you like to go?"

Earlier she had wished to find Berenice. Instinctively she shied from leading Crouch to the singer. Her mind drifted instead to the room where she had first watched, in a mirror, Berenice's perfect face as she described the women she'd seduced and wished dead, as she pictured girls playing pattycake on a Rorschach card, as she dreamt of the soldier who stole her voice.

"I want to go to Leo's flat," Nora said.

She accepted Crouch's hand.

6

They stood, side by side, before the largest mirror in the room: a circular one, three feet across.

"Do we have to transform?" Nora asked, because she had last seen him use the mirror as a beast.

"You can, but it isn't essential," he said. "I am I, whatever I imitate. Cloud the mirror with your breath. The cloud needn't be very large, just the width of your hand."

She obeyed, and raised her hand to the misted surface.

"Thinking of where you want to go is sufficient to take you," he said. "Provided the mirror at your destination is uncovered."

The space beneath her fingertips felt more like the air on a damp evening than brittle glass. She let her hand pass through, then her arm. The rest of her collapsed in on itself to fit through the gap. Crouch still held her other hand tightly; he followed her without letting go. They did not emerge on the other side immediately. Nora could see nothing, and felt weightless, though a persistent sensation of moving through space reminded her of vertigo. She would have asked Crouch if he was still there, had she been able to speak. She thought the question instead, and tried not to panic when she received no sign of his presence. Then she felt her hand slip through into ordinary atmosphere, and her arm, her shoulder and her head as they emerged from the long mirror in Leo's apartment, until she stretched full length upon the floor, with Crouch seconds behind her. As they lay he needlessly raised a finger to his lips. The success of their passage had already left her uncertain what to say. Unlike the days of Berenice's analysis the curtain no longer divided Nora from the rest of the consulting room – the rail appeared to have been taken down altogether. But the other features of the room were just as she recalled them. The couch was positioned as it always was, with Leo's chair angled away from it. She realised this was the first time she had ever entered at night.

"He doesn't sleep here any more," Nora told Crouch at normal volume. "He bought a house when he married Berenice."

But Crouch silently pointed at the line of light beneath the one internal door.

Leo must have stayed after seeing a client; maybe he had been completing work late, and decided he was too tired for the journey home. Or maybe he had been feeling nostalgic, for the days before his marriage. Nora supposed the discovery that one's wife is unfaithful might sour a man towards the family home, though she had little remaining sympathy. It would be delicious, in confrontation, to reveal that she had been right all along about her nature. He had persuaded her she was deluded, but here, by her very presence, she had demonstrated he was wrong. She was a monster, in the company of another monster.

Her voice hadn't summoned him, so she assumed he had fallen asleep. But she was unconcerned about waking him, and stood, neatening her sleeves.

"We should say hello," she told Crouch, who was watching her intently.

When she entered the bedroom she saw Leo sleeping in his suit above the covers, with a half emptied brandy bottle in reach on the floor. His face was pink and his tie loose. The sight was pitiable. She watched him, without trying to rouse him, long enough for Crouch to say: "You followed Miss Oxbow to win him; but you don't seem happy with your prize."

"No." She considered. "It wasn't him I was trying to win."

Crouch nodded. "Then when are you going to bite?"

"Bite?" Nora's head shot up. She laughed. "I'm not going to bite him."

Leo was stirring. He opened an eye, looked unsure of his surroundings and why he wasn't alone. The way he couldn't focus told Nora he was very drunk.

"It's a good kill," Crouch pointed out. "The meat is better when you have a reason to want them dead."

Still she delayed.

"You and I are different from each other," Nora told Crouch. "I never wanted to be like Valery. That was why I tried to confess when we met in the woods. I didn't want to be a hyring."

"But you are," Crouch said.

Nora stared at Leo, on his back, as he struggled to speak.

"Oh for God's sake," Crouch said impatiently. He seized Leo's hand and bit into it deeply, tearing flesh from the bone.

Leo made no attempt to get away.

Crouch swallowed. "No drink would make him that docile. What's he taken?"

"Nothing. He doesn't feel pain."

"I bet he does. Something broke how he reacts to it. Eat."

Slowly, slowly, time seeming to run at half its normal pace, she knelt on the bed. She straddled Leo as Crouch returned to flaying his hand. Leo made eye contact.

"Nora?" he said uncertainly.

She placed a hand upon his face. Her thumb hovered over the pulse in his neck. It grew more erratic as Crouch fed. Eventually she bent towards Leo, his face still concealed, and bit him sharply in the neck. The blood sprang so fast he was dead within a couple of minutes. The bed, and Leo himself, and Nora's face and blouse were sodden. She licked her lips, and the taste was sweet, though she didn't return for another bite.

"Should we wash here?" she asked Crouch.

"No, I think not. Better to leave sooner. If we're disturbed, I don't want to fight on a full stomach."

"The neighbours like to pry," she remembered, thinking of the man with the trident. "But they can't have heard anything remarkable."

"All the same."

"It might be a long time until they *do* find him," Nora thought aloud. "I wonder if news will reach England before Berenice sets out for Zurich."

Crouch swiped at his mouth with his cuff. "Were you planning to let her return?"

"No, I don't know," Nora said swiftly, fearing she would forego her claim.

"What *is* this cowardice? You must be cajoled into

eating a man who tried to degrade you. You must be cajoled into eating his slut of an accomplice. I hoped I was mistaken that you were sentimental for her. I can see now I wasn't. You must know she will betray you as she betrayed her husband. While you were looking for her in the streets, I saw her back at the hotel, all over that crude Italian like a rash."

"Merlini?"

"Perhaps you don't believe me? She went into his suite. I watched her, and she didn't care that I saw."

"No, she wouldn't. I don't care either," because Nora knew Berenice's flaws better than her own, and it was easy to love what you truly understood.

"You should. She has made a fool of you, once with this drunkard and this very night with her lover. If you had any dignity you would gut her on our return. Are you so squeamish that I must fillet Miss Oxbow and present her on a plate for you to take dainty bites?"

"No."

"I might just take her for myself."

Nora slapped him, and he caught her wrist almost as soon as she'd broken contact. He showed his teeth, still red-stained. "I wouldn't do that if I were you. Which of us would come off worse from a fight?"

"You don't want kinship," Nora said. "Not with that kind of taunt."

"I had high hopes for you," he jeered. "I knew you were Valery's daughter; I could see when you arrived that you were hunting; you kept *coming* to me, and I thought you must sense that you are like me underneath. But every time you have managed to disappointment me by disavowing what you are. It is the worst hypocrisy and I am tired of it. Eat Oxbow or I will eat you both."

Even Valery had never threatened to destroy her.

"All right," Nora said, and Crouch nodded as he released her wrist. He made for the door as she considered her form. She had never assumed her true state, and would not have said she knew how. But it was simply another act of mimicry: of Valery, of Crouch. Her spine arched and her snout protruded and her teeth elongated. Crouch turned to face her. He did not seem alarmed. She had accepted his terms: it was inevitable that she would look less human, and more beast.

Her maw dropped and she leapt with the force necessary to fell him.

She had the advantage of surprise. Her hooves pinned him to the floor at the hind arm, and he struggled to throw her off. He succeeded in biting at the nearest of her limbs, but the adrenaline helped her withstand the injury. Before he could get in a second attempt she tore at his face, blinding him, and ate the eyes from their sockets. He screamed, and then he grinned, which told her the cry was as much vengeful as anguished. The neighbours would hear. She would have less time to kill him and make her getaway. So next she snapped through his neck. The bones crunched in her mouth. She paused to listen out for anyone raising the alarm outside the flat. Nothing yet. They may be creeping by silent, fearful of bringing attention on themselves before the police could be notified. Leo's flat had a telephone. She didn't know whether that would be true of the other residents.

Hurriedly, she tore what flesh she could from Crouch's

face and swallowed the pieces whole. It would be impossible to identify him now. She wished to linger, because he tasted good. But he had made sure she must leave. Reverting to her human shape, she scrambled to collect the clothes that had torn from her back, and checked the cupboard in the consulting room where she knew Leo kept basic medical supplies. She took Carrel-Dakin solution, Vaseline, bandages and a pair of bird-beak pliers. Dogs were barking out in the shared stairwell and she could hear raised voices too. She ran to the mirror, bent to breathe upon the glass and pushed her shoulder through the cloud, the rest of her folding and slipping through, with everything she held in her arms.

7

On the return the darkness didn't scare her. Partly she enjoyed the thrill of escape. She knew, too, that the Regent she was returning to was more fully under her control. Crouch had served a purpose. He had punished Leo when she had failed in courage. He had forced her to examine herself. But he was a liability, because he so thoroughly prioritised his own desires, and whatever fraternity he might have offered her was not in the end worth her deference. She would re-enter a hotel which was no longer his territory.

It was her own hotel room – not Crouch's, and not the pineapple suite – that she had envisioned in the darkness between mirrors. It was there that she emerged, naked, bloody, and with her belongings spilling out from her arms. Initially she sat in the dark room catching her breath. The patch on her arm where Crouch had bitten her was throbbing and she suspected that it had bled very freely. She didn't know how much of the blood on her skin was hers and how much belonged to her victims. It had dried tightly on her face. She placed the medical equipment on the bed and dropped the ruined clothes in the empty hearth. It

would be best to wash standing in the tub. Starting at her
scalp she methodically rubbed at each inch of bloodied hair
and skin, watching the pink water collect at her feet. She
was careful around her wound. Once the water ran clear she
had a better idea of how badly hurt she was. Crouch had
left a neat impression of teeth marks and entirely removed
her tattoo. It had been part of her for twelve years; too long.
She was glad it was gone. Her memory of Miss Lowrie had
grown dispassionate. Now the slaughter among the nettles
was the first murder, not the only murder, that Nora had
enabled. Miss Lowrie took on a similar status to Nora's old
maths tutor: an awkward first romance, from when she was
very young and did not yet know herself.

She dried herself and returned to the bedroom. She lit the
fire, partly to burn the clothes, but also to sterilise the pliers.
The desk by the window would have to do for dressing the
wound. She disinfected it as best she could. Bites were best
left unstitched, which was just as well; she could only use
one hand. Dressing the wound would be sufficient.

As soon as her arm was bandaged, she put on fresh
clothes, being careful to pick a dress with long sleeves. She
winced as she tugged down the cuff. The fragrance of charred
cotton and blood drifted from the coal fire, prompting her
to push up the sash window and let in a shock of cold air.
By the moon, she could see that the water outside had fully
drained. Over by Needless Alley two police lanterns were
still visible. When the burnt smell had dissipated Nora drew
the curtains closed.

She left the room to knock on Harvey's door with a
request. The housekeeper answered promptly, wearing
small round spectacles that made her look older.

"Are the kitchens providing drinks?" Nora asked.

"Certainly, Dr Dickinson."

"Might I have two glasses of Hokey Pokey?"

"I'll bring them to you directly." Harvey's eyes lowered. "I think we can see to it that they are complimentary."

That was an odd remark. Nora returned to her room to wait for them. She sat down and did nothing but look into space.

The hotel didn't rest while she waited. Outside, the porters were hoisting Louis Vuitton cases, cabin wardrobes and bentwood trunks into a juddering lorry, because the next morning passengers would finally be departing for their ocean liners. The young guests with minor titles were already leaving, their chauffeurs collecting them in Bentleys and Daimlers, after the wilful damage to their rooms had been discussed. Quarrington had the right to retain their luggage as a lien, but he waived the bill: high jinks didn't matter while violent deaths were still under investigation. The hotel's reputation depended on the patronage of socialites, and that was truer than ever now the Regent faced scandal. On the ground floor of the hotel the silence cabinets were operating again and fully occupied. Pretoria Block telephoned the haunted sites of England to cancel the onward stops of her tour. The MP for Warwick and Leamington telephoned his mother to reassure her of his good health. Calls within five miles cost two shillings; within fifteen miles, six. After snowstorms and murders the guests would pay much more to hear voices from the outside world. Thirteen shillings for Rome; eleven for Berlin; ten for Paris. A newspaper mogul had a mistress in France with septic poisoning. His secretary called the nursing home for a report, pretending to be her sister. Fourteen shillings for Belgrade, ten shillings for Prague, eight shillings for Zurich – but no one, today, telephoned Zurich.

Time passed. Nora didn't know how much. Harvey brought a silver tray bearing the two beautifully curved glasses, brimming with the green drink. Her eyes darted, in the expectation of there being another person in the room, though she was too tactful to enquire why Nora had two drinks and no company. The hotel workers would assume there had been a falling out – they would gossip that Berenice was fickle and didn't pay any one person attention for too long. This was somewhat accurate. Nora wondered whose bed Berenice was sleeping in.

Harvey made for the door, and as she grasped the handle she said: "The bridges have been checked. Trains will be running from Snow Hill from the morning."

"Thank you. A shame the police might need me for longer." The needs of the police ceased to matter as soon as she'd stepped through Crouch's mirror – she could come and go anywhere she liked by that means and they would be none the wiser. But she would mimic a normal person's worries well enough.

"The police *are* dependent on your testimony, then?" Harvey asked.

Nora folded her hands in her lap. All the hotel workers stood to suffer from Westall's smearing; an under-manager assaulting several guests and murdering one would taint his colleagues' prospects. But Harvey faced a higher risk. She had a motive to kill Reid, and the police might discover it if they looked away from Westall. No wonder she was being conciliatory.

"The police insinuated it had been difficult to verify the note, so it will be very important if I can confirm Westall was entering rooms uninvited," Nora said. "But my recollection of what I could see in the dark is hazy. It comes back to me in fragments and flashes. I haven't, yet, regained a full memory of that night, though I'm sure it will come."

"Do let me know if there is *anything* we can assist you with for the rest of your time here."

"Thank you. I do have one rather delicate request."

"Oh?"

"Might you let me know if any telegrams arrive for Miss Oxbow? It is important that you notify me before they are delivered to her. And I'd also like to know if she makes plans to depart." There was a chance Berenice would leave as soon as she was notified of Leo's death, neither informing Nora nor bidding her goodbye.

Harvey deliberated. "I'd have to call in a favour from the telegraphist, but I think that can be arranged with discretion."

"Very good. I'm sure, after a good night's sleep, my memory of the intruder will have improved."

Harvey nodded and left.

Nora downed the first glass of Hokey Pokey, which fulfilled two functions. She wanted her arm to hurt less, and she had a final procedure to perform which would take some Dutch courage. She was slower with the second glass, letting herself enjoy it more. The feast in Zurich had heightened her sense of taste in the most preternatural, and delightful, way. She could discern the precise proportions of crème de roses to anisette to absinthe.

"Absinthe is only a kind of brandy," she said to the empty room. "Infused with herbs."

The herbs were distinct to her. Star anise and liquorice; calamus and almonds; peppermint and juniper. Angelica root. All as warm as the sunlight they'd distilled in. Wormwood. And stinging nettle, though it held no more meaning for her than the other ingredients. She could imagine the nettles being gathered from a woodland floor, in Pontarlier or Tarragona, somewhere she'd never been and had nothing to do with her. Countries all over the world had a village like Alspath, enclosed by woods.

When the lines of the world had comfortably blurred, she took the sterilised pliers from the kettle over the fire. She returned to the bathroom. The face in the mirror was soft-edged. Nora opened her mouth. It would have been sensible to decide, before the absinthe, which tooth she needed least; instead she must make that decision with compromised faculties. She shrugged and the pliers gripped a smaller molar on the bottom left. It came more easily than she anticipated. Eating Crouch had made her strong. Her mouth flooded with the taste of iron and salt mingling with the nettles. She released the pliers into the palm of her hand, and closed her fingers round the tooth. The gap in her mouth, when she looked again, was in the exact same spot as her mother's.

Postscript

It was the fourteenth of February – mid-morning on a Thursday. In an early harbinger of spring, the sun was out as Nora walked down the steps of the hotel. She wore a petal-brimmed turban made from rayon, and a coral coat with a standing collar. A small travel case contained everything that she deemed essential; the remaining possessions had been abandoned to her hotel room. Normal traffic had resumed: half a dozen streams of cars and buses motored past her. She saw Enid approach from the opposite direction. As they drew close to each other, the older woman stopped, opened her mouth to greet Nora, then let the words dry on her lips in confusion when there was no returning smile. Nora trained her eyes on the passengers' entrance to the station.

Inside, the light falling through the trusses cast pale diamonds on the floor. The train was waiting, which meant many had taken their seats already and the platform bore a handful of passengers bidding family farewell. It wasn't quite time for departure. Nora had time to walk along each carriage, looking for a particular face. Inevitably her search was fruitless. Berenice was never early.

Nora inspected her gloves, brushing away smuts left by the station smoke. According to her arrangement with Harvey she had learnt of Berenice's imminent departure, and was ready to leave Birmingham herself. She intended that today would be the last day she ever gave Westall or Reid a second thought. Minutes ticked by on the station clock, and Nora grew impatient. Finally she saw an elegant figure by the entrance, trailed by hotel porters with her luggage. Nora strode briskly to meet her. By the time she reached the right carriage Berenice was already seated, and she shot an apprehensive look as Nora let herself in.

"You're travelling light," she commented, puzzled, as she saw Nora's small case.

"Never mind that. Why did you give me the slip for Merlini?"

Berenice shrugged and shook her head irritably. "You were wrapping me up, stopping me from acting as I wanted. It's stifling. I hated it. Leo does it too. *Did* it too."

"Did?" Nora asked blandly.

"He's dead." Berenice's expression was cold – harder than Nora had ever seen it. She didn't speak with a hint of her usual preciousness.

"He won't be stifling you any more, then. If I vowed never to try controlling you again, if I said the very idea horrified me, what would you say?"

They heard the whistle. The train heaved into movement.

Nora took Berenice's hand, and asked: "Did you feel, when we met at the hotel, how different we were from everybody else? I kept waiting for you to acknowledge it. Do you feel how separate we are?"

"I don't recognise your voice," Berenice murmured. "Something happened to you."

Only that Nora had spent years caring that she was believed, and hearing that her own beliefs were false. Now she would do neither.

"Don't you like my new voice?" Nora asked.

"It is interesting," Berenice granted. "Did you eat Reid and Westall?"

"No. But I ate the man who did. Among others."

Through the window the Birmingham skyline unfolded, passing into view and out again.

"I don't like people who delude themselves," Nora said. "There's something snivelling in their guilt. I prefer the travellers who are without remorse, who believe the only rules that matter are the ones they set. Particularly if they are honest about that fact."

"You'll tire of me, then," Berenice said. "I need a little delusion."

Like the belief she could tame a beast.

"Where are you travelling to?" Nora asked.

"Zurich," Berenice said. "Isn't that where you're going to?"

"No. Anywhere but there. Come with me somewhere else instead."

"Such as?"

"We could stop in Paris. Go to Rome. Athens. Constantinople."

"You're right. Anywhere but Zurich."

Berenice let go of Nora's hand, and examined her wedding ring. She slid it from her finger.

"Are you going to throw it away?" Nora asked.

"No. Never. It will be a good reminder, not to get married, if I keep it hidden somewhere safe. For now…" She took a dainty handbag from the neighbouring seat, unfastened the gilt clasp, and dropped the ring inside.

Nora took her tooth from her pocket. "Hide this with it."

Berenice threw back her head and laughed. It wasn't a widow's laugh. "That's a disgusting thing. Is it one of your victim's?"

"If you like."

"What a macabre thing you are, my baby." She let the tooth fall into the bag, too.

"Your Russian song…" Nora said.

"Yes?"

"I put the English words to a tune."

"Sing it."

"*The girl pretended to be the grass,*" Nora sang, remembering the blood in the hokey pokey. "*She pretended to be the weeds. She pretended to be the fields. I pretended to be a scythe. I have to tell you, I'm thousands of years old, and this is the pretence of love. The girl pretended to be a story. She pretended to be a page. She pretended to be a book. I pretended to be a storyteller. I have to tell you, I'm thousands of years old, and this is the pretence of love. The girl pretended to be bread. She pretended to be milk. She pretended to be meat. I pretended to be teeth. I have to tell you, I'm thousands of years old, and this is the pretence of love. Are you asleep, my baby?*"

Berenice's eyes were closed. Ever since Nora cured her,

she'd slept the sleep of the guiltless. Nora silently watched her tranquil features. It was a shame there was no corridor on the train; all the passengers were divided from each other. But one of them might have a compact mirror. The journey was long, if you didn't eat.

Author Note

Birmingham has several historic hotels, including one with its own spring and another with a cathedral view. Although some of these businesses have archives, they weren't available to the public at the time of writing. Accordingly, I invented the Regent, a fictional hotel situated in the real streets of Birmingham. My depiction of hotel life in 1929 was informed by hospitality literature, including interwar copies of *The Hotel Review, Restaurant Gazette & Catering News* and *The Hotel and Restaurant Diary and Year Book* produced by Practical Press. I consulted Ed Burrow's *British Hotels* (Burrow, 1923), W. Bently Capper's *Licensed Houses and Their Management* (Caxton, 1926 edition) and Ernest M. Porter's *Hotel and Restaurant Careers for Women* (Pitman and Sons, 1931). The pandemic put paid to my original plan of consulting trade archives at the British Library and the Bodleian Library. Fortunately I could get relevant ephemera at little cost from hotels and private individuals across Britain: old receipts, guest books, menus and advertisements. I was also interested in how hotels were written about by novelists in the late twenties and early thirties; my favourites were Arnold Bennett's *Imperial Palace* (1930), Elizabeth Bowen's *The Hotel* (1927) and Vicki Baum's *Grand Hotel* (1929). I let Nora make a reference to reading *Grand Hotel*, though she must have been quick off the mark and bought the original German edition for it to squeeze into the time frame.

The Holzberg is also imaginary. The following books were helpful for checking that the building and its day to day running were appropriate for Zurich in the period: *The Routledge History of Madness and Mental Health*, edited by Greg Eghigian (Taylor & Francis, 2017); *Treating People with Psychosis in Institutions* by Belinda S. Mackie (Taylor & Francis, 2018); *Material Cultures of Psychiatry*, edited by Monika Ankele and Benoît Majerus (Verlag, 2020); and *Behind Walls: Photography in Psychiatric Institutions from 1880 to 1935*, edited by Katrin Luchsinger and Stefanie Hoch (Scheidegger & Speiss, 2022). While thinking about the role of women in such hospitals – as psychoanalysts, the wives and lovers of psychoanalysts, and patients – I found it helpful to read *Mad, Bad and Sad: A History of Women and the Mind Doctors from 1800 to the Present* by Lisa Appignanesi (Virago, 2011), Catrine Clay's *Labyrinths: Emma Jung, Her Marriage to Carl, and the Early Years of Psychoanalysis* (William Collins, 2016), and Susan Baur's *The Intimate Hour: Love and Sex in Psychotherapy* (Cengage Learning, 1997). The inkblots used by Leo during Berenice's analysis are based on the images in *Psychodiagnostik* (Hans Huber, 1921) by Hermann Rorschach.

Lastly, a note on Nora's place of birth. The village in the woods roughly corresponds to Meriden, which is about twelve miles from Birmingham. The intersection of roads at Meriden was once believed to be the centre of England. Crossroads are significant in vampire lore; depending on local superstition, they're meant to be places where vampires are especially dangerous, and especially vulnerable. It is, then, exactly the kind of place you might find Valery caged. On this occasion I was deliberately anachronistic: the story uses the village's archaic name, Alspath, as recorded in the Domesday Book, because Nora's coming of age feels dream-like and out-of-time. Nothing in her childhood has unfolded quite as it should.

Acknowledgements

Thank you to Oli Munson, Madeleine O'Shea, Clare Gordon, Laura Palmer, Sophie Whitehead, Helen Crawford White, Tamsin Shelton, Kathryn Colwell, Amy Watson, everyone at Head of Zeus who worked on the novel without my direct knowledge, Elizabeth Lee, Cara Attwood, Richard Beard, Stephanie Butland, Tracy King, my mom, and Matt.

About the Author

KATE MASCARENHAS is a part-Irish, part-Seychellois Midlander. Since 2017, Kate has been a chartered psychologist. Before that she worked as a copywriter, a dolls' house maker, and a bookbinder. She lives with her husband in a small terraced house which she is slowly filling with Sindy dolls. She is the author of two other novels, *The Psychology of Time Travel* and *The Thief on the Winged Horse*.